Ryan Cousins, aged 39, was born in Johannesburg, South Africa and currently resides there. He is married with no children but treats his two beagle girls as if they were his own. He holds an undergraduate degree in Human Resources and an Honour's Degree in Business Management with a successful career in Talent Acquisition, spanning in excess of ten years. He is currently the Talent Acquisition Lead for Sub-Saharan Africa for a Global FMCG company. He is an avid reader and only recently ventured writing himself where he tends towards easy description and uncomplicated characters, but not to the point where it feels superficial. He lives every moment of the stories he builds, almost reading it as he writes it.

My sister Kelly Cousins, who inspired me to give this writing thing a go and to my mother, Joy Cousins, who read every chapter I sent her and who kept encouraging me all the way. Finally, my wife, Taryn, who put up with listening to several hours of ideas and musing but never once gave up in her support of me.

Ryan Cousins

HOLLOW PUPPETS

AUSTIN MACAULEY PUBLISHERS™

LONDON • CAMBRIDGE • NEW YORK • SHARJAH

A CIP catalogue record for this title is available from the British Library.

ISBN 9781398468412 (Paperback)
ISBN 9781398468429 (ePub e-book)

www.austinmacauley.com

First Published 2022
Austin Macauley Publishers Ltd®
1 Canada Square
Canary Wharf
London
E14 5AA

Mrs Lorraine Emmett for taking the time to review and edit my manuscript.
Thank you for time and feedback, it is greatly appreciated.

Table of Contents

Chapter 1 – Dreaming

Blood is splattered on the walls. Not random blotches but regular crimson spurts travelling the length of the room, as if child were playing with a water hose, stoppering and unstoppering the flow with his thumb. Although decidedly unsettling, it is nothing compared to the atmosphere of the place which has a physical aura of pulsing darkness. Echoes of screams, prayers and begging, mixed with the smells of shit and piss produced an emotional soup. A soup you could taste like a tangible memory and you could swim through. As always, it's the nausea he feels first, rapidly followed by an all-consuming fear. An indescribable fear-inducing panic; a rolling black mass forcing all before it to flee, leaving no room for rational thought. Like a phantom limb, he remembers the fear. It is this indistinct, but real, memory that forces him to stand his ground and take stock of the situation. Even without clear direction as to why he must, he knows he must. Putting aside the unanswered questions of, 'how did I get here?' and 'where is here?'. He boxes the fear and starts looking at the whole so he might later recall the pieces that made it up.

The floor is uneven and unpaved. A piece of raw flattened earth pock-marked with inky black puddles of various sizes, impossible to avoid if you tried to walk from one end to the other.

The room itself was no larger than a 5x5 metre square space that could have served as anything from a dining room to a storage room. It had no other fixtures that could provide clues as to its original purpose. In the centre of the room stands a three-legged stool, listing slightly to the left as a result of a broken leg. On each side of the stool, the blood splattered walls exist; one second as pure darkness and the next as the blood-splattered, metallic scented horror they really are. It was the bare, exposed light bulb hanging by a black cable from the roof directly above the chair, swinging first left and then right in a never-ending metronomic madness that allowed for this effect. Why it is was in motion in a closed, windowless, doorless room with no moving air was not important, he knows that! It is what the swinging arc of light was revealing that needed to be focused on. Darkness, then light. Darkness then light. The creaking cable supporting the bulb continued to swing. He stood with his back to one wall, the stool right in front of him and the pair of gory walls on either side. Staring to his left he waited for the light to reveal the secrets of that side. Light then dark. Light then dark. He keeps looking. Light, nothing, or something, then darkness. It wasn't what he saw, but what he felt. His heart rate quickened and sweat beaded the top of his lip in contrast to the dry desert that was the inside of his mouth. Light, nothing, then dark again. Light, nothing then dark... then it was there. Hiding in the dark, but not visible in the light. Heart rate climbing higher, he swallowed convulsively and continued to stare. It was a man but not a man, dressed in a suit, black on black with a white tie. Light again swings into *view, nothing again. Darkness returns and so does the man that is not a man. Is he closer to the stool now? Light returns and the bulb swings away again. The man that is not a man is faceless, like store mannequin; he is definitely closer now. The cable with the bulb stops swinging with a dramatic suddenness, allowing the darkness to remain in place. Now the man is moving in a jerky imitation of walking, stock motion. The fear builds to an impossible crescendo. The aura of pain and terror follow the man who approaches the stool. It is now occupied by what he can only imagine must have been a woman. Her face is a frozen mess of blood, bone and ooze. She has no ears or nose and her mouth reveals missing teeth, evenly spaced, as if each 'other' tooth had been removed as some sort of sick joke. Holes filled with congealing blood have replaced her eyes and her top lip is cut off. He can't watch anymore. It is shocking and the fear too all encompassing; he tries to run but he can't. He is stuck in a VR horror movie screening, purely and solely for him. He tries to scream but can't. He tries to turn and can't, so watches on in dread. The stock motion man is suddenly a frenzy of slashing arms with knives attached, leering and looming over the woman. Blood is flying in all directions and the woman in the chair is screaming in soundless agony and horror. It is too much. The walls seem to be closing in, his vision narrows as he seeks to escape this windowless hell. In the moment before the world winks out of existence, an instant between breaths, the frenzied slashing stops mid-slash, as if frozen. The silently screaming woman turns her eyeless gaze upon him, lifts her hand and points one long broken-nailed finger at the suited mannequin and says, 'But he was so nice.' The other fingers on the hand then slowly open to reveal a man's finger-ring in her strangely white palm, untouched by blood.*

His vision zooms in as if looking through a telescopic lens. He doesn't want to see. An inexplicable sense of that if he looks, he is bound. There, in microscopic detail on the silvery bulbous ring are the words, 'vocare ad regnum'. There is an echo of a scream, all goes black and is no more.

Jackson awoke with a start. He was drenched in sweat and lying in a little puddle of the same stuff which formed a damp ghost version of himself on the sheets. Why was it back? He had just begun to hope, just begun to live. He rolled off the side of the bed and opened the little window overlooking the main street of his second-floor apartment. He needed the air, he needed to think. The sounds of early morning traffic and construction work assailed him in a familiar and comforting way. It was a fresh, still morning, promising a hot day ahead. He knew the headaches would soon come and he had to prepare. Without further thought, he returned to his bed and stretched across to the mattress to pull out the well-worn leather notebook and pen from the side table. He always kept the notebook close by. His practiced hand made sure to record the dream in as much detail as possible. He left nothing out, regardless of how minor or ridiculous it might seem. He took the time to draw the ring and the inscription as well. Writing it down brought back all the fear and anxiety he had just experienced and as a result, it took several attempts to complete. He would usually re-read everything to ensure he didn't miss any detail, but he was emotionally out of practice and didn't think he could take himself back into that space.

He needed a beer, which always eased the shakes of the dream withdrawal. Silly thought – he had been sober for over six years now, but even imagining opening a drink had the desired effect and he started calming down.

Notebook in one hand, imaginary drink consumed, Jackson made his way across the hall to the kitchen to prepare breakfast – a much healthier, and more real option than the beer. He mulled over the dream as his hands mulled over the scrambled eggs in the hot pan. Why now? What had changed to make the dreams come back? Nothing immediately came to mind but the anxiety of the impending headaches was an unwelcome friend that he knew he would have to live with once again. With breakfast done, he checked the wall-mounted clock, 08:30. He had plenty of time for a walk before his shift at the bar downstairs. His daily work routine started at 11:00 and went through to 21:00. It kept his hands busy and his mind occupied, just the way he liked it. He got up, put the finished plate of eggs in the dishwasher and went to get ready.

Walking down the street on a warm June morning, an extra cup of coffee in hand from the local across the street, Jackson tried to clear his head. This effectively got him thinking even more. He spotted a bench and headed towards it. There were no cheery 'Good mornings,' or other greetings from the people he walked past (even those he sees everyday) and that was the way he preferred it. He purposely kept to himself and avoided any form of interpersonal relationship – it is just easier that way. He had learned many hard lessons throughout his life but he knew, that prime amongst all of them was this; people got hurt around him. This was the foundation he had built his life on. He never knew his parents and had never connected with some of the foster parents he had been placed with. Several of these foster parents had often wondered if he needed medical or even psychiatric attention. Even as child, without a full grasp of what he was, he remained apart. He never made friends, he always played by himself. It was just that Jackson just naturally avoided people and even though he was never truly happy, he was always more content when alone. As he had gotten older he never changed in this regard, instead he just made more of an effort to be polite about it. He found that constantly rejecting any sort of advances from everyone, had the desired effect of pushing them away for good. No one had the patience to pursue Jackson as a friend and he could outwait them all with his polite declines, day after day. Girlfriends were few and far between. In fact, Jackson never had a 'real' girlfriend, not one that he thought of as a girlfriend at least, regardless of what she thought of it. Like any other man, Jackson had, had a few sexual conquests but nothing to write home about. In truth, he hardly thought of sex, it just wasn't something that interested him as much it did many others. In his late teens, around 16, 17 or so, he pursued girls just to add that level of normality to the way people perceived him. It was all an act, he did it because it was expected of him. He did it because not doing it would have singled him out and given something for people to notice. Instead, he just played the part of a horny teenager doing what teenagers do. The girls he managed to win over didn't stick around though. To them Jackson came across as gloomy and uninterested which, after a fashion, he was. To anyone walking past him sitting there on the bench, Jackson would look no different to any other middle-aged man drinking his morning coffee. This was an image that he had spent years cultivating. Taking a sip of rapidly cooling coffee, he reflected on the first time he could remember having 'The Dream'. There might have been many more incidents before, but this was the first time he came to understand it and actually acknowledge it as a real thing. He must have been six or seven; it wasn't precise but he remembers being 'nearly' seven. At this stage in his life, Jackson was between foster parents and living in a home for children that wasn't great, but better than others. To this day he can clearly remember that particular dream – mostly because he nearly died shortly afterwards.

Jackson was playing on the roof of the building that the orphanage occupied. It was about four stories high, with the home taking the top two floors. It was here, between the cages of the caretaker's pigeons, that he would often find himself. Even in his dreams, Jackson was a loner. *Looking around, he couldn't see the usual door opening onto the roof and he briefly wondered how he had got there. Stepping back he realised that the waist-high walls around the edge of the roof had grown considerably higher as he could no longer see over them. His heart started beating rapidly and the little hairs on the back of his neck stood up. Something was wrong. The air was heavy, sitting on his shoulders like the friendly python one of his foster parents used to let him hold. He looked for an escape from the encroaching fear but there wasn't any and he knew he had to watch. The sun suddenly seemed unbearably bright and while Jackson squinted, figures suddenly appeared. Three of them, all boys and wearing the standard garb of the home, white t-shirts and black shorts. All three were faceless, just hollow puppets and all the more terrifying for it. Jackson tried to run again but found his feet glued. He had become an immovable fixture, a staring gargoyle on the roof of the home. It felt like his heart was trying to escape his chest and he was battling to breathe in the thick air. The puppet boys started moving towards him, jerkily, just like puppets on a string. Jackson was staring at them as they approached, his mouth agape with as much fear any six-year-old is capable of feeling or imagining. They were now right in front of him and still moving.*

Jackson screamed but nothing came out; the figures passed right through him. When the tears and sudden fright abated, he found himself turned around, looking away from the maintenance box and straight at the pigeon cages. With the strong intuition that all children possess, Jackson became concerned for the pigeons, his only friends at the home. The puppet boys made it to the cages and with wooden movements, each of them caught a bird. Jackson's heart stopped beating and began to sink. 'Please don't hurt them,' he tried to scream, but nothing came out. Each pigeon was manhandled in such a way that its wings were extended to the top of its 'down-push' of flapping. Elastic bands were then placed over them, effectively holding the wings trapped in that position. Crying, Jackson knew something bad was going to happen and his fear heightened exponentially. The boys took their manacled pigeon prisoners to the edge of the roof. The wall on that edge had regained its normal size as he could see the building across the road. Jerky movements brought the boys shoulder to shoulder at the edge and the pigeons were held extended over the drop below. Jackson was panting, hyperventilating. As he watched, the middle puppet boy's head turned 180 degrees and stared straight at him while his body remained facing the edge. Thick black horn-rimmed glasses suddenly appeared on the otherwise featureless face and, even in the midst of terror, recognition of the glasses flickered across his consciousness. 'We are all the same, some can't be better than others,' said croaky voice that somehow escaped the blank face. The sound conjured up pictures of dampness, peeling wallpaper, moth-eaten carpets and low hanging blue smoke gathering on a ceiling. The head resumed its proper place at which point, time stopped, he knew. The hands of all the boys opened at the same time and the struggling pigeons dropped. Suddenly unglued, Jackson ran towards the edge wall; it was growing again. It was getting darker and he had to save the pigeons, somehow. The darkness grew until he could only see a pinpoint of light at the edge of the roof – the edge he could never reach. Just before it all went dark, he thought he heard splattering thuds. Then there was no more.

Six-year-old Jackson lurched up from his position in the bottom bunk bed in the corner of the room. He was screaming, uncontrollably. It took a while for him to gather his bearings but when he eventually stopped screaming, he lay back and tried to control his breathing. He had woken up the dorm, although not too much concern was forthcoming from any of the twelve other boys. Mostly, 'Shut up weirdo!' or 'Quit it!' Jackson waited for any response from the night matron but she never showed. It felt like a million years later, but he finally managed to go back to sleep.

When the sun came up the next day little Jackson stumbled out of bed, bleary-eyed and anxious. He unobtrusively looked under the covers and was immensely relieved that he hadn't wet the bed. He could remember the dream with perfect clarity, but was finding it difficult to distinguish between what was real and what was imagined. What he did know was that he was scared and didn't know what to do about it. After washing he lined up with the rest for breakfast. Jacob was behind him. He didn't need to look to know as it was painfully obvious the moment he felt his underpants tear before being pulled straight up his bum. Jacob was the dorm bully and Jackson had, had plenty of attention from him before. This particular wedgie was by no means a 'first contact'. Bending over to pick up his tray, Jackson quietly wiped the small tears that escaped his eyes and tried to hide his face from Jacob and his sniggering comrades. After some mild abuse (standard daily fare from Jacob), the bully pushed his glasses up with his middle finger and theatrically thrust past Jackson to the front of the line. As was his way, Jackson lowered his head and looked away, retaking his place in a slightly longer line. Not long after he had eaten and because it was a Sunday, he managed to sneak away from all the people and deposit himself in a secluded corner of the playroom. He loved drawing and the room provided plenty of kid-sized tables and a large variety of coloured pencils that suited him just fine. He had almost finished the first of the day's masterpieces, a pigeon in flight, when it started. A dull ache behind his eyes. Jackson brushed it off and continued to draw. A few hours later he put down the pencil, balled his fists and rubbed his eyes. The pain was a thing now; branching down from his eyes over his cheek bones and then wrapping itself entirely around his head and meeting at a point where the spine attached to the skull. Although he hated doing it, Jackson forced himself to get up to find the matron to ask for something to help with the headache. Leaning slightly against the wall along a drab grey corridor, he was walking to the kitchens (that's where one usually could find the matron) when a blinding light of pain lanced though his head. This caused him to double over while holding his temples with both hands. He eased slowly down the side of the wall until he was sitting and waiting for the lightsabre pain to pass. Once it eased, he got up, just in time to see Jacob and his cronies, their heads lowered together, scurrying around the corner and heading for the stairs to the roof. He knew. Somehow, little Jackson knew exactly what Jacob and his two friends were going to do. There was absolutely no doubt in his mind whatsoever. He had prophesised the event and with childish certainty, believed it with all his heart. Past experiences had taught him to avoid getting mixed up in Jacob's daily torture and scheming, so he turned away and tried to forget what he had just seen. He was going to pretend it was all made-up and go back to his drawing. It made him sick to the stomach and added to the pain behind his eyes which now felt like it was trying to push his eyeballs right out of his head. Jackson ran into a bathroom stall and sat with his feet curled up below him on top of the toilet seat and tried to massage the pain away from his head. Try as he might, he was not able to avoid thinking about what Jacob and his buddies were doing right now. Each time he thought of them, the lightsabre struck at his eyes. The massage wasn't working, so he got off the toilet and walked out the stall. There was small window against the bathroom wall looking out onto the street. He was on the 3rd floor and had no reason to look out. It was so small that all he could really see was the regular brick pattern of the building across the road. He was drawn, however, to the window as a moth to a flame – not wanting to go but going anyway. Also, much like the moth, instinctively knowing that it might be to his demise.

Standing on his tip toes, Jackson propped his chin on the lip of the window frame and stared out of the window. As expected, he saw only the brick wall but as he watched further, he could feel his anticipation growing. Suddenly, three small shadows dropped right past his nose. With a fright he tried to look over the edge but he was too short to peer further over. It didn't matter, he knew what it was. A breath later, he heard the same sound he had heard in his nightmare last night, three, sad, spluttered, thuds. Pain. Jackson blacked out for what felt like the second time that day.

Back on the bench, adult Jackson looked down to see he had squeezed the paper coffee cup in his hands. The plastic lid was sitting on his knee above a spreading dark stain on the leg of his pants. Cursing, he got up and brushed himself off. The memory was as constantly fresh as a Twinkie and just about as wholesome. Walking over to the water fountain next to the bench to try and clean up the mess left on his leg, he reflected on the days spent on hospital after that event. The pain, nausea, endless tests, the uncomfortable hospital bed and the confused doctors. All agreed he was dying but none could agree from what. Further to that, none could agree how to treat him. All the different meds and painkillers had no effect. Jackson remained in hospital in a semi-conscious (at times painfully, violently conscious) trance for what felt like an eternity, but in reality was two weeks. One day he woke up feeling great and asked for some scrambled eggs, as he was starving. He could feel nothing of what had been ailing him for the past two weeks. He was the talk of the hospital staff. Doctors were mightily confused and he had to remain in hospital for an additional week for more tests. All came back inconclusive. Eventually he was released back into the care of the orphanage amid much head shaking on the part on the doctors. They didn't know what Jackson knew. He almost died because he turned his back on a task that he was given. He almost died because he was too scared to act when he should have. On the day that he left the hospital with a belly full of warm scrambled eggs, six year (nearly seven) old Jackson Brandt vowed to never turn away; he would act next time. One wet pants leg later, adult Jackson sighed loudly and made his way back towards his apartment and the bar beneath his humble abode. His shift was about to begin. The work required busy hands and thoughtless conversation. It was exactly what he needed to forget the dreams, at least for a while. Hopefully there were still some Twinkies remaining under the counter, he thought he could do with a few.

Jackson was at home amongst the early day drinkers. They were a quiet, sullen bunch with not too much to say. With last night's dream firmly in mind and not seeming to want to disappear, Jackson used the bar phone to call the owner.

'Randall, it's me. Just wanted to check who's working the night shift this evening?'

'Hey Jackson,' a bleary-eyed Randall replies, 'Give me a moment to check… why?'

"I wanted to find out if I could work a double today? It would be help in keeping up with the rent and stuff." Randall was silent for a moment, and if he was giving away any hint of what he thought of this development, Jackson wasn't picking it up. This was Randall though. He had owned the bar, 'The Grimm Repo', for over 15 years and it was now a firm fixture of the neighbourhood. He had seen it all, which seemed to have drained away any last remaining excitement he might have once felt for life. The Grimm Repo was so named after he ran into some money trouble in his earlier years. After most of his worldly belongings were repossessed, he agreed to run the place for his brother to earn something to live off. At the time, the place was called simply called 'Barts'. When his brother passed away Randall inherited Barts and promptly changed the name in honour of his past financial difficulties.

Although it was never going to make him rich, the bar did provide a decent living. Jackson learned this over the course of the past five years that he had been working here, but mostly from one whiskey-sodden evening when Randall decided to drink at his own establishment. The bar counter ran for the length of the narrow room, with a set of male/female/unisex bathrooms at the end. The dim interior revealed large bay windows with deep amber coloured glass allowing you to see outside, but not letting too much light come through. I suppose this was the effect whoever had designed the place was going for. Below each window squatted maroon leather booths that circled brown tables, each with its own little green lamp in the centre. Between the booths hung pictures of families and various celebratory events, but these weren't clearly visible in the dingy room. Large industrial-styled lamps were suspended from the pressed ceiling between the booths and bar counter. The counter itself was a magnificent piece rustic oak that had, over the years, soaked up all the joy, happiness, melancholy, and depression from the numerous visitors; along with thousands of ash and drink spillages. It might sound like a depressing place, but it actually combined to create a sombre but cosy environment, a drunken library of sorts.

"Shelley is scheduled for tonight. Should I call and ask if you can take her shift?" Randall suddenly announced on the other end of the line.

"No don't stress, I'll give her a call from here. Cheers." Shelley picked up on the first ring. "Dammit Randall! I told you I can't work this morning…"

"Shell, it's me Jackson. Sorry to bug you."

"Ah fuck, sorry. I thought it was the boss man trying to get me to do a double." The relief in her voice was noticeable.

"Speaking of doubles, how would you like to have the night off?" I asked casually. "Things are pretty slow around here today, anyways I could use the extra shift tonight if you would be willing?" There was a brief silence on the other end of the line before Shelley responded.

"Bad dreams, rough night?" Sometimes people got to know you no matter how hard you tried to avoid it.

"Maybe, but it's more about the few extra bob if you know what I mean." I tried to make it as light as I could to avoid any further discussion.

"Of course Jack, you can have my shift." A brief moment of thoughtful silence followed before she went on. "You know you can talk to me if you ever need to, right?" Jackson was truly touched by her sincerity but thanked her and hung up, as he always did.

The day went by as others had before it. Looking up past the bar and out the window, Jackson realised that the evening had crept up on him. Drinks were served, drinks were consumed.

Contrary to what he had told Shelley, the bar had filled up quite nicely and was becoming relatively festive. Jackson managed to lose himself in the work and was beginning to enjoy the evening. It was around 21:30 when the door opened and she walked in. Despite the warmth of the evening, she was dressed in blue jeans with a hoodie pulled up over her head. Jackson noticed that her hair was blonde, tucked behind her ears and was spilling out over her shoulders. She was carrying what looked a full ream of paper and approached Jackson at his 'waiting' post behind the row of beer taps.

"Are you the manager, are you in charge of the place?" It came out rather breathless and straight to the point.

"I just work here but since its only me, the cook and the waitress in tonight, I guess that would leave me in charge. My name is Jackson, how can I help?" Jackson smiled in response.

"Alex. Alex Harver," she smiled back. "Apologies for jumping right into things like that but it been a long day, long week really." The smiled faltered. "Do you mind if I hang a couple of these up?" She handed Jackson a flyer with a picture of a happily smiling teenage boy crouching next to a golden retriever. Above the picture the words, 'HAVE YOU SEEN THIS PERSON?'

"No problem, we have a notice board there between the doors to the ladies' and men. You can put on up there if you like. Also, if you have enough you can leave some with me and I can keep a few to on display on the counter?" As bars were places people often visited, Jackson would get these sorts of requests all the time and he tried to sound as sincere as possible. She thanked him and moved off toward the notice board. To Jackson, she seemed exhausted. On her way to the board with her shoulders slumped he couldn't help but empathise. When she was done, she turned back the way she had come and as she passed Jackson, she looked up and smiled.

On a whim, Jackson said, "You look like you have had a rough day. Could I get you a drink, on the house? I do a wicked Pina Colada…"

She stopped and looked back up at him and then back at the door, seemingly calculating. Finally, with an air of resignation said, "You know what, I'll take you up on that offer." She dumped her bag and pile of flyers on a stool and then slumped down on one of its neighbours.

"Great," replied Jackson as he made his way across the other side of the counter to prepare the drink. Adding ingredients to a glass Jackson looked over to see the woman resting her head in her hands which were being propped up on the counter by her elbows. "Do you know him?" he asked.

"Who?" she replied looking up. Jackson nodded his head in the direction of the notice board. "Oh, of course. He's my brother," she said shrugging.

"I'm very sorry to hear that. Has he been missing long?"

Dropping her hands from her head she looked Jackson straight in the eye and said, "It's been just over two weeks now. He is nineteen years old and although the police say kids do this all the time, Freddie is just not like that. He has never been gone this long without at least letting someone know. Everyone keeps telling me he will turn up soon but I just know something is wrong, that something bad has happened and there is nothing that I can seem to do to help. I am going crazy just sitting here…" It all came out in a rush and by the time she had finished she had tears in her eyes and was looking embarrassed and upset. Jackson was shocked into silence. It wasn't the outburst from Alex that affected him so, it was the lightsabre of pain that lanced through his eyes. Not the slow, steady build-up that he had become accustomed to, but straight into the main event. He faltered and with one hand reached out to steady himself against the counter while with the other he clutched at his eyes. Alex, no doubt thinking she had caused this sudden trauma, tried to lean over and grab at Jackson before he collapsed.

"Are you OK? I didn't mean to upset you. Should I call someone for help?" It came out with genuine concern. Jackson managed to catch himself before he fell over but as immediate as the pain had been, it had disappeared.

"No, no… I'm alright, I just got a bit dizzy there for a second. Nothing to worry about I assure you." Not looking entirely convinced, Alex lowered herself back onto her stool. "I really am sorry about your brother. Is there anything else you can tell me that I could possibly use to help you in your search?" Jackson said as he tried to lamely dismiss the near-fainting episode. Looking down he realised that he had spilled the near compete cocktail and set to cleaning it up and preparing a new one. He wasn't just being friendly or polite, he was now convinced that he had become a part of this missing boy's story and he would be damned if he let the headaches put him back in hospital again.

"Thank you mister, uh Jackson, but I hardly even know you. Not sure why you would even want to help?" Alex wrinkled her nose in what looked like a mixture of confusion and possible suspicion. When she grimaced like that, Jackson couldn't help but notice the one dimple that formed on her cheek next to her mouth on the right side.

Forcing his attention away from the dimple, Jackson looked up into her eyes and in what he hoped was a convincing tone said, "Listen, you're right. You don't know me and I don't know you. I could tell you I am a good guy and that I truly have no other motive but to just try and help someone who looks like they need it, but that wouldn't necessarily convince you I'm sure. So can I propose this? You sit and drink this near perfect Pina Colada." He pushed the second, complete attempt across to her, "And I will tell you a story that might help you to get to know me or maybe even understand me a bit better. If you are enjoying the story and you finish that drink, I will gladly provide you with another free of charge. Free drinks and what I think is an awesome story, what do you say?" That wrinkled-nose-grimace remained on Alex's face while she considered what Jackson has said. In the end, it was the first sip of the white coconutty drink in front of her that finally settled it.

"Sure, why not. If your story is as good as this drink, it can at worst serve as a good distraction."

"Excellent!" Jackson said. "Let me quickly get old Bob over there a refill and I will get stuck right in."

While Jackson continued to work the bar from behind the counter, he started telling his story. "I was a foster kid growing up, moved between families and children's homes. More in children's homes that out I suppose. It had more to do with my winning personality than with the people I was placed with, to be fair." As Jackson narrated, he felt himself becoming lost in the story. "When I was in the tenth grade, I didn't have many friends and I generally kept to myself and my drawings. People didn't really connect with me in any way even though they tried. I eventually started discouraging any sort of interaction by being rude or dismissive, because I knew I couldn't have friends like normal people. I was different and I knew it. I had no one to tell my secret to and truthfully I didn't want to tell anyone what I believed was going on with me. I was perfectly healthy and had no real physical issues but, I was prone to bouts of headaches. Headaches I thought, and still think (know) today what caused them. It was the dreams you see, nightmares really. I would see things in my dreams, horrible, wicked things. Horrors of bullying, torture and awful, inhumane pranks. They didn't come around often but when they did, I would wake up in panic and have to wait several minutes for my heart to return to a normal beat. Also, I would sometimes have to change the sheets of my bed, the fear was that real. Anyways…" Jackson motioned down at the drink in front of Alex. She looked surprised to see she had finished it already. "May I get you another?" Jackson asked, smiling.

"Please, but can you make it a Jameson's on the rocks, double I think? I don't expect it for free, happy to pay for it. There are only so many sugary drinks I can handle in one day." She reached for her bag.

"Don't be silly, I offered you more and I intend to keep to that. Besides, it's not often I get to tell stories to listening ears. Actually, come to think of it, this is a first." Jackson moved off to prepare the whiskey while continuing with his story. "I remember the dream of this story quite clearly but I am not going to go into too much detail. I will try and stick to the general outline. I remember it started with me standing in the hall with my back against the lockers. No one was around, the closed classroom doors interspersed regularly in front of me. I remember the fear being a real thing, coming inexplicably from all directions with no clear source. Just a sense of ice-cold terror. Then the length of the corridor narrowed suddenly and the entire space around me became an area shrunk by a portion of lockers behind me, and two closed classroom doors in front of me. There were dead-end blank cream coloured walls on my left and right. There was no way in or out." Jackson motioned to her glass and with a little of her head Alex agreed to another refill. Jackson topped up her drink while she waited for the story to resume. She was spellbound by now and folded into the story as much as Jackson was, so he continued. "A moment later the boys appeared, there were four of them and normal in every way, until your eyes moved up to their faces. These were horrifying in that they had no features at all, just smooth white skin where eyes, ears, nose and mouth should have been. They were standing in circle around something below them, as if staring at their feet. At first I couldn't see what they looking at but within a moment my angle of perception altered so that I was viewing from above the boys' heads. It was weird. I hadn't moved (couldn't actually) and could still feel my feet on the ground, but from where I was looking down from, I should've been about nine feet tall. Anyways, what I saw was a younger boy but unlike the others, his features were clear. I recognised him. He was younger than myself by two years and could often be seen sitting alone at the cafeteria during lunch. I can't recall his name. He was cowering on the grass below the bigger boys, trying hard to stare at them all at the same time, when suddenly they all started moving in a frenzy. Their movements were jerky and robot-like but that didn't deter from the ferocity of what they were doing. They kicked and taunted and spat on the child who, by now, was curled up in a ball and crying. It was horrifying to watch, watch and not be able to do anything." Jackson checked up on Alex, he was very much into his story and he just wanted to ensure she was still listening. She was, although the Jameson was starting to have an effect. He reached out behind himself and plucked a bottle from a slot on the shelf. He gave it a little shake in front her.

"Uh, no thanks. Seems like I might have had enough two drinks ago already," Alex said with a smile. Jackson was just about to put the bottle back when Alex reached out across the counter and grabbed his arm gently. "You know what, one more won't hurt. These drinks and your tale have been so wonderfully distracting and I am not sure that I want to it to end." Jackson took her glass, refreshed the ice and poured her a double, but he was concerned.

When Alex had touched him, the pain behind his eyes spiked, not as painfully as before, but certainly enough to take notice of. That had never happened before and he was still mulling over its potential meaning when Alex brought him back to the present. "Hey mister, so what happened then? Did the faceless boys keeping kicking the smaller kid?" Alex asked with a slight slur.

"No, they stopped the beating as quickly as they had started it and they remained in that stationary pose, just like in the beginning of the dream. The smaller kid had also stopped moving. He wasn't so tightly curled up; his muscles had relaxed and his limbs had spread out slowly in a pool of his own blood. He was clearly unconscious or dead. Then my perception altered again and was suddenly nose-to-skin face with one of the boys. I then saw eyes that slowly formed on the skinless face. Piercingly blue, with heavy brows. The left brow had two thin stripes shaved out. Although it was popular amongst the seniors on the basketball team to shave those little lines in their eyebrows, the combination of that and the blue eyes was unmistakable. It was Trent, the school Basketball Captain and local neighbourhood bully." Jackson looked up from inside his head and noticed how quiet it had become. There was only Bob and Alex left in the bar, but Bob was a permanent fixture anyways. Alex had fallen asleep on the counter with her head resting on her arm. Jackson walked around the counter and tapped Bob on the shoulder, "Time to go guy," he said. Bob mumbled something but got up and laid a hand on Jackson's shoulder in thanks as he passed him on the way out. Jackson then went about closing the place up for the evening. By the time he had finished, Alex had roused to a state of semi-consciousness. Jackson moved over to her. "Listen, it's quite late and you are in no state to get yourself home in one piece. My apartment is upstairs and you can nap on the couch. If I am still too much a 'stranger' to you, you are welcome to try and stretch out in one on the booths. I can go up and fetch you a blanket and pillow."

Alex surprised Jackson by replying, "I think I know you better than most others you have come across," she slurred, "and also I think I trust you enough to sleep on your couch, if that offer still stands," she smiled crookedly while leaning at an alarming angle on the bench.

Jackson smiled back and offered her a steady hand while she tried to pull herself upright. She brushed him off, not rudely, just matter-of-factly. "Point the way to my evening abode Master Jackson." Jackson did, turning off the lights on the way upstairs with a slightly wobbly Alex trailing behind.

Jackson awoke to the smell and sound of frying eggs. It was unusual and disorientating for him as he hadn't had someone else in his house for a very long time. Sitting upright, he stretched and yawned until he felt his jaw hinge and creak. Pulling on his jeans he made his way down the short hall to his little kitchen. Alex, obviously still dressed in the same clothes she was wearing yesterday, had her back to him and was poking a pan with two frying eggs sizzling in it. She didn't hear him approach. Jackson could also smell coffee brewing.

"Morning!" he said while still a safe distance away so as not to alarm her. Alex spun around, spots of oil flying outwards from her spatula.

"Wow, you move silently. Morning to you too. I hope you don't mind," she said spatula pointing at the eggs, "but I wanted to make you some breakfast for putting me up for the night." She seemed embarrassed and completely ill at ease.

"Thanks so much but you really didn't have to. I enjoyed chatting with you last night." Jackson moved over to pour a couple of cups of coffee. "Do you take milk and sugar?" Jackson asked. He was trying his best to appear as if everything was not completely awkward to help ease Alex's embarrassment.

"Yes please, one sugar. Take a seat, I will be ready with these in a sec." Jackson took the coffee to his little two-man breakfast nook. Alex came over and flopped two eggs and a plate of toast in front of him. She returned the pan to the sink and then moved over to the nook to sit across from him.

"You not having any?" Jackson asked nodding at his plate.

"Nah, my stomach is a little unsettled after last night. Haven't had that much to drink since college." As she spoke, spots of colour appeared on her cheeks. Jackson broke the eggs with his fork and scooped a mouthful.

"Yum!" he said while chewing and smiling. Alex laughed and relaxed a little.

"Really though, thanks so much for last night. I really don't make a habit of drinking myself comatose and crashing on a stranger's sofa."

Jackson brushed it off. "Please man, don't stress, I already told you, you were excellent company… at least while you were awake." They shared a laugh while Jackson mopped up the remainder of his eggs with a piece of toast. Looking up he caught Alex looking at him intently. She immediately glanced away as if caught in the act of doing something she shouldn't have been doing. "We are old friends here now," Jackson said smiling, "Something is obviously on your mind so go ahead and ask it?"

Alex made her wrinkled-nose grimace at being caught out, then smiled and said, "I can't stop thinking about your story. Honestly, I'm not so sure what I remember correctly or what I dreamed, but it's killing me not knowing what happened next. I know you just woke up and have a nosey stranger in your kitchen but I would really love to hear the end of it."

Jackson pushed his plate to the side. "So, up to which part do you remember?"

"Right to the end, when you recognised Trent," she replied with strange amount of excitement.

"You weren't kidding, you really were into the story," Jackson said.

Alex shrugged her shoulders and replied, "I don't understand my own excitement and I feel like a kid checking under her pillow to see of the tooth fairy has left her anything in the morning." Jackson laughed and said that he just wanted to get cleaned up and would join her in a second.

"On second thought, would you like to freshen-up before me, only got the one bathroom?"

"I think after such a magnificent breakfast it would only be fair that I tidy up here." Jackson could see the indecision on her face. She really wanted to hear the end of the story, but as she ran her fingers through her hair she obviously made up her mind. "Thanks Jackson, I think I will do just that." Alex pushed the chair back with the back of her legs as she stood up.

"The bathroom is just there opposite my bedroom. Also, there is a new toothbrush in the cabinet you can use if you want. Mi casa su casa!" Jackson was surprising himself at his own display of hospitality. For everything he told Alex of being a loner, he was acting in the complete opposite manner.

Alex smiled, "Thanks Jackson. Thanks for being so nice to me." She briefly laid her hand on top of his before making her way to the bathroom where she shut the door behind her.

Jackson sat at his breakfast nook for a while before getting up to tidy the kitchen. He smiled inwardly as he cleaned up. For such a simple breakfast of eggs and toast, she sure had made quite a mess. When everything was packed away and the dishwasher turned on, Jackson wiped down the counters and moved to the coffee machine to pour another cup. Coffee in hand, Jackson moved back to the breakfast nook and took a seat while he waited for Alex to finish up in the bathroom. For someone he had just met, he marvelled at how comfortable he felt around her. He realised that something wasn't quite right this morning. It took him a while to put a finger on it but finally he understood. He was feeling content, bordering on happy. He hadn't felt like this in forever.

After Alex returned looking clean and fresh, Jackson took her place in the bathroom and got cleaned up himself. When he came out of the bathroom he spied a very impatient Alex trying her hardest not to look so. Jackson sniggered quietly to himself while he made his way back to the table opposite her.

"So where were we?" he said as he settled in. Alex curled her legs underneath her and blew on a fresh cup of coffee. She looked at him expectantly. "Ok so I had just recognised Trent and the other boys, who were likely his hanger-on goon friends that were the ones beating the kid. That morning I woke up in my dorm, shivering all over. I could hardly remember eating breakfast or the walk to school. I just kept replaying the dream in my head, over and over. I knew that I would have to deal with Trent otherwise the headaches would come. You see, over the previous few years I came to understand that failure to act on The Dream would bring crippling headaches. When I was much smaller I almost died of such a thing, confused the hell out of the doctors."

"So are you saying that when you have this 'dream' you are compelled to action, like some sort of reluctant hero?" Alex asked speculatively and not without a little scepticism. "Yes, exactly! I know it's hard to believe and I am not going to try and prove it to you.

Let's just say it what I believe, regardless of how insane it sounds. As I kid the duality of the concept really got me. You know, the shepherd and the wolf, predator and prey, dark and light, angel and demon…? You know, good and evil?"

"So you think you are some sort of dark avenging angel out to protect us innocent lambs?" Alex sniggered, but not unkindly.

"Not at all. Those were simple concepts I imagined when I was small. I was referring to a balance, one force can't exist without the other or else the tables tip. There is balance in all things and my way of thinking is that I might just be a counter force to the events in the dreams."

"So an avenging angel versus the demonic forces of evil?" Alex smiled.

"Sure, why not?" Jackson admitted ruefully. "The description fits as a metaphor; except I don't have wings and I am not religious in any way. Also, I would not be an avenging angel in this case, more of a warrior prophet out to stop harm from occurring before it happens." They both laughed companionably at the image that description conjured.

"So I am sitting in the kitchen of a warrior prophet who has a day job of a barman and escorts drunk women to his apartment every evening. That sound about right?" Alex asked cheekily.

"The perfect description of me didn't exist until right now!" Jackson laughed. "Anyways, would you like to hear the rest of the story?" Still giggling Alex nodded motioned for him to continue. "Ok. So I got to school lost in thought and worried as to what I had to do. I was not the biggest kid in my grade, but also not the smallest. However, I was in no way a match for Trent, who seemed to have done all his growing from the 6th grade to the 8th grade. He stood just short of six feet and had a wiry, lanky look which in no way dispelled the sense of brute strength emanating from him. It was not difficult to understand how he came to wear the captain's armband on the basketball team. I was no match for him physically, but that was not about to stop me. Any potential beating from Trent would pale in comparison to the headaches. Ok, I am starting to drift away from the story here. So it all came to head when I was walking to third period. I still didn't have a clue as to what I was going to do when events overtook me, as they always tend to do. I rounded a corner and bumped into the back on Trent, who was leaning against the lockers with his arm extend for support. I was so lost in thought that I managed to knock him hard enough to make him drop the basketball from the crook of his other arm. I still remember the intake of breathe from the person Trent had been talking to when this happened. Any kid in our school knew that I had just crossed a 'no-crossing' line. Trent staggered and then righted himself. Someone had already caught the ball and was handing it back to him when Trent turned and zeroed in on me. Not gifted in witty repartee, Trent huffed and pushed me hard enough to send me flying and sliding backwards on my ass for about two metres. It was right then that I lost myself a bit." Jackson looked up to see the rapt face of Alex looking back at him. I stood up slowly and put my bag and books down next to me and then quite nonchalantly walked over to Trent. I put a finger on his chest, stood on tip toes, so as to lean close to his face, and quietly whispered so only he could hear. "I know what you and your knuckle-cracking friends are planning to do to the little kind with the glasses and the green backpack. Now I can't stop you, but I can make you rethink some of your life choices." I took a second to enjoy the genuine surprise that lit up his dull features before I took the biggest swing of my life and punched him squarely on the point of his chin. He dropped like a stone. It was pure exhilaration and fear that drove what happened next.

Trent was out cold lying on his back with his arms spread. I jumped on top of him and continued raining punches down on his face. I had no idea how long I had been doing this before someone pulled me off and held me back. After a while I stopped struggling and looked around. A bunch of kids had formed a circle around us and were staring wide-eyed at me and at Trent, who was lying in an expanding puddle of blood around his head. I think I had scared the shit out of everyone there. Trent was a well-known bully but the pure violence I had unleashed on him had spooked everyone. Anyways, I was expelled later while Trent was still recovering in hospital. I never managed to find out if I stopped the future beating the small kid with the glasses, but I know one thing, the headaches never came after that dream!'

There was a momentary pause while Alex caught her breath and considered his story. "This isn't an isolated incident?" she surmised, "These dreams have occurred before?

Does it always follow the same pattern, dream, headaches, action, repeat?"

"Yes, always. Until recently that is," Alex replied.

"So something happened recently that changed, have I suddenly become a player in this this?" Jackson liked how quickly she came to that understanding.

"Yes, I think so," he answered. "Last night when you started telling me about your brother I suddenly got this intense pain behind my eyes…"

"That's when you almost collapsed?" Alex cut in.

"Yes precisely. It's never happened like that before, there is usually a slower build up to a climax of sorts. With you it was instantaneous." Alex smiled at the imagery. "Another thing that was different," Jackson continued, "was that I have never had separate dreams, or sequences, occur simultaneously. The night before I met you I had another of those dreams and I was actually trying to distract myself when you walked in. It's always been one story at a time."

Alex was contemplative for a time before asking, "What changed? What different this time?"

"I don't know, this is new ground for me," Jackson answered. "What makes it worse is that I am out of practice with this. It's the first dream I have had in about five years." Jackson went on to tell her about the last few years recovering from alcoholism. He didn't want to go into too much detail on that score but he thought it might be relevant to the situation.

Embarrassing as it was, his recovery period was almost the precise amount of time the dreams had stayed away.

'Would you be willing to tell me more about the dream you had last night, I want to check if there is any connection between it and my brother?' Alex asked. Jackson could see the gears moving in her head. She was working this through the same way he would have done. The dream was still quite raw, but right off the bat, he had felt a connection to Alex he couldn't explain. He wanted to include her in this. It went against all the barriers and lies he told himself about trying to remain completely independent, about not needing people in his life, about protecting people from potential harm. He nodded to Alex, got up and went to his bedroom to fetch his notebook. He had a feeling that if he tried to fight against this in anyway, it would still happen regardless. With notebook in hand, he returned to the table and started his account of The Dream from the night before. It was mid-afternoon when they both agreed to take a break. Alex needed to go home for a change of clothes and check in with her family. Jackson himself was exhausted. He had not had this sort of intense one-on-one conversation with anyone in a good while. He felt emotionally drained and was considering a nap. He called a cab for Alex while she collected her things. On her way out the door, she paused, turned towards Jackson and put both her hands on his shoulders to pull herself and then planted a soft kiss on his cheek. Jackson was caught off guard but before he could say anything Alex beat him to it, "Thank you for looking after me last night, but what I really wanted to say is thank you for sharing your stories with me. I know it must have been hard, possibly painful, but I am glad you decided to include me. Call me when you are ready, I think there is more to this than we both might think." She slipped a card into his hand, turned and walked away toward the stairs. Jackson was left watching her walk away, with the card held out before him.

Later that afternoon, after a nap, Jackson got up off the couch and prepared an early dinner. Tonight it was going to be mac n cheese, not because he had any fondness for it, but rather because it was all he had beside eggs. He would usually just eat at the bar. He couldn't help but glance at the card Alex had left behind. He had placed it on the fridge with magnet. He couldn't get over the feeling of how empty the place felt without her, how different everything suddenly now was. He took his gourmet dinner over to the nook but on his way decided to turn on the TV. He needed something to quell the silence that his little apartment was throwing off. It was the news; the talking head would be good company while he ate his meal. It was the usual mundane rubbish they were reporting on, weather, sports and a political analyst breaking down an even more mundane speech by one of the local big wigs running for higher office and so on. Jackson was not really paying any attention; he was only in it for the companionable noise. Toward the end of the bulletin, something did grab at his consciousness. The anchor was detailing a missing person's report. The person in question was female, blonde, 5'4 and approximately 32 years of age. She was last seen five days ago and was reported missing when her office had called her next of kin inquiring as to her whereabouts. At that point, the family had called the police. It seemed rather early, to Jackson, to launch any investigation but this was cleared up by the news anchor when a picture of the victim's car was posted on screen. It was a blue Toyota Tazz parked in a well to-do neighbourhood driveway. It must have been a crime scene photo as it detailed an open driver's door with a lady's handbag still on the passenger seat. It looked like someone was just about to go for a drive before they suddenly vanished. It was obviously the same conclusion the police had come to, hence the manhunt. The screen changed to a tearful relative, Mother of Victim, flashing in the text bar below, holding a picture of her daughter. The camera zoomed in on the face and Jackson nearly choked on a forkful of his mac n cheese. The woman was a perfect likeness of the one he had seen in his dream last night.

Chapter 2 – The Flutes

On the drive home Alex tried to go over everything she had experienced during the last 24 hours. It turned out that ten minutes in the car ride home was not enough time and she was properly exhausted, partly still hangover. It might have been the previous night's drink but since she had left Jackson's apartment, all the anxieties and fears over her missing brother returned in full force. They seemed to have taken a break while listening to Jackson's stories and she was very thankful for that. However now that she was at home and alone, she had to contend with both anxiety and now the guilt. Guilt at forgetting about her brother, even if it was only for a bit. She found herself staring at her door with the key extended towards the lock, but couldn't even remember leaving the taxi and taking the elevator up. She shook herself and muttered something about losing her mind before opening the door and entering apartment. She dropped her keys into a little bowl next to the phone and an assortment of mail atop a small entrance table. Hanging her coat up on the hook behind the door, she made her way to the kitchen and put the kettle on. She felt exhausted and was leaning one hand on the counter below the kettle with the other rubbing the back of her neck. She actually decided on moving into this place because of the kitchen. Unlike most modern places, this kitchen was a separate room, not open to a lounge or dining area. It had a cosy old-school look about it and was tiled in light lime green with unpainted wooden cupboards which had been treated to bring out the natural soft browns. It was a small, narrow room with a fridge taking up one end of it. A wooden counter top, with cupboards above and below which ran the full length to the other end of the room, before ending in a built-in breakfast table that filled a hollow around a window looking out onto the street. Naked, floor to ceiling, shelves covered the other wall of the narrow kitchen allowing a view of an assortment of groceries, spices and other kitchen paraphernalia. The space between shelves and cupboards was only wide enough to fit two people squeezed next to each other, shoulder to shoulder. A small sink and combination oven and stovetop took up a portion of the counter closest to the fridge. She spent a great deal of time reading or looking at pedestrians on the street below from the little comfy nook at the end of the kitchen. That's where she found herself now, drinking her tea and thinking about her brother. Suddenly she remembered her parents and got up to call them from the phone by the door. She spent a few minutes, updating her them on her search and alternatively being updated by them on their search. She put the phone down, nothing had changed. Freddie was still missing and no one knew anything more than they did yesterday.

She returned to the kitchen, finished her tea and took the mug to the sink. With a little sigh she turned the light off and made her way to bed.

The next morning was Sunday and Alex was up early getting ready for a run. While locking up, her neighbour, an elderly woman with a bit of a habit for snooping, caught Alex by her door.

"I noticed you didn't come in on Friday night. I only mentioned it because someone came around looking for you." Francis said. It seemed she permanently had her hair in curlers with a cloth draped tightly over them holding everything in place. Alex put on her best, most accommodating smile.

"Morning Fran. Did this person leave a name or contact number?" Alex said, ignoring Fran's question.

"Nope, he just banged on my door and when I opened up he asked if I knew you and if I knew where you were. I said yes, I did know you but even if I knew where you were, I wouldn't tell a complete stranger. He seemed very upset, well angry, actually. He just glared at me, crumpled this piece of paper and threw it past me and into my house. The man stalked off and said nothing more. Do you know who he could be, I have not seen him around before?' Fran couldn't help but be nosy as she passed Alex the creased (although attempted smoothing-out was obvious) piece of paper. Alex's breath caught in her throat as she noticed the picture of her brother smiling back at her, in her hands. Alex grabbed Fran roughly by the shoulder.

"Are you sure he didn't leave any contact details? Is there anything else you can remember about him?" Fran shoved Alex's hand off her and rubbed one of her shoulders.

"No, I told you everything." she responded. "However, and mind you, I don't do this very often but because of how upset he looked, I ran to the back of my apartment to see him drive off. He was still stalking towards his car, people were giving him a wide berth, and he reached it just as I was opening my window to get a clearer view. It was quite the

46

scene as he sped off tires screeching. I could hear the neighbours gossiping about through the open window."

"Fran!" Alex said. "What car was he driving, what colour was it?"

"Oh that's easy. It was a 68 Ford Mustang, black. I know because my husband, bless his soul, would talk about that car incessantly when he was still alive."

"What did the man look like?" Alex pushed.

"Well he was slim, brown hair and about your height. He was wearing a green jacket over black jeans and safety boots, which thumped loudly when he walked away. Oh yes, he had very bad teeth and the front upper two crossed over each other slightly." Alex was already moving. As soon as she had what she needed from Fran, she was bolting back into her own apartment. She slammed the door in Fran's startled face. She would apologise later, but right now she felt a strange sense of exhilaration that was too hard to ignore. This was the closest she had come to a lead since she started looking for her brother. She almost knocked over the phone in her haste and then stopped with the receiver held up to her ear. What was she doing? A real lead and the first thing she wanted to do was to call Jackson, a man she just met. She realised she didn't even have his number and with an embarrassed chuckled she dropped the receiver into its cradle. What could she do? She quickly made up her mind and left the apartment again. Fran was still standing outside her door, suspiciously close by, as if she had had her ear pressed against it, trying to listen in. Alex apologised for being rude as she ran past her to the elevator. She was going to go to the police.

"Dear, you didn't lock your door!" Fran called out behind her, but Alex hardly noticed.

She was already behind the closing doors of elevator.

The officer behind the desk of the 79th District of the New York City Police Department, stared back exasperatedly at Alex.

"Ma'am, as I told you on your last visit, the case has just been opened. If we hear anything we will call and update you."

Alex, herself exasperated, replied, "I am not looking for an update, I want to provide the investigating officer with information that could be important..." This was going nowhere and in a theatrical huff, she turned on her heel and stalked out, straight into a small balding man with frameless spectacles. For a while it was just spinning arms and grasping fingers, but eventually they both toppled over in a heap.

"Excuse me, really, really sorry." Alex mumbled while she rolled off the man and got up. The man himself stood and straightened his glasses that had miraculously remained perched on his nose.

"Uh, no problem. You OK? Were you helped by someone?" He had a friendly, enquiring voice and the side-parted, thinning grey hair added a touch of maturity to his question.

'No, not really. I just wanted to talk to someone regarding my case but no one seems to want to help.' Alex answered. She hadn't realised how upset she was. Her original excitement had turned into a festering anger since no one would take her seriously.

"My name is John Levi. I am a detective here at the 79th. Is there something I could possibly help you with?" Alex jumped at this sudden turn of good fortune and rapidly brought the detective up to speed on her brother's case. As she talked, he guided her to his desk upstairs and had her sit across from him, while he listened. John seemed much more invested in this than the person she had given a statement to when she initially opened the case. He often would stop and ask some small detail that Alex believed irrelevant but at least proved he was listening to her and seemingly taking her seriously. "OK, OK, that's good for now. Let me go and find out who has been assigned this case and see what I can do. By the way, please don't get too excited at your mystery caller. The way he was acting doesn't sound like someone who is wanting to help. It may be completely unrelated, but a couple of days ago a car matching your mystery man's, was reported stolen. If he shows up at any point, call me straight away as he could be dangerous." The detective passed her his card and guided her back downstairs and out the building. On the pavement outside, Alex looked around and wondered what to do next. The whole day was ahead of her and she was filled with a buzzing energy that she needed to release. She caught a cab back to her building and decided to pick up some more flyers to hand out at any restaurants, shops and businesses she might have missed on her previous expeditions across the neighbourhood. This would later prove to be dull and unrewarding. If she had been playing closer attention, (however), she would have noticed a black 68 Mustang with shaded windows, parked on the corner, a block away from her house. It remained there all day. It had been waiting for her to return and only left once Alex turned all the lights off in her apartment before getting into bed. In the apartment next door, Fran scurried over to the window when she heard screeching tires but only saw the tail lights of a car speeding away into the dark.

A few kilometres away, Jackson was following a hot lead of his own. Seeing the victim of his most recent dream on live TV last night really brought home the urgency of the situation.

This was going down fast and he had to move. He managed to track down the mother of the victim through a police contact he had from previous 'adventures'. It turns out the family he was looking for a was living only 30 minutes away and quick ride on a train and a cab drive later brought him to the front door of his target. While standing like an idiot on the landing in front of the house's white door, he realised that hadn't yet decided how he was going to introduce himself. The door suddenly opened without him having to knock.

"Oh hi, Mr… Gerard! I was just about to knock," Jackson exclaimed.

"May I help you?" the man asked. He was wearing jeans, a sports coat over a collared golf tee and loafers. He looked to be in a hurry. While he was speaking he kept looking over his shoulder back into the house.

"My name is Jackson Brandt and I was hoping to talk to you about you missing daughter."

"I'm very sorry mister, uh, Jackson, but now really isn't a good time. You see, I was just on my way out and we have already told the police everything we know."

He was trying to close the door behind him when a voice from inside called out, "Honey, who's at the door?" Mr Gerard stopped. Closing the door mid-shut, screwed his eyes closed and mumbled something under his breath.

Jackson, spotted an opportunity and quickly shouted out, "Hi Mrs Gerard! My name is Jackson. I sometimes do side jobs for the 79th precinct in Brooklyn and I wanted to see if you wouldn't mind answering a few questions about your daughter?" Mr Gerard scowled at him but didn't say anything.

He looked to be calculating something when he said, "Kelsi, do you mind chatting to this gentleman while I run out to the office? I just want to pick up some additional... stationary," He didn't wait for an answer. He ushered Jackson into the house and then bolted for his car in the driveway.

"I must apologise for my husband. He hasn't been coping well since Linda's disappearance and has been finding all sorts of things to do but be in this house. It's hard for him you understand?" Mrs Gerard flowed into view. She was a slim woman in her sixties.

She had her hair done up in a bun behind her head and was wearing a cream, sleeveless dress with buttons down the front and a shawl draped across her shoulders. Her naked toes poked out from beneath the hem of the dress. When she spoke she smiled, although sadly and gentle wrinkles bunched up in the corners of her eyes. They shook hands. She motioned to the living room. "Could I get you something to drink?" she asked.

"Oh no thank you, I won't hold you up too long. Just a few questions and I'll be out of your hair. I know this isn't an easy time for you... and your husband." Jackson took a seat on a single seater couch and pulled out his notebook. Mrs Gerard took the double seater opposite him. There was an oval coffee table between them with an ashtray resting on a doily. Quite a few dead soldiers filled the bowl and Jackson could smell the lingering scent of cigarette smoke in the air. Looking towards a sound that caught his attention, Jackson recognised the noise from a TV in the family room. It was on the other side of the hall in a room that opened out into kitchen, the two areas separated by an island counter top. The house had a wonderful open plan feel to it, a nice family home.

"So how can I help you? What would you like to know about my Lind?" Mrs Gerard asked.

"Well I wanted to ask you about her friends, where she would hang out... that sort of thing. I am hoping I can link stories from police reports and other people that have been interviewed so far. Like I said, I'm running an independent investigation and I often help the police where they allow." Jackson said. It was a well-rehearsed story he had used on previous occasions when necessary. If needed, he could pull out his police contacts details. They had an agreement where he would provide a reference for the more sceptical folks he came across.

"I see, well, where to start..." Mrs Gerard spoke uninterrupted for twenty minutes or so, all the while Jackson scribbled furiously in his notebook. When Jackson had exhausted his prepared questions he asked if he could see Linda's room. Mrs Gerard obliged and led the way up carpeted stairs. At the top, they turned left and she opened and held open, the first door on the right. Jackson walked straight in. Mrs Gerard poked her head in briefly but with tears in her eyes, moved back out and said, "Take your time in there, if you need anything let me know." She walked back down the stairs, lost in thought. Jackson was very thankful he was left alone because as he was walking up the stairs the pain behind his eyes flared and was intensifying each step he took closer to the room. In fact, he probably didn't need Mrs Gerard to show him Linda's room because he almost passed out the moment she stopped next to it. He could hardly speak and was truly worried he might black out as soon as Mrs Gerard walked away. He pushed on deeper into the room and luckily the pain eased enough for him to focus properly. It was a typical teenager's room, with a desk pushed up against the wall with the door, a shuttered closet on his right and entry to an en-suite bathroom in the far corner. A double set of windows looked out to the cloud spotted sky, with a chaise long below it. A three-quarter bed with a white bedspread took up the left side. The most striking feature of the room were the posters, rock bands mixed and overlaid punk bands that mixed with an assortment boy bands. Linda had varied tastes. The posters covered every visible piece of wall except above her desk. There Jackson found a cork pin-up board with Polaroid photos of her friends, tagged up at random. An old white MacBook was powered up on the desk.

Jackson ignored the laptop and instead focused on the pictures. Most of them included Linda with two other girls in different locations making various hand and finger gestures. Looking out the door, Jackson pocketed a couple of the pictures, ones containing the most people so he could look at them a bit more closely when he got home. Nothing in the room jumped out at him and he was just about to leave when his hip caught the corner of the desk and bumped the top drawer open. He pulled it open all the way and with his hands, ruffled amongst the bits and bobs inside. Right at the back of the drawer, by now his arm was in up to his elbow, the tip of his fingers touched something hard and cold, taped to the underside of the desk inside the drawer. He grabbed at it, ripped the tape and pulled it out to look. It was a small flute of sorts. Basically it was several hollow reeds bound together with glue and a leather strip. The top of the flute sloped down in an arc so there was a high point and a low point.

The bottom of the instrument was flat and even. The police obviously didn't think it was important (maybe they missed it) or else they would have taken it in as evidence. He pocketed the flute as well. When Jackson first started trying to stop the headaches, he felt bad about taking things he thought could help him discover what he needed to do. Now however, with greater experience, it wasn't a problem, and any clue, especially something he thought might help someone down the line was fair game. He left the room and walked downstairs to find Mrs Gerard crying and dabbing at her eyes with a tissue.

"Did you find anything useful?" she asked.

"No, not really, unfortunately. I spotted quite a few rock posters, was Linda a musician, did she play any instruments?" Jackson asked in return.

"Not that I know of. Why? Could it be a clue, could it be something that could help you find Linda?" Mrs Gerard had grabbed his arm with both hands as she pleaded.

"No, not really, just wanted to make sure I leave no stone unturned. But I promise you, should I discover anything, I will be in touch with you straight away. In fact," Jackson pulled out his notebook (carefully so nothing dropped out) and ripped a small piece of paper to write down his phone number, "this I my number. You can call at any time if you think of anything that might help the investigation." Mrs Gerard took the paper, thanked him and led him outside the house. Jackson took a last look back and saw Mrs Gerard in the window, crying as she watched him walk away. He gave her a friendly wave goodbye as he walked to the bus stop two blocks away.

Back home, Jackson sat down at his breakfast nook and pulled out his notebook. He quickly scanned the pictures he had borrowed from Linda Gerard's room. He didn't expect to learn too much from them, but you never knew. The flute, however, was something else entirely. Not just because of its exoticness but mostly because it had been hidden away. Linda obviously thought it important enough to keep and conceal; the question Jackson needed to answer was why? Mulling over it for a while but coming to no real conclusions, he moved over to his couch to retrieve his laptop. If for nothing else, he would at least attempt to learn a bit about this weird looking instrument. He lifted the lid of the laptop and typed 'Flutes' into the Google search bar. He selected 'images' and scanned through the pictures until he found something similar to the one he was holding. When he spotted what he was looking for, he clicked on it and discovered that he was now in possession of a pan flute. This, according to Wikipedia, '*is a musical instrument based on the principle of the closed tube, consisting of multiple pipes of gradually increasing length (and occasionally girth).[1] Multiple varieties of pan flutes have been popular as folk instruments. The pipes are typically made from bamboo, giant cane, or local reeds. Other materials include wood, plastic, metal and ivory'.* With his interest now peaked, he continued on down the page to understand more of its history. Although not in any way helpful but interesting nonetheless, Jackson learned that the pan flute is named after the Greek god Pan, the god of Nature and Shepherds. It is also widely associated with the character Peter Pan, of which the god Pan being the inspiration. With the image of Peter Pan firmly in his mind, Jackson tried to think of where else he had recognised the flute from. Tapping his finger on the edge of the computer he had a sudden flash of inspiration and typed, 'The Pied Piper'. Images came up of man playing the flute while leading children away. The flute the Piper was holding was more of the standard variety so it wasn't the same instrument. However, Jackson felt it was worth exploring a little further and managed to unearth an interesting fact; the pan flute, Peter Pan and the Pied Piper were all theorised to be connected. '*The connection to the Pied Piper may seem stretched until you recognise the theme,*' the article reported. In both of these stories the Pan character (Peter Pan and the Pied Piper) leads children into a magical world. In fact, a third story was highlighted as an example – 'The Lion, the Witch and the Wardrobe,' where one of the main characters was a Mt Tumnus; a strange half man, half goat like creature who plays his pan flute and convinces Lucy to go home with him. Three stories connected by the fact/thread of leading children away, three stories connected by a similar pan flute and most importantly, three stories directly connected or having originated from a single source – the god Pan.

Although very interesting, it wasn't particularly helping him with his investigation. Jackson shook his head, trying to clear it. He went to pour a whiskey, then checked himself. No booze for five years and he still felt like it was almost a normal thing to do. He instead prepared coffee and took it back with him to his laptop. He was unsure as to why he was researching ancient gods and flutes but on the premise that he had nothing else to do and was actually finding it all quite interesting, he pressed n. He typed in Pan, and checked the results. He clicked on the most relevant link and read: '*The most elusive of all the gods is a half-human, half-goat deity known as 'Pan'. A nature god, Pan is usually depicted with the legs of a goat, horns and carrying a pan-pipe. Pan is mostly forgotten in our modern world, a footnote in history, lacking the rich mythology enjoyed by most of the old gods. And yet, Pan is pervasive in the collective unconscious. He pops up in all sorts of unexpected places. The remaining myths of Pan paint him as a sort of happy-go-lucky character, frolicking through the forests having sex with nymphs (tree spirits), singing and dancing. What's more telling is what Pan doesn't do. He doesn't really do anything. Pan doesn't engage in power-struggles. Doesn't fight the other gods. He's not really in charge of anything, and he lives down on Earth, not up on top of Mount Olympus with the other gods. Pan acts more or less like the half-man and half-animal that he is: minding his own business and just doing what he does.* Jackson absorbed everything and continued to take notes in his book. He had been at it for quite a while. The coffee, untouched, had gone cold and he was getting drowsy. He stood up and stretched and went to close the blinds as it was getting dark. Moving back to his laptop, he bookmarked the page he was on and then closed the screen. On his way to bed he glanced at his phone and thought about calling Alex, but with nothing more than mythology to update her on, he wouldn't know be able to tell her why he was calling. Shrugging his shoulders, he got underdressed and climbed into bed.

The next morning Jackson awoke all groggy and confused. He had fleeting images a goat-man playing the flute in a meadow. It was not like any normal dream he had had, and it certainly was not like The Dream, as those tended to be very detailed, and he could always remember everything. This was very different. He remembered the strong emotions associated with it, confusion leading to acceptance then sadness/depression but finally anger, all-consuming anger.

"Teach me right to read up funny things before bedtime," Jackson mumbled as he made his way to the kitchen. Strangely, he did not end up and there but found himself in the entrance hall standing above the phone. "Ah hell, why not?" Jackson said to no one. He might as well call her and get it out of the way, he would not be able to concentrate otherwise. He checked his watch to make sure it was not too early and was pleasantly surprised to see that it was already 09:00. Jackson was normally wide awake by 05:30 every day. He retrieved the card from the fridge and punched in the numbers on the phone.

It did not even finish the first ring when Alex picked up, "Hello... hello?"

Surprised, Jackson responded, "Hi, Alex. It's me, Jackson. Um, everything all right, you sound a bit distressed."

"Oh, thank God, Jackson. I am so happy to hear from you. Something has happened and I am a bit spooked. Do you think we could meet up, say in an hour?" Jackson agreed and they discussed meeting at a Starbucks roughly mid-way between each house. Jackson put down the receiver and immediately dialled the bar where he professed to be feeling ill and said that he would not be able to make it in. Randall huffed and puffed but eventually accepted that Jackson would not be able to work. Forty minutes later, cleanly shaved and dressed, Jackson had ordered two coffees and was seated at a table near the entrance of the Starbucks. Alex arrived shortly after looking a little harried, but she immediately spotted Jackson and headed for him. He pushed a cappuccino in front of her to which nodded her thanks. She grabbed three of the sugar packets he'd brought to the table, plopped them in her cup and stirred and then sipped with her eyes closed. Jackson watched the whole affair/process quietly and waited for her to compose herself.

After a bit, she said, "Well it is good to see you. It was an… usual night."

Jackson shared the sentiment and said, "So, what happened, do you want to fill me in?"

"Sure, sure, just give me a sec." Alex got up and walked around the small, warm coffee shop. She paid extra attention to the passers-by in the pavement outside. Eventually she returned to her seat and leaned in confidentially towards Jackson. "I think someone is messing with me," she said quietly. "Last night after I went to bed, around about 09:15, someone knocked on my door. I got up and looked through the peephole but did not see anyone, so I went straight back to bed, this was around 10:00. I shrugged it off thinking it was those kinds from 3C playing a practical joke. Then it happened again at 11:00, then 12:00, then 01:00 and continued until 03:00. I am sure you can imagine, but I was freaking out by now. That last door-knock really got to me and in a panic and not knowing what else to do, I yanked the door open and screamed, 'Leave me alone!' at the top of my voice. There was no one there. I looked up and down the hall, but nothing. As I was closing the door, I saw this on the floor," she pushed a small package across the table towards Jackson. He nearly spat out his coffee. With trembling fingers, he reached for the object and slowly picked it up. It was an exact replica of the flute sitting at home next to his laptop. "Are you OK?" Alex asked. "You look like you are about to throw up."

Rather roughly, Jackson stood up and pulled Alex with him. "Come with me, I need to show you something." The abruptness of the action did nothing to make Alex feel any better but without saying anything, she grabbed her bag and followed him out the shop. She stood and watched as Jackson hailed a cab and ushered her in. He gave the driver his home address and they drove off. Not a word was said between the two of them during the short commute. They arrived back at Jackson's apartment (Jackson tried to cover his face as he walked past the bar) and used the back entrance and fire escape stairs to get to his house. Once inside, he pushed her towards the lounge where she dropped onto the sofa. Without a word, he took Alex's flute, put it on the table and then took his own recently procured one, and lined it up next to it. They both stared at the pair of flutes on the table before them.

Nothing was said between the two of them for quite some time while they both stared at the flutes laid out before them. It was undeniable, they were a perfect pair and no way could be a coincidence that they both came across the things, separately, but at about the same time.

"What could this possibly mean?" Alex said quietly, without taking her eyes off the flutes. "I have absolutely no idea Alex. I am completely stumped and extremely concerned."

Jackson said while sitting down. His headache was starting to pick up and he did not want to think of those implications just yet. He popped a couple of Advil into his mouth and chewed thoroughly to allow him some time to think. He always had a bottle of painkillers on him, always. "Well one thing is for certain, it isn't just you and I in this anymore, there is a third party involved now, and perhaps always has been." Jackson finally said after he swallowed the bitter pills.

Now looking properly alarmedAlex asked, "What do you mean? Who else could possibly be part of this? I mean, all I have to go on right now is a missing brother, why would anybody else have an interest in this, apart from some sort of sicko?" Alex asked as her mindraced.

Jackson was silent while he watched her get up and pace to and from across the front of the TV. He had come to his own conclusions about her brother now, but that could merely be because of his previous dark experiences of a similar nature. As far as he knew, Alex had never encountered a situation quite like this before. He waited for her to make up her own mind before saying anything further. Eventually, looking more tired than worried, she flopped down in the single seater next to him. "I don't know, I can't make heads or tails of this." she said.

Jackson turned as faced her, "Alex, do you merely think your brother is just missing, or do you think that some horrible accident occurred that no one knows about? When we first met you told me that you were so scared, that you just knew that something bad had happened. Do you still feel the same way?" Alex turned her head to look at him over her shoulder with big, teary eyes and nodded in agreement. "Then the flutes turn up for me and then for you. I haven't even told you where I found it yet. That's not important right now, but it is certainly not a coincidence." Jackson let that sink in a bit before going on. He really wanted Alex to come to the same conclusions as himself, but he didn't want to force his own thinking on her. He wanted her to figure it out as he thought he had. "The flutes indicate a third party and knowing what you now know of my Dreams and what you experienced last night, I doubt we are dealing with a person of benevolent intent. Lastly, the flutes link you and me that is obvious."

Jackson was just about to continue when Alex interrupted him. "You mean to say that this person has something to do with my brother, that he kidnapped him or… or… murdered him?" Alex said, horrified. Jackson moved over to her and sat on the arm of the chair.

"I am not saying that, but we can't count out anything like that out either. There is something going on that hasn't become clear to me yet, but I am sure this other person doesn't mean any good." Alex said nothing but leaned sideways and rested her head on his chest. Jackson put an arm around her while she covered her face with her hands. She cried quietly while Jackson did his best to console her. He could tell that she agreed with what he had said. After a short while, she gently pushed away from Jackson, stood up, smoothed her clothes, wiped her eyes with a tissue she produced from nowhere and redid her ponytail before sitting back down. Jackson returned to his own seat.

Composed now, Alex looked at Jackson with a resolve he had not previously noted and said, "Ok Jackson, tell me how you found the flute and anything else you think is relevant." Nodding to her, Jackson pulled out his notebook and told her everything that had happened since (and including) the Dream that precipitated the events of today. Alex listened closely and did not say anything until he was finished. After a quick bathroom break, Alex moved into his kitchen and made them both a cup of coffee. Jackson noted the ease with which this was done, how comfortable she seemed in his place. For that matter, Jackson reflected on his own ease at having her there. It was as if they were old friends reminiscing. Alex handed the hot drink over to Jackson who accepted with thanks. "Ok, I think it best I tell you of my own progress and then we can compare notes." Alex settled back in her chair and curled her legs underneath her before telling her own story. Jackson listened and took notes in his book. He would often interrupt her and ask a question before taking note of her answer. Alex noted how similar he was in this regard to Detective Levi. After she had finished her story and Jackson had finished with his questions and notes, they mulled over this new information in comfortable silence. Eventually Alex turned to Jackson and said, "So what do we do now?"

The man with the clunky, heavy, black shoes walked ahead. He enjoyed walking, he enjoyed moving. While you were moving you were always placing yourself in a position to observe something new. While you were sitting still you let the world pass you by, you missed things. If there was anything in the world that the man with the clunky shoes hated, it was missing things, not being a part of things. The man listened as his shoes clunked on the dark tarmac as he walked. It reminded him so much of ages past, half forgotten, partially remembered hooves on pressed dirt and stone. Unlike his near forgotten brethren, this was where the man liked to find himself, in and amongst the frail human world, in amongst the activity of the living. He loved the epic and constant plays of emotion, the individual and slow unravelling of stories, the great unveiling of the larger collective stories. He loved that feeling of being part the Alive. Most of all, he craved and revered his own influence on such events, this was his essence, what defined him, what drove him. This is what forms at the core of the man walking down the road in the dark. He chuckled to himself in the darkness and he remembered things no else ever knew. The great power struggles of the gods, the never-ending quest for power and dominance which, as it always did, would lead to their own downfall. The constant ladder climbing while ignoring the real stuff of importance, the stuff of everything. The man with the clunky shoes knew better, knew why he was he was still around while all the others, who were remembered and revered for the great deeds and accomplishments, were no longer around to enjoy them. He was everything, he was all encompassing for he was what life was; experience, the sentient ability to acknowledge your surroundings and manipulate it, to create your own story. While he did nothing and observed, the other gods waged their battles and quests but in the end, unwittingly, became but mere actors on a stage, a play directed by him, the director, the spectator and the consumer. The man brought out a little flute and whistled a mindless tune as he continued walking, each footstep making a clear 'clunk' as it landed, one after the other. If anybody had happened to be on that same road in the dead of the night they would have noticed nothing more than the rhythmic tapping of footsteps with no clear indication of where they were coming from. Had they possessed the ability to see however, they would notice a man dressed in a large, black overcoat reaching to the mid-point of his shins, black ankle boots under faded black jeans that would seem grey. A non-descript and thoroughly unmemorable face sat beneath a large wide-rimmed, black hat that would have, under normal circumstances, cast a large shadow hiding any possible feature that might have existed. The man would been seen playing an instrument that only he could hear, but one that everyone could feel. It was panic-inducing and forced anyone who sensed it to flee in any direction away from it, with no conscious thought as to why. The man clunked along contentedly. He was of no age as it would be impossible to try and determine, for he had no idea when it was that he suddenly became aware. He had no starting point as a reference. If pressed as to what he thought his age could be, he would answer in the only way that he understood, in the number of experiences he had observed, in the number of emotions he had watched and in turn felt. Putting a number to that would mark it in eons, centuries, thousands upon thousands of years. The man continued walking forward, lost in thought and playing his inaudible, mindless tune. In the beginning, he had enjoyed being part of the great world events, drawing in all the experiential values of the massive collective effort of human beings. The learning of speech, the learning of written speech, the great treks, and the sea voyages of great discovery. Mostly however, the greatest emotion was experienced during the times of great conflict, wars, this is what the man loved above all else. He had played his small, but hugely influential, part in all of the great events. He had whispered into unwitting ears and left clues to follow for some of the great conquerors and leaders of the past. He remembered fondly, Alexander the Great and another (the wonderfully violent Mongol emperor) that between them conquered most of the known world at different stages. He was there for the great world wars, the cold one included (he giggled at this) and played his part in everything. He stopped mid-tune while he remembered the advent of Christianity, the so-called religion that had killed him off, according to the world as it now stood. The same Christianity that had stopped the world from believing in the pantheon of old gods and in some way had managed to kill them all off. This angered the man but in a way that human beings would understand. However, the man was still around, he hadn't moved on like the others. He existed, was nourished by something different to the rest and although believed to not be around anymore, he was strong and as vital as ever. In the human context, he had recently changed his way of existing. He had moved on from the great events and now found massive satisfaction in the manipulation of individuals. To his great surprise, the experience of individuals, gently or forcefully pushed just at the right moment, had the same sort of experiential value as the great collective events. He had many names and cared for none of them. To get along in the modern world he had adopted the name of Robert, or Bob. He liked the imagery of a piece of flotsam bobbing up and down in a river that the name conjured. Always moving, always floating downriver. The man in black walked on, lost in the most recent thought in his current endeavour, remembering and savouring all the moments he had already been involved in, and all the moments yet to come. This particular story still had a way to go, and he was looking very much forward to it. Clunked footsteps faded and echoed into the dark evening.

Chapter 3 – The Breadcrumbs

Alex and Jackson spent the night, once again, in each other's company. Alex was too afraid of being home alone and Jackson agreed that it would be better for her to stay with him until they had a better idea of what was going on, if they were in fact, in any danger. They had gone over each other's stories several times but still had no clue as to what their next step would be.

"Ok, I'm calling it!" Jackson announced. "I am beat and by the looks of it so are you." Alex sighed and agreed reluctantly, unable to keep a huge yawn from escaping. "You take my bed and I will take the couch." There was a mild argument about this but in the end fatigue got the better of Alex and she agreed. Jackson was unloading blankets and pillows from the hallway closet when a sudden thought occurred to him.

"You know Alex, I feel like I know you so well, but thinking on it now, I hardly know you at all. I mean, in the normal way of things, like what you do for work, where do you come from." Alex smiled at how the normal sort of questions (not so important to have considered until now) seem so abnormal right now. She had the spare toothbrush in her mouth, which was now hers all things considered, and had to spit toothpaste into the sink before answering.

"Nothing special. I got an undergraduate degree in journalism from Columbia in the hopes of becoming an investigative journalist. Things didn't quite work out that way, unfortunately, because I realised not long into it that my passions lay elsewhere. My parents didn't think too much of me resigning within the first month of employment at the Herald as it was they who paid my tuition and organised me the job in the first place. My dad is a senior accountant at the paper and apparently he was properly embarrassed by the whole affair. It was quite the family fight at the time and truth be told, I still don't see eye-eye too much with my dad. Anyways, that was about seven years ago. I am now thirty years old andI own a little bookstore in Vanderbilt Avenue, the Tasselled Bookmark. It keeps me busy and financially in the black. I also get to read as much as I want." Alex smiled at the thought. "My friend Susan is looking after the place while I am away and she doesn't expect me back anytime soon. Luckily enough for me, I trust her and am now free to get drunk with strangers and sleep in their houses." Alex was laughing as she slipped under the under thecovers.

"And your brother, what about him?" Jackson asked tentatively. The smiled instantly dropped from her face as reality of the now struck home.

"He is such a darling, I adore him. Freddie was always quiet, preferring to let others make the choices. I think he looked up to me as a sort of bastion of sanity with my parents being as they are. They are quite eccentric and loud, everything Freddie is not. What he is, is very smart. He had just finished school, valedictorian and was going study

68

engineering. On my last call with him, about 15 days ago now, he was telling me that he was waiting to hear back from Stanford and MIT. He had already been accepted at Yale but wasn't that keen. I think his heart was set on MIT. Anyways since his disappearance, my parents have been a combined wreck. My dad works like a maniac and is never home. I think he prefers the order and understandability of the numbers he works with and can't cope with Fred not being around and not knowing where he has got to. I think he believes that any day now Freddie will just turn up as if nothing has happened and things will go back to normal. My mom just cries and is either ringing the police every hour for an update or is actually siting in the police station every day. She is inconsolable but at least she is pretending everything is OK. It's her that I call every now and then." Alex was staring at the ceiling while lying in bed. Jackson still had a blanket and pillow in one arm and was leaning against the bedroom door frame.

"What about you then, how are you handling all of this?" he asked gently.

"I am not quite sure, to be honest. I go between manic panic and manic depression. I am so worried about him that it is hard to breathe. I feel this really strong desire to keep moving, to do something, anything. It's really the not knowing that is killing me. I dread what could be happening right now." By now tears had appeared in her eyes and she was trying her best to keep them from spilling over.

"I can only imagine Alex. I'm so sorry." Jackson told her as he started making a move towards the couch. He stopped and turned back and out of nowhere said, "I will help you wherever or however I can Alex. I want you to know that you can trust me." It was imperative that she understood that, but he didn't understand why.

"I know Jackson. Think I knew that the moment I agreed to that Pina Colada. I also want you to know something. It's easier with you, it's not so scary when you are around. Dealing with this is almost bearable knowing you are here. Thank you Jackson." Alex smiled up at him from his bed.

"Night Alex." Jackson said.

"Night Jackson." Alex replied. Jackson turned the bedroom lights off and went to make his bed on the couch. He lay there for a while trying to sort out the tangle of thoughts in his head. He was still trying when he fell asleep. In the room across the hall, Alex had fallen asleep almost immediately. It was the first time she had allowed herself to relax fully and her body was grateful.

Randal was not happy with Jackson. He was still swearing profusely when Jackson hung up the phone after informing him that he was, once again, not going to be able to come in.

"Is he always like that?" Alex asked.

"Pretty much," Jackson said while pocketing his notebook in a fresh pair of jeans he had dressed in this morning. They had decided to go through to the police station to check if there had been any progress in Freddie's case. First though, they caught a cab to Alex's place where she changed and packed an overnight bag, enough for several evenings. Looking around the place, Jackson could see no evidence of a break-in. He had silently been quite worried that something of this sort might have happened while Alex was with him, so he was inwardly relieved that it hadn't. Bag in hand, they jumped into her car, a white Tesla. Jackson was thinking that she had undersold how well that bookstore of hers was doing judging by the car.

Alex noticed him checking the car out and said, "I might not always see eye-eye with my dad but he still tries to look after me as best he can. I got this as a gift from him last year. In fact, my brother also got one at the same time." She was smiling as she dropped the shifter into gear and drove off silently. At the police station they got exactly what they expected.

There was however, one small change, the investigation had been formally moved over to Detective Levi. This was the first bit of positive news to come from the police so far in Alex's opinion. Alex introduced Jackson as a friend as they sat on the other side of the detective's desk.

"I think I know you Mr Brandt," the policeman said, "I have seen you around. You have come in often and like to chat with what's-his-name? Um, yes, Ben, Ben Hasset." Jackson looked back at the cop and smiled, feeling rather embarrassed.

"Please call me Jackson. Yup. You are 100% correct. I have a good friendship with Ben.

We met in the army," Jackson said. The detective smiled back.

"Likewise. Call me John. Good friends eh, I have heard that you somehow wiggled into several investigations in the past, a bit of a nuisance according to some?" Jackson shrugged his shoulders and said nothing. "It's not an issue as far as I'm concerned. From the bit I have heard, the nuisance you made of yourself provided some good assistance to this department and these days we can use the help we can get," Jackson let out a breath he was aware that he was holding.

"Anyways Alex, no further update from my end. It's actually quite bizarre that we haven't been able to ascertain anything of use at all, I'm embarrassed to say," John said while shaking his tired, grey head.

"Do you know anything about the Linda Gerber case? I saw her on the news the other night," Jackson said off-handily. John stared at the Jackson intently.

"Nuisance indeed Mr Brandt," Jackson smiled apologetically. "Strange that you mention it. We got a call of a disturbance in an old office complex downtown. Reports of someone screaming. Why it's associated with the Gerber case is unknown to me but that what I heard. Strangely enough it came from a conscientious vagrant living across the street," John said shaking his head wonderingly. "However," the detective said coming back to himself, "it's got nothing to do with your case so I shouldn't have even told you that. Please keep it to yourself!" They discussed little bits and pieces for the next 15 minutes but in the end they were still no wiser for the conversation. They shook hands with the detective and left him staring at their back as they walked down the stairs.

"Just a minute. I need to check on something quick, I'll meet you back at reception," Jackson said.

Alex could see he intended to get something without her so she just said, "OK," and continued downstairs without him. Not even ten minutes later Jackson found Alex sitting downstairs leafing through a magazine without any real interest. She looked up as he approached.

"Come," he said, "I managed to find something out that could be interesting." Alex wanted to ask him what he was on about, but only did so once they were back in her car.

"Remember that contact I said I had in the department, the one detective Levi mentioned?"

"Yes, Ben," Alex said.

"Well, he was in today and I managed to get the location of that screaming report that the vagrant mentioned. It's only a few blocks from here. Keen to check it out?" Jackson asked her. Alex was. She punched in the address on car's navigation system and the screen lit up with the route. They arrived there five minutes later but they were not alone. Jackson asked Alex to park a little ways up the block so they could watch the scene from the car. The police were there in full force. Chevron tape blocked all the roads leading up to the abandoned office complex and there must have been about seven marked police vehicles parked around, blue and red lights flashing. Looking up at the building itself, they could see scores of people moving around through the broken windows. Jackson returned his attention to the street below when he noticed people coming out the entrance of the building pushing a gurney toward the flashing ambulance. As he watched, he could see that a body, covered in a white cloth, was strapped down atop the gurney, holding the body in place. There was a short staircase leading from the building entrance and as the gurney hit it, an arm dislodged from the white cloth and flopped out. A sudden, intense pain hit Jackson behind the eyes and he passed out.

He was back in the dream. He was staring at the figure of the woman being assaulted by the puppet man. Knives were flashing and blood was flying. He was, once again, consumed by fear and panic; he tried to fall but of course was stuck, unable to move. As he watched he realised that the scene was playing in reverse. He was amazed he could think as clearly as this through the panic and fear, but he could. Blood wasn't spraying out from the woman's face but rather being drawn towards it. Jackson watched on in sickening fascination as the features of the girl's face came into focus. Suddenly he could see her, he could see Linda Gerber. He tried to scream but couldn't. Even in the Dream he could feel the pain behind his eyes. The macabre scene in front of him stopped reversing and sped up in forward motion. It was all a blur until the final moment, when the puppet freezes all movement and Linda holds out her hand to Jackson with the ring in it. It all starts to fade to black as Jackson once again see's the words, 'vocare ad regnum' highlighted on the ring.

Sitting up suddenly, Jackson took stock of his surroundings and tried to figure out what had just happened and where he was. He was still in the fancy Tesla but it was moving now. The moment he had sat up, the car screeched to halt and he turned over to see a very concerned Alex looking at him with relief and confusion.

Jackson tried to gather his thoughts and softly said, "I'm all right. I'm alright. Just passed out. Where are we, why did we leave?" Jackson asked. Alex had a hard time coming to terms with his strangely calm demeanour.

"What do you mean you are OK? I thought he had an aneurysm or something. I left because I thought you were dying. I shook you and you would not wake up. I was on my way to the hospital for help." Jackson could see how worried Alex was.

He took her hands and said, "I'm fine, really, just had a Dream, or re-had a Dream. That's never happened while awake before but apart from that, I am perfectly OK." Jackson tried to sound as convincing as possible and he hoped she was buying it. He was quite concerned himself. Alex still looked unsure but a lot less panicked. "Do you know this area; is there somewhere we can go to talk?" Jackson asked while letting go of Alex's hands and looking around. Alex checked the map on the car's display screen and located a hotel nearby that held a restaurant and bar. They drove on in silence until they found themselves a booth as far away from the other patrons as possible. Alex ordered a Jameson and Jackson asked for a Cola Tonic. While they waited for their drinks to arrive Alex looked across at Jackson who held up his hand to indicate, 'not now'. The waiter returned, offloaded their drinks and then left them alone.

"Now tell me, what the hell just happened?" Alex whispered intensely.

"That body that we just saw being pulled from that building belongs to the late Linda Gerber," Jackson whispered back.

Alex went green but quickly asked, "How, how do you know?" Jackson took a sip of his drink and told her what had just happened. She took a while to digest the story and had forgotten her drink entirely. Jackson was quite jealous of her as she remembered it. Then watched as she downed it all in one slug. "We need to understand the significance of the *vocare ad regnum* slogan you saw in your dream," she said matter-of-factly. Jackson agreed and said his laptop was in the car, so they could research it quickly now. While he went outside to fetch it, Alex ordered another drink. Jackson noted that she didn't dispute the validity of his Dream at all. In fact, she had taken it all in her stride and was now fully in business mode. Trying to figure the clue as to what next, Jackson found himself admiring her resolve. When he got back to the table, he saw that she was sipping her second drink, a little slower this time.

A few taps of the keyboard later he shared his findings with Alex saying, "*vocare ad regnum* is a Latin phrase meaning *call to fight* or alternatively*, call to kingdom*."

Alex immediately replied, "That's quite a strange phrase. It shouldn't be that hard to trace as a possible motto or something, don't you think?"

"Maybe, let's have a look," Jackson said as he turned his laptop back to himself to continue the search. The next ten minutes of googling didn't provide them with anything solid except for one thing. There was a gym about 40 minutes away that used the same phrase as its motto, however, it was written in English. The name of the establishment was 'Jyms.' It was a family owned local and had been in operation for the last nine years. According to the official blurb on its website, it 'caters for the middle aged, busy individual with minimal time but a strong desire to regain their former physique. Those that hear the call to take back their life, a call to fight.' Jackson found it thoroughly cheesy and Alex agreed. "Well, we don't have too much else to go on, wanna take a drive to go and check it out? Jackson asked."

"Sure thing, but let me finish this first," said Alex holding up her drink. "Jackson, what are we doing? I'm running around the country with you chasing ghosts and dreams. It feels like we are nowhere closer to finding my brother and the whole thing just seems so messy and confusing. I'm scared but I don't understand why and it feels like there is a clock in my head, ticking and counting down to zero. It was only three days ago that I was handing out flyers for a missing person, now I am squatting at the house of someone I just met, effectively leaving my business to a friend. I am chasing up dreams and actual murders and the most solid thing we have is a pair of flutes. What are we doing?" Jackson could understand the frustration, as he was feeling it himself but he had no comforting words to give.

"Alex, it's a lot, I know… perhaps I know better than most. This is my life so I suppose I am more used to it than someone who just recently dropped into the middle of it. I can tell you this though, what seems vague, what seems completely unbelievable, what seems to be leading us in circles, is all just superficial. What counts is a bit deeper inside," Jackson said pointing to his heart. "I have learned to trust, or rather have faith, in what is put in front of me, otherwise why would it have been presented to me? The real thing you need to consider is what you feel, what is your gut telling you? Rationally I agree, this is a wild goose chase but I feel like we are doing the right thing. I strongly feel like we just need to keep moving and following the evidence, no matter how far away from the original goal we seem to be moving. Things don't always happen in straight lines but rest assured, there is always a starting point and definitely an ending point!" Without realising it, Jackson had grabbed hold of and was squeezing Alex's hands. He let go immediately and took an embarrassed sip of his drink. He hadn't spoken that much in one go in… forever.

Alex smiled back at him. "I know you are right; I feel the same. Maybe I just needed to hear it said out loud." She reached across and squeezed his hand in return. "You know, have you ever consider motivational speaking?" she asked cheekily.

Jackson smiled and stood up. "Well, let's follow this yellow brick road to see where it goes," he said. Alex took the last sip of her drink and followed Jackson out of the hotel bar. The drive over to Jym's was surprisingly pleasant. Not a word was said about their little adventure. It was by some unspoken agreement that neither of them brought it up. Instead, they spoke as friends would, taking the time to get to know each better. They traded stories of their lives (at least the happy ones) and laughed together at the funny things remembered and shared. Jackson was almost disappointed when they eventually pulled into an empty spot in front of the gym. The little shopping centre formed a 'U' around a mostly deserted parking lot. There were, however, a few cars parked nearest to the gym. The other stores all looked worse for wear, some empty with newspaper stuck to the windows in a final declaration announcing their end. Jackson waited in front of the car while Alex collected her things.

Jym's positively glowed in comparison to the other stores around it with its posters, decals and motivational quotes plastered all over the floor to roof windows. The luminous colours and the garish, bolded, large-font quotes complimented the techno music you could hear pulsing from the building. Jackson remarked how it would be almost impossible to miss this place if you were looking for it. When he pushed open the door, the music assaulted them, and he winced but, nonetheless held the door open for Alex to enter. They approached the reception where a bored looking, gum-chewing, teenager was filing her nails. The desk was backed by a freestanding wall with three large posters showing trainers proudly displaying their muscles. Looking around the block of a wall, he could see patrons running on treadmills, pulling on cables, pushing weights and chatting in groups around what looked like a little tiki bar mid-way down the room. It was one large room with mirrors on all three walls apart from the one looking out to the street. Immediately on his left was a small staircase leading upstairs. Jackson had never seen such a display of spandex and prime human beef in his life. In fact, the scene before him had a surreal quality about it, almost like a caricature of what someone might imagine a gym to be like. He shook his head and focussed on the receptionist in front of him and who was trying her best to ignore them.

"Excuse me, do you think you could help us?" he said. Without looking away from her nails, she motioned to a stack of papers and folders on the counter before her.

"New membership applications are here," she said. Then pointing to another stack, "upgrades and cancellation forms are over here." She switched the emery board to the other hand and started on those fingers.

"No, we aren't here about the gym. We actually wanted to ask you a couple of questions if you wouldn't mind?" Jackson replied smoothly.

With her interest finally aroused, she looked at them both in turn then said, "What do you want to know?" Jackson was amazed at how she managed to continue chewing, filing, and talking all at the same time, and that the gum hadn't managed to escape her mouth. He reached into his pocket and pulled a picture from the notebook he had on him. It was one of the polaroid's he had borrowed from the Gerber house, one that clearly showed an alive Linda pulling what he still thought of as a peace sign with the fingers of her right hand. He held it up in front of the receptionist's face.

"Is this person a member at the gym, or have you seen her around here at all?" Jackson asked. The teenager leaned forward, squinted at the picture then sat back and shook her head.

"No, I have never seen her here before. Why do you want to know?" Jackson was ready for this and he spewed out one of the many concocted stories he had made up and used many times before. This one, had him as a private investigator helping parents search for a missing child. In fact, it was not too far from the truth. The receptionist did not question his story but asked to have a look at the picture again. "No, I don't recognise her, but let me check with the manager, he has a memory for faces like you wouldn't believe." She leaned over the counter again and looked towards the stairs. "Rob! Robert, please come down here, there's some folks wanna ask you some questions!" she yelled. Jackson winced again at her screeching which had managed to hurt his ears even more than the blaring music. A few moments later, Jackson and Alex heard the sound of heavy, rather amplified footsteps as they echoed down from the stairwell.

"Dammit Janey, how many times have I asked you to use the phone to call me. That scream of yours could wake the dead," he said as he appeared at the bottom of the stairs. Upon seeing Jackson and Alex, he immediately ignored Janey and approached them. "Hi there, apologies for that." He swung his arm vaguely in Janey's direction and continued, "How might I be of assistance?" he said but did not offer to shake hands or introduce himself.

'Robert is it?' The man nodded. Jackson repeated his fabricated story of being a private investigator. To emphasise his sincerity, he produced a fake PI license he had managed to secure a while back. Putting his wallet back into his pocket, Jackson asked, "Have you ever seen this person around, could she possibly be a member of this gym or maybe a friend of a member?" Robert took the picture and seemed to concentrate on it. It was rather difficult to describe how he looked. His features were so ordinary and run-of-the-mill that a person would forget seeing him the moment he was out of sight. He had a rather roundish face with brown hair neatly parted at the side. His build was average but obviously well-toned beneath the green golf shirt and black gym shorts, as you would expect of a gym manager. He was wearing well-worn sneakers with tube socks pulled up evenly on both shins, both white.

"No sir, can't say I have," he replied non-committally. Alex suddenly pushed herself ahead of Jackson and held up one of the flyers with her missing brother in front of Robert's face.

"I know this is weird, but I can't help asking as Janey here mentioned that you have a thing for remembering faces. Do you perhaps recognise this person? Has he ever been here before?" Alex had no idea why she had decided to pull out the flyer then, but she was just acting on a hunch, or perhaps from desperation. There could be no rational explanation as to why Freddie would have come to a gym this far from home. Particularly one as 'colourful' as this.

"Now this face I recognise," said Robert in his bland sort of way. "He is not a member but came in with one. He didn't stay very long, just hung around the juice bar watching people use the machines. In fact, he came back on one other occasion the same week. Must have been about six days ago." Robert pointed to his office upstairs that overlooked the single-room gym below. 'I can see most goings-on from up there.' Alex was shocked into silence; she had grabbed onto Jackson's arm again without realising it.

Jackson spoke up before she had a chance to. "Did you speak to him, did he seem OK to you, and did you notice anything worth remembering? Anything you can tell us might be of help," Jackson finished. If Robert was surprised by the sudden intensity of the questioning, he did not show it.

"No, I can't tell you much more apart from that I saw him here, although I do remember wondering what he was doing. He seemed to be interested in the equipment but never tried anything out. He looked a bit like he was lost, which was why I was surprised he came back the next time." Jackson peppered Robert with a few more questions while Alex stubbornly held on tightly to his arm. She was quite happy to let Jackson take the lead on this as she instinctively knew that he had a good handle on what needed to be asked. Realising they were not going to get too much more from the manager, Jackson thanked both him and the receptionist and led Alex out of the gym and back towards the car.

"Want me to drive?" Jackson asked. Alex handed over the keys and settled into the passenger seat without saying a word. The car started silently and Jackson drove away from the brightly coloured building. From the office upstairs, Robert watched from behind the blinds, as they drove away.

The atmosphere in the car on the way home could not have been any more different from their ride to the gym. It was sombre and thoughtful with not too much being said between the two of them. Both Alex and Jackson had wordlessly agreed to go over this new development once they got home. As they were pulling into an open parking slot across the street from the bar, Alex's cell phone rang. Such was the quiet nature of their drive, they both jumped with fright at the jarring ringtone. It was almost as if they had completely forgotten the outside world while in their little mobile bubble; it was a rude reminder that a world outside of the Tesla still existed. Alex dug in her bag and pulled out a little, black iPhone. She checked the display before answering.

"Hi Mom, is everything OK?" she said. Jackson watched as Alex listened with the phone pressed to her ear. After a few moments, she mumbled something back into the phone and then dropped it in her lap. She brought her hands up and covered her face before breaking into tears. She was shaking all over, wracked with sobs. Alarmed, Jackson put the car into park and was reaching over to her when she suddenly looked up at him smiling. It was in such contrast to the tears that he froze halfway out of his seat while leaning over to her. "He's back! Freddie is home!" Alex burst into tears again. Jackson sat back in his seat and tried to gather his own thoughts.

After a while, when the tears, which had turned into happy giggles, had subsided, Jackson looked at Alex and said, "Well, should we go see him?"

Alex laughed happily again and said, "Lets!"

Chapter 4 – Back Home

Freddie sat on his parent's couch in the lounge. With him on the either side were his mom and dad. Mom continuously hugging him as if afraid to let him go. Across the coffee table was Detective Levi. He had his notebook open on his lap. There was a uniformed police officer standing guard at the entrance to the lounge. Several more were gathered in the kitchen and standing next to marked cars in the driveway. On the other two-seater to his left were his sister and a man he didn't recognise. She was holding hands with him, squished between their legs on the soft seat. Freddie caught his dad not-so-subtly watching the little silent play between his daughter and this stranger and despite everything, had to stifle a laugh. Fred had never been so confused in his life, but he answered all the questions thrown at him since his return. In fact, the more questions he answered, the less confused he became and the clearer the picture of the last few weeks was. Something he wouldn't tell anyone, was that at first, he did not know how he came to be outside his house that evening. It was only later, after the telling of his story that he thought remembered what had happened. While speaking, the mists cleared and he started to become more confident in what he was saying.

He was told he had been gone for sixteen days but to him it didn't feel like that. All those days ago, he explained, he had been sitting in his room reading when he received a text from a friend asking if he was keen on going for a ride to the beach. There was a girl his friend was keen on meeting. Fred had agreed and went downstairs to wait. His parents weren't home at the time and he saw no reason to inform anyone, besides, he thought he would be home before dark. So, he went with his friend to meet this girl at the beach. It turned out to be a party, which lasted late into the night, and no, he didn't know why he didn't tell anyone, it hadn't crossed his mind. At this, both his parents and his sister frowned as this was not at all like Freddie. The story continued with a mad idea to move the party to a friends' yacht at the marina. Well his friend's dad's yacht. The next day, Freddie woke up on the boat with Miles, his friend, fast asleep next to him on the deck. There were several other boys and girls spread out on the deck with them, all soundly asleep. Fred said that he wasn't a regular drinker and he remembered feeling sick to his stomach as he looked around. They were out on the ocean, land not in sight. Fred said he couldn't remember how or why they were where they were. He had also lost his phone. All together there were eleven people on the yacht. Luckily, the boy whose father owned the yacht, knew how to pilot it and swiftly made their way back home. It took the majority of that day to do so and with no means to get home that late, stayed over with Miles at the boy, Phillip's house. At this point in the story, Detective Levi asked why he hadn't alerted his parent as to his whereabouts, but Freddie said that he once again couldn't explain why. Frowns were shared by all listeners. Freddie continued his story saying that one thing led to another and that he agreed to go and watch a band up state with Philip and his friends. Miles left to go home. He spent the next few days partying and following that band across the country with Philip, as they had been invited to join them on their tour bus. All of this, not once thinking to call home. Eventually the tour bus dropped him off at the seven eleven a couple of blocks away after which he walked home. The story had been told without elaboration but with true sincerity. Freddie truly believed that his is what happened despite the glaring holes and inconsistencies. Apart from his parents, who were just happy to have him home, all other listeners shared looks of concern. They could all sense that something, everything about this wasn't right. Freddie noted this but was just glad the holes in his memory were starting to fill up. He did not once think that what he had just said was highly unlikely, even bordering on absurd. The alternative for him was just too frightening. After a while, his parents ushered the cops outside while his sister remained seated in the lounge.

After many hugs and kisses from his family, Freddie went upstairs to his room. He was exhausted and desperately wanted to go to sleep to clear the fuzziness from his head. Upstairs now, he looked outside to the street below and saw the cops chatting with Alex's new friend among the flashing lights of the patrol cars. He didn't feel like watching more, it was dark in the room and he was so weary. He felt heavy so he moved over to his bed and collapsed, asleep before his head hit the pillow.

"Does this make any sense to you?" Jackson asked Detective Levi once they were outside. Everything about the story Freddie had told him just didn't add up. Also, from everything Alex had told him about Freddie, it just wasn't in the kid's nature to behave the way he did.

"Not in the least," Detective Levi replied. "It almost felt like he was remembering lines that someone had fed him, but what really weirded me out was that he seemed to believe it all. Let me tell you Jackson, I have made a career out of watching people lie while trying to cover their tracks, but that kid was not lying, at least he believed he wasn't lying!" Detective Levi said perplexed.

"So, what are you going to do now, what's the next step?" Jackson asked while rubbing his temples with his thumbs. The flashing lights were starting to give him a headache.

"Nothing at all," the detective said shrugging. "This case revolved around a missing person that is no longer missing and nothing in his story constitutes involving the law in any further way."

"Apart from fabricating the whole story!" Jackson responded more sternly than he intended to. Why was this whole thing bothering him so much?

"That maybe be so, but that would be for him and his family to address. It's got nothing to do with the police any longer." Detective Levi responded calmly, while holding out his hand. Jackson reached out and shook it.

"Thanks John. It has been a strange day," Jackson said smiling.

"We can't solve them all Jackson, let's just be content that the boy is back safely with his family. Just between you and me though, I think I am going to check how Fred's story checks out with…" he consulted a notebook very similar to the one that Jackson was carrying, "Phillip and Miles." Jackson thanked him again and watched as he and the other cops drove away, the flashing lights now turned off. As he was turning around to head back towards the house, he spotted Alex coming down the front steps towards him with her hands in the pocket of her jeans. She had a broad, rather shy smile on her face. Seeing her like that, without all the worry of the past few days, brought a smile to his own face, despite all his own misgivings about the whole situation.

"So, we solved the case?" she asked.

"It would seem so," Jackson responded as he held his arms apart, inviting her in for a hug.

Alex accepted eagerly. Jackson wasn't sure when they started behaving like a couple, but it seemed completely natural and comfortable. They stood and embraced in the driveway for a few moments saying nothing.

Looking up at him with arms maintaining their tightly wrapped position around him, she asked, "I know that I should want be here, celebrating with my family, but if it's OK with you, I would like to stay the night, above the bar?" Jackson looked down and saw how exposed she had suddenly made herself, how small and scared she looked while waiting for him to respond. He leaned in and kissed her.

"Nothing would make me happier." They walked hand in hand back to the house to wish her parents goodbye. The rest of that night was the most exhilarating, nervous, and wonderful experience of Jackson's life. Later, lying in bed with Alex with her arm draped across his chest, her one leg over his, Jackson listened to her slow, regular, deep breathing. For the first time in his life he felt truly happy, content – it was a novel experience. Since he had kissed her for the first time, he hadn't given any thought to his previous anxiety from the day's events, he just wanted this night to last forever.

Everything seemed perfect, except for the nagging, hardly there, pain behind his eyes. Jackson took a deep breath himself, looked to the ceiling and gave thanks to anyone who would care to be listening, and fell asleep.

It was too dark to see anything. He didn't know where he was but he was terrified, completely alone in the darkness, listening to his own breathing, waiting for something to happen. The panic engulfing him was overwhelming and his breathing quickened along with his heart rate. Jackson recognised the Dream and started to focus. He put all the fear and panic in a small box at the back of his mind. Without realising he was practicing a learned habit, he partitioned his emotions and everything that made him what he was, from the rest of himself. He made himself hollow, like a puppet being pulled in the direction he needed to be. All the fear, panic was acknowledged, but not entertained. Jackson had become an observer; the Dream was showing something he needed to see. Something he needed to see to help people. In the Dream, Jackson was aware of what he had done with his mind but he was even more aware that if he focused on it, that place where he partitioned everything, would break down the walls he built around it and flood him with unrestrained terror. With a mental push, Jackson placed the partitioned box into his mental peripheral vision, so that without focusing on it, could still keep track of it. The darkness was suddenly lit up from an unknown source, and in the circle of light, he stood alone and waited. The light circle slowly expanded around him and his vision revolved, as if he was standing on a turntable, to show him where he was. It was a clearing in the woods, the trees pressed so tightly together as to offer no way through. Besides not being able to move, Jackson knew the scene before him offered no escape. A bonfire suddenly appeared before him with several older teenage boys and girls lounging around it holding beer cans and marshmallows on sticks. All their features were clear in his vision but they were still as statues. Jackson looked around and noticed the small details always so explicitly clear in the Dream. He saw the unmoving smoke amongst the individual pine needles of the overhanging trees. The silent, still, beautiful sparks from the bonfire scattered randomly above the fire. The terror and panic suddenly pushed at the walls of his box. Acknowledging it, but not losing himself it, Jackson sensed to horror to come. It happened suddenly as it always did. People began moving, talking, drinking and roasting their marshmallows. Then they were still again. To the left the air seemed to become thicker, radiating out in a circle. The trees and the fire leaned away from it but none of the kids saw it. Jackson knew it would do no good but he tried to scream at them to look, to run, and to do something. The sense of wrongness and evil was palpable and Jackson didn't want to have a look at whatever it was. The evil thick air he was watching suddenly collapsed, like a popped balloon, and a man was in its place. He was slim, wearing khaki shorts above a pair of expensive hiking boots. A red and black, long-sleeved shirt was collared all the way up to his chin. As he had become accustomed to, the face was a blank white orb below a woollen beanie with tassels that hung over where the ears would have normally been. The fear-box was starting to break its walls. A tiny trickle of the emotion it contained escaped and Jackson screamed. He screamed at nothing at first and then at the kids. He screamed for them to run, to just look up and see what was coming. With *a monumental effort, Jackson forced the fear back into the box and mentally strengthened it. Then pushed it back to that place in his peripheral mental vision. Panting with effort, Jackson returned to the scene before him.*

Everything suddenly sped up. A pair of machetes appeared in the mannequin man hands and then he was amongst the still unmoving teenagers. At once there was chaotic movement as everything jumped into motion. The mannequin man was swing his weapons without any apparent direction. He hit skin, he hit bone. Blood splattered on Jackson's face and he had to wipe it away in order to see what was happening. A dislodged arm was spinning towards the fire like a macabre comet with a pulsing red tail. In a matter of moments there were five still, bloodied and dismembered bodies lying in a random mess, with blood expanding around them. The puddles were all joining to form a pool linking all the bodies. The screams were still echoing in Jackson's ears when his vision shifted back to the mannequin man. He was chasing the last remaining survivor who was running as though hounds of hell were nipping as her heels. As he watched, the mannequin man leaped onto the back of the girl. With fascinated horror and impotence, Jackson watched as the mannequin man threw one of the machetes away and brought the last remaining one around toward the girl's neck. He was now straddling the teenage girl's back. With his left hand he pulled her hair back to expose the soft stretched skin of her throat and slowly drew a red, wet line with the thin blade across that sensitive patch below her jaw. With a nearly decapitated head in his hand, the mannequin man slowly turned his head and looked at straight Jackson. Jackson felt his mental box started to break apart. The mannequin man was still looking at him when the box burst and unadulterated fear and terror assailed him in a deluge. The last thought that went through Jackson's head before the darkness took him, was that the mannequin man was smiling, although he had no mouth.

"Jackson! Jackson wake up! Jackson!" His eyes opened suddenly. It took a moment for him to understand where he was and what was going on. When his heart rate calmed and his breathing evened, he turned his head and saw the blurry face of Alex looking down at him. He sat up in the bed and wiped tears from his eyes, his hands were still shaking. He threw back the covers and stood up to open the window. The fresh air on his naked skin was immediately soothing.

With his eyes closed and his back towards her he asked, "Alex, please would you pass me my notebook, it should be in the bedside table there on your side?" Alex leaned over and after a bit of rummaging, tapped his back with the book. Jackson turned around and took it, trying his best to smile in thanks. He suddenly became aware of his nakedness at the same time as Alex. Before they both could become embarrassed, Alex grabbed him in a fierce hug.

"Last night was so... perfect! But when you started screaming this morning I was so scared, I didn't know what to do. You wouldn't wake up!" Alex cried against his chest. Jackson stroked and smoothed the hair on the back of her head while mumbling something he hoped was soothing. He was quite touched by her worry for him.

"I'm quite OK now, thank you. Just so you know, last night was the best thing that has ever happened to me to me!' Alex leaned back from him to look him in the eye. When she was certain he was being serious, she smiled and stretched up to kiss him.

"Ok, let talk about what just happened," Alex said as she pushed away from him. She scrounged awhile in her over-night and pulled out a large white t-shirt that she dropped over head. It had a Columbia College logo printed on the top left.

"Ok, let me get some coffee brewing and I will tell you about it as I take my notes," Jackson replied. Later, with a steaming mug in front of both of them while sitting at the breakfast nook in the kitchen, Jackson told her of the Dream and took down all the important bits in his notebook. Once done, he put the cheap pen on the most recent page and closed the book over it before slipping the attached elastic band over the cover to hold it closed.

Looking a little green, Alex asked, "Is this how it has always been? Have you lived you whole life like this?"

The question got Jackson thinking and he took a while to answer her. "I told you of my first Dream I remember and since then the have been many more. The older I got, the more violent the Dreams became. Perhaps it was evolving with me as my view of the world changed, as I matured. It went from small animals being hurt, to bullying incidents, to assault, to murder and so on. I suppose the Dream took whatever I thought the most awful at that age and focused on events in line with that. I remember the first actual murder I 'witnessed'. It was just before I had enrolled in the army. I dreamt of a mugging that went badly wrong and the victim had been killed. When I woke up, I didn't have too many clues to follow up on and in short order the headaches started. It must have like three of four days after the dream that I was parking someone's SUV – I was a working as a valet then –

in the underground parking of the Hilton. I clearly remember the sudden intense burst of pain behind my eyes as I was driving down the ramp. I must have closed my eyes for a split second but it was enough. I bumped something in front of me hard enough to deploy the airbag. I hit the brakes and the car skidded to stop. My eyes were watering and my nose was bleeding from the impact of the airbag but it was nothing compared to the pain behind my eyes from the Dream. Anyways, I got out of the car and walked over to the bundle of clothing lying a little distance away from where I had hit it. The car behind me had its bumper caved in just on the left and the windscreen was a mass of shattered glass. On closer inspection, I realised I had hit a person. He was wearing a dark trench coat that had covered him as he fell, which I why I didn't recognise him as a human being a first. I clearly remember my panic.

The man was obviously dead and I was in a full panic. I was only eighteen and this was probably the most traumatic (at least physically) thing I had ever experienced. I tried to turn him over to check if I could help and as I did, the trench coat parted to reveal the man's chest. His shiny purple shirt was unbuttoned almost all the way down to his belly button. He obviously worked out and was a muscular a man, but that not what was important. What I immediately noticed was the tattoo of an eagle with its wings spread covering the entirety of his upper body. You see, it was one of the men who had mugged the person in my Dream. It was like a switch went off in my head. One moment I was battling to see because of the pain behind my eyes and the next it was gone. The panic and remorse I had felt and killing someone, even if it was unintentional, disappeared. I had served the Dream's purpose and I like to think I had saved a potential mugging victim, although I would never be able to find that out." Jackson was quite breathless after telling all this.

"So what happened to you? Were you charged with anything; did you have to go to jail?" Alex asked.

"No, it didn't quite pan out like that. After they had secured the scene, someone took me to the local PD where they questioned me about the events. While they were doing that they were able to review the CCTV footage that was installed in the underground parking. It turns out he had not been paying attention to where he was walking and had stumbled right into the path of the vehicle I was driving. It was quite clear that there was nothing I could have done. Also, the post mortem later revealed the man was quite drunk, but what he was doing in the parking lot is still a mystery. Interestingly though, it turns out that the speed I was driving at should have done nothing more than bump him off his feet. He tripped at exactly the right moment so that his knees connected with the lower bumper and flipped him. His head connected with the windscreen of the car and cracked his neck so perfectly it couldn't have been done if planned. Anyways, I decided I didn't want to work driving cars anymore. I enlisted not even a week later." Jackson concluded.

After a moment of contemplation Alex asked, "So did the Dream happen while you were in service?"

Jackson could feel his mood darkening at the subject and before he fell back into those his memories he responded, "Yes, but that's not something I really want to talk about right now." Alex immediately noticed the change in Jackson and didn't continue that line of questioning. She rather got up and refilled both their coffee mugs.

"So about last night, did the dream give you anything to look into, to follow up on?" Alex asked.

"Not much unfortunately. All I can remember is a tasselled beanie on the murderer but that's all." Jackson took a sip of coffee as he wrote another point he wanted to remember into the notebook. Something about what he said had struck a nerve in Alex, something about it really worried her but she couldn't put her finger on it. It had the effect of ruining the atmosphere in the little kitchen for her. She got up from the table and sat in Jackson's lap, forcing him to stop writing.

"Ok mister. I am going to clean up and go home to check on my brother. Then I think it would be a good idea to pop into my bookstore to see that it hasn't burned down. What are your plans for the day, can we meet up later for dinner?" Jackson had noticed the sudden change in Alex's mood but didn't question it. It would play out in time.

"Well, if I still have a job, I will have a shift from eleven to eight. Want to meet me at the bar around then?" Jackson asked. Alex agreed, kissed him and moved off to the bathroom.

Jackson returned to his notes and tried to draw the picture of a beanie he had seen in his Dream.

Alex grabbed the door handle and tried to push against the door with her shoulder to open it. Her parents never kept it locked and although it might seem rude since she didn't live there anymore, she would usually just enter without announcing herself. This time however, the door didn't budge and she was still rubbing her shoulder when her mom eventually opened for her.

"Sorry Al, Freddie wanted it locked, and bolted," Alex's mom said. She looked haggard.

There were dark rings under her eyes and her hair was a mess of loose blonde stands hurriedly tucked behind her ears. It was already 10:30 and she was still in her bathrobe.

"Is everything alright, Mom?" Alex asked with concern as she closed the door behind her. "Oh, oh, lock it quickly please!" her mom said while shooting a worried glace up the stairs. Alex turned around to lock the door.

"What's going on, Mom?" Alex was getting very worried.

"It's your brother. He didn't sleep at all last night. He was having terrible nightmares, kept us up all night. Do you want some coffee?" she asked. Alex declined and started heading up the stairs. "He won't talk to you Alex; he hasn't said a word to us since you left last night." Alex was terrified at the sound of wearied defeat from her mom's voice that followed her upstairs. Outside Freddie's room, Alex paused and knocked. There was no answer so she softly pushed open the door and went in. The room was a mess. The desk chair was turned over and the remains of breakfast had spilled out across the table. The duvet from the bed was on the floor. Freddie was lying with his back to her in the fetal position and was viciously hugging a pillow. He was slowing rocking on his shoulder, head pointed towards the closed window. He was wearing only his boxer shorts. The air was stale and laced with sweat so Alex made her away around the bed to open the window.

She had put her hands on the edge of the window frame and was just about to pull up when Freddie suddenly screamed, "Don't! Don't open that, please, please just don't!" Alex almost jumped right out of her skin; she had thought Freddie was asleep.

"Hey Fred, of course, but don't you want some fresh air in here? Your room is starting to smell like your socks." Alex smiled as she spoke while sitting down on the edge of the bed, close enough to lay a hand on Fred's brow. He was feverish and hot to the touch; a fine sheen of sweat covered his naked upper body. If Freddie heard the mild jab he took no notice of it, he just kept slowing rocking on his side, staring wide eyed out of the window. Alex picked up a towel that was lying on the bedside table and started wiping the sweat from her brother face. "Rough night, Fred?" She asked. He didn't answer, just kept rocking. "Mom tells me you want the doors locked? What's that about, why are you scared, who are you scared of?"

Alex asked. Still no response. She tried several other questions, all with the same result. Frightened, Alex tried another approach and started telling Freddie of Jackson. She spoke of how they met, what they had been up to while searching for him, and how happy she was.

She had been taking for several minutes before she realised that she had started telling Fred of Jackson's dreams, of how he was forced into some terrible situations because of them.

While she was talking Freddie became still and had stopped his unblinking stare out the window. He was looking straight at her. Alex looked down and caught herself with a gasp. The fear radiating from her brother's eyes was heart-breaking and frightening. It was scary how similar it was to what she had seen that morning when she woke Jackson up.

Swallowing a wail, she leaned down and hugged her brother as hard as she could.

She was still holding him when he spoke, "Nightmares Al, they were terrible, can't sleep."

"What did you dream about Fred, tell me, maybe I can help?" Alex asked while leaning back and holding his shoulder.

"I don't know, I can never remember the details but I do remember how they make me feel. I am so scared Alex and so confused. The story I told everyone last night has me all tied in knots. I can close my eyes and I can clearly see and remember everything I said I did, I know it happened but I… I can't explain it." He was shaking his head from side to side on the pillow. "I can remember it happening but I can't *feel* that it happened. Like I'm watching a movie remembering the scenes from an actor's point of view." Tears were streaking down his face as he talked. Alex wiped them away and hugged him again. She was crying along with him. She had never felt so helpless in all her life. After a while, Freddie's sobbed lessened and he started to fall asleep.

"Freddie, why did you want the doors locked, what's that about?" Alex looked down but it seemed as if had fallen deeply asleep. She retrieved the duvet and tucked it around him.

She righted the tipped-over chair and cleaned up the breakfast mess.

She was closing the door behind her when Fred softly spoke as if from far away, half in and half out of dream, "The door… it's not to keep anyone out, it's to keep me in." Alex scrunched her face in a grimace that Jackson would have recognised.

"What do mean Fred, why would you want to lock yourself in?" Alex asked, but Fred was already long gone into a deep and exhausted sleep. Alex backed out of the room and closed the door behind her.

Downstairs she found her mother asleep on her arms at the kitchen table in front of a cup of coffee. As she had done upstairs, Alex quietly cleaned and tidied up as best she could before waking her mom.

"Mom, Mom?" Alex said as she shook her mother gently.

"Ah Alex. Goodness me I was more tired than I thought," she said as she came fully awake. "Did you have any luck with your brother? I am so concerned, maybe I should take him to the doctor?" she mused to herself. Alex found herself reluctant to tell her mother about her conversation with her brother. For some reason she couldn't quite yet understand, she was scared more now than before she was when her brother missing.

"I'm sure he'll be fine. He's sleeping now, maybe you should get into bed yourself." Alex said smiling at her.

"Really, he's asleep? Ah that's good news." her mother sighed with exhaustion.

"I am going to pop into the bookstore to see how things are going. Please call me if you need anything or if Freddie says anything more." Her mother said she would as they hugged and Alex left the house. The happiness and excitement she had woken up with after her night with Jackson was slowly fading away and a sense of dread was creeping in. There was too much unanswered and there was something she had missed in all of this. Something Jackson had said in the morning that was lying in her mind like a fisherman's lure. It was right there but too slippery to catch. She kept trying to grab at the elusive lure all during the drive to work but to no avail. Putting that nagging, unremembered thought away, she parked her car in a little, dedicated slot in front her of her store and went in search of some normality. Once inside the store the million unattended things that were required to keep it running, beckoned and she found that normality. At least for the next few hours, life went back to how it had been before. She managed to push thoughts of dreams, murders and her brother away as she focused on the tasks at hand. Jackson, however, still remained in the front of mind through all of this. Susan looked over her shoulder at her friend and wondered why she was smiling.

Despite the ache behind these eyes, Jackson was enjoying himself. He was in an uncharacteristically good mood which hadn't gone unnoticed by his regulars, and by Shelley. She was sharing his shift for the day.

"I don't know what's got into you Jackson but I like it," she said while handing Bob another beer.

"Hear, hear!" Bob said smiling and saluting Jackson with his new drink. Jackson waved them off with his cloth that usually lived on his shoulder while he worked. Mentally though, he made an effort to keep his mouth from curling up in the corners. It didn't last long. His mood had effected a rather happy atmosphere. Jackson was looking forward to seeing Alex later and was wondering where he could take her for dinner when Bob called him over. This was unusual in itself as he would normally just wave an empty bottle in Jackson's direction when he wanted a refill.

"What can I do you for Bob?" Jackson asked as he stopped in front of him. Bob was holding a flyer in his hands and motioned Jackson closer to him. Leaning up from his chair Bob flapped the flyer down on the counter but left his finger pointing at the picture of the missing boy.

"I saw him not so long ago, maybe about four days past' he said.

Jackson trying his best to hide his shock asked, 'Where Bob, where did you see him? The boy has since been found but I would be interested to know regardless."

"It was outside the rent a car place, you know, near the bus station? I was doing a part time handing out business cards. I remember it clearly." Jackson highly doubted this as Bob had been in the bar nearly every day at different levels of inebriation, "The kid had the same specs and everything. It was strange because he stood holding the card awhile before speaking, like he was asleep on his feet. He asked where this gym was I and told him the address was printed right there, on the card. I'm glad he was there because the bus station was rather empty and I was not sure I was going to be able to get rid of the all cards I had been paid to pass around. I didn't manage to hand out all the cards in the end, a few of 'em found their way down into gutters, so I got paid anyways." Bob finished his story with a wink and waved the empty bottle to Jackson who quickly replaced it with a fresh one.

"When exactly was this?' Jackson asked taking notes. He hadn't even realise he had the notebook in his hands.

"Like I said, about four days ago," Bob replied. Jackson didn't need to check his notes to know that either Freddie or Bob was lying, the two stories didn't have matching timelines.

A thought suddenly occurred to him and he asked Bob, "That rent a car place, why did they ask you to hand out cards for them?"

"Oh no it wasn't them; it was someone else. Didn't catch his name but the cards were for a gym called Jyms. Hee-hee, go figure." Bob was still laughing as he took another sip of his beer.

"This man who paid you to hand out the cards, anything you can tell me about him?" Jackson asked.

"Nope! I's sitting on the bench on the side of the road and the next moment he was there, asking me to work for him. He paid me a fifty and when the cards were finished I returned to the bench. The man was already waiting there with my other fifty." Bob shook his head and sipped from his bottle. "Easiest money I ever made!" He finished with a slap of his hand on the counter in front of him and laughed loudly. Jackson retreated to his waiting spot behind the bar to think. He opened the notebook and wrote; Jackson then Dream then Linda Gerber, circled each of them and linked them together with a line. Then he checked his earlier notes and wrote; vocare ad regnum then ring, circled this together and linked it to the other two circles. Next he wrote Alex then Freddie then business card then Jym. He circled each of them as well and linked Freddie and Jym through the card. Lastly he wrote pan flute and boxed it with solid border. The flute connected with Alex and through her connected to Freddie. The flute also connected with Linda and himself through the Dream. He was tapping his pen against his notebook thinking this all through when he felt eyes on him. He looked up and was alarmed to see the very lucid, seemingly calculating eyes of Bob watching with a hint of smile on his face. When Jackson met his eyes, Bob held his gaze for a moment before losing the smile and waving the empty bottle at him. The whole thing was so unusual and out of character for Bob that it made Jackson's hackles rise. He shook himself as if from a weird dream. Then he went over and fetched Bob another beer.

Alex came into the bar about ten minutes after eight. She saw Jackson talking to someone at the taps so made her way over to him. He looked so comfortable behind there, so at ease talking and pouring drinks. So at odds to the screaming man she had woken up next to that morning. Jackson saw her coming and held up a hand indicating he would be with her in five minutes. Shortly, she found a double whiskey on the rocks pushed in front of her and the smiling face of Jackson hovering just over it.

"Now I know that you like Jameson's but this is next level," his eyes looked down at her drink. "Let me know what you think. I am just going to chat with Shelley before packing up. Enjoy!" Jackson left and disappeared through arch out of site from the patrons.

"Are you the person that's got our boy Jackson in such high spirits today?" Shelley said as she slid along the bar to sit next to Alex. "Shelley," she said holding her hand out smiling. Alex took her hand in her own.

"I can't claim to be the one to have done that but I am his friend. We are going out for dinner later," Alex replied in a friendly tone.

"Well it has to be you. You are the only friend of Jackson I have ever seen," Shelley laughed. Alex joined her, Shelley had a really easy-going manner and she liked her straight away.

"You know, I think Jackson went off looking for you," Alex nodded her head towards the archway behind the door.

"I know," she said smiling cheekily. "I saw you come in earlier and noticed Jackson's face nearly split in two from the size of his smile. So I jumped the bar and came to investigate before he caught me and tried to hide you away." Alex laughed at this as she saw Jackson return from wherever he had been.

"Oh, so I see you have met Shelley. Don't get caught up in that friendly smiley shit of hers. It's a ploy to lure you in so she can steal all your shift!" Jackson joked. Shelley punched him playfully on the shoulder. "Ok, so we're off Shell. Let me know if you need anything?" Jackson said in goodbye. While Alex was getting up, Shelley grabbed her, forcing her to stop what she was doing and look up at her.

"I hope I see you around again. You are really good for him... he needs it." Shelley said this with such earnest sincerity it left Alex a little stunned not knowing what to say. "Have fun you two. Shell will just stay here and work the rest of the night on her own while you gallivant," Shelley smiled and moved away. Alex took one last look at her talking to a large man waving an empty beer bottle at her then she left the bar and walked to her car with Jackson.

There was a small café that had a few tables placed on the sidewalk of a quiet street not far from the bar they had just left. The Tesla had them there in no time and once the waiter had taken their drinks order, Jackson and Alex fell into an easy conversation about their respective days. The air was warm but not uncomfortable. There were no clouds in the sky and if you looked behind the small umbrella over their table, you could actually see a few stars shining down on them. Little string LED lights were looped and strung up between all the tables to make the café feel like they were sitting in Paris or some foreign, exotic location. They were holding hands across the table.

"So Freddie is a mess and has the whole household worried," Alex said before taking a sip from her glass of the bottle of red standing to attention between them. Jackson had an untouched diet coke. She went on and explained what happened at her parents' house.

"He said the door must be locked not to keep others out but to keep him in?" Jackson asked and Alex nodded her response. "Do you have any idea why he said that?" Jackson probed.

"Not a clue, but he is frightened Jackson. I have only ever seen one other that scared before… and that was this morning after you woke up from your nightmare." Jackson looked at her worried face and thought for a bit. Why should he be scared? Why didn't he want to be let out? Jackson was so deep in thought he didn't hear Alex speaking to him.

"Huh, what? Sorry Alex, I was in another world." he said as Alex repeated her question. "Have you thought anymore about the Linda Gerard murder, do you think they have identified the body yet?"

"No not really, it was very busy at the bar today. I think by now they would have identified her and informed the family. We will probably see something on the news about it tomorrow," Jackson said. It reminded him of the police department and particularly of Detective Levi. "Maybe I will pop in at the PD tomorrow morning and check in with that detective… also with Ben if he is around." They enjoyed the rest of their dinner in happy discussion of things more normal.

The night had an ethereal quality to it, like the evening before Christmas for a child. Jackson and Alex were in no rush to go anywhere else but to remain in each other's company.

Eventually Jackson noticed the time and the grumpy waiter leaning at the entrance to the restaurant waiting on only them. The restaurant had emptied while they had been talking. Jackson called the waiter over and paid the bill. Alex said she needed to head to her apartment. Jackson asked if she wanted to stay over again but she politely declined. She wanted to be at work early and her apartment was closer. Rather sadly Jackson agreed and said he would walk back to his place. She kissed Jackson long and hard before jumping into her car and driving away leaving Jackson standing behind watching. When the car rounded the corner, Jackson crossed the road and started walking home. It was about a fifteen-minute walk, plenty of time to work things through is his head. Why the flutes, why those two random instruments? More importantly, why did the flute turn up at Alex's door? He understood the flute as a piece of evidence in the Linda Gerard case but Alex had nothing to do with that, why did she have one? Then the way Freddie was acting up, that was the most disturbing of all. It was all so confusing but Jackson couldn't help but feel everything was linked. He was completely lost in thought while walking and didn't notice how empty the street had become. A thick fog, completely out of place and out of season, was rolling in along the ground at ankle height, wrapping around light poles, red mail boxes and bins fluidly and soundlessly. It was only when the street lights started flickering that Jackson stopped, looked around and took notice. With wide eyes he found himself in an urban bog, the road on his right seemed like a river of flowing white smoke. The bank of this river had telephone pole trees with wire vines running between them. A sense of panic, normally associated with his Dreams took hold of him. Jackson took a quick moment to make sure this was real and that he was not asleep, but a quick hop (he could move) to the left and a slap to the face confirmed that this was indeed real. The fear was wrapping around him in a claustrophobic blanket that would soon leave him completely incapacitated. With more than a little apprehension, Jackson tried to do something he had never done in the waking world, he attempted to partition his mind, to take control of the fear. He closed his eyes even as the mist licked at his ankles with cold and wet promise. He created a box, reinforced with steel sheeting around the edges, held tightly in place against the box with round bolts, a decidedly medieval looking thing. He imagined the top of the box with the lid opened up like a hungry mouth waiting to be fed. He pushed this imaginary box to that place he could just about see in his mental peripheral vision. He did this all in the space of a single breath. Just as he did while dreaming, Jackson gathered all his fear, all his panic, but also all of his other emotions, the very core of himself, in an imagined whirlwind. He pushed the whirlwind of himself towards the box which sucked at it greedily. When nothing remained outside the box, Jackson gave a mental push and closed the lid, securing the box away from his direct attention.

Jackson opened his eyes. He didn't feel anything, he didn't care about anything. He had become like the observer he was in his Dreams, a hollow shell.

"That's a neat little trick you have there, Jackson, I don't think I have ever seen it done so well." The voice came from everywhere at once and its vibration sent ripples along the fog river in all directions. The feeling of being in a bog was suddenly greatly enhanced by the smell of vegetation, cloying, moving, and a pulsing green. The sound of footsteps, heavy in the silent white world, came to him first from the left, then from the right, then from behind him and once again the fog rippled in all directions along the ground.

"Who are you, what do you want? How do you know my name?" Jackson shouted out in no particular direction. It was not a shout of fear or apprehension, it was purely inquisitive, questioning and loud enough to be heard all around him.

"I know all Jackson I have existed in this plane for countless experiences. I have seen all and played a part in it all. I have played my tune for witting and unwitting ears." The voice echoed mysteriously across the street. The nature of the voice was impossible to define, neither old nor young, neither gruff nor light, it just was. "You intrigue me Jackson. I have not seen the like of you in millennia and I wonder at your presence. What are you doing here Jackson, what role are you playing? Are you sent? Why, why, why… so much to find out." Jackson listened on impassively, not knowing how to respond, he merely waited. The most unlikely of giggles bounced off the fog. "Listen to me, musing to my puppets, perhaps I am losing my mind." The giggling cut off immediately. "I am very excited to see this play out Jackson. Very, very, very excited. I will be keeping a close eye on you. Before I go, please accept a small gift!" The world around Jackson started to spin. Much like he had earlier imagined, everything solid before him suddenly became like a gas as it swirled around him at speed against a solid black backdrop. It went faster and faster until Jackson started to feel nauseous and dizzy. Still it continued to speed up, all the colours now compressing into a smaller and smaller white line spinning around him. It all froze so suddenly that Jackson lost all sense of direction and fell over, hitting the ground with his shoulder painfully. After a moment, while he waited from the nausea to subside, he opened his eyes. He was lying on his side on the pavement before the road, the fog had gone and he could hear cars driving around on other streets nearby. Right in front of his eyes was a little wooden pan flute. The box in his mind broke and all the fear escaped and hit him without warning. He got up and was violently ill. After he had emptied all the contents of his stomach, he wiped his mouth and picked up the flute. It was strangely warm on his palm. He had a sour taste in his mouth and his headache was back. He pocketed the flute and looked around to see that no one had been watching. No one was. Jackson headed home thinking the world had gone mad on him or perhaps he had gone mad on the world. He was an extremely worried man by the time he got home and climbed into bed.

Jackson was immediately out of bed the next morning. The events of last night washed over him and filled him with a sense of purpose. He spent the morning researching and learning as much as he could about the pan flute (his growing collection now had three), its significance and its associations. Gradually, through many broken links, metaphors and mythology, Jackson started drawing a picture of what he could potentially be experiencing. There was one article that really stuck with him and he summarised it in his notebook;

Pan, the god of nature, is the only god that doesn't do anything. Why? Because Pan is the founder, the creator. Zeus, the king of the gods has to maintain his position as king, and he has responsibilities. He has a job to do. He's playing someone else's game... Pan's game.

And it makes sense. Pan is all. Pan is everything. Pan is the one true god. Pan created the 'game' we are in, the Matrix, this reality. It is Pan's Labyrinth.

And Pan, the storywriter, the author of this world, doesn't play the game, but is the game master. Pan wrote himself into the story, gave himself a character who does nothing but play so he himself could walk within his own creation. Everyone else is busy working, and Pan enjoys the show.

Was he really dealing with a god? Some sort of mischievous all-encompassing being playing within a world of its own creation. It seemed completely absurd and Jackson took a moment in his research to laugh quietly to himself. Dreams he could believe in, but this sort of mythology nonsense was going a bit too far. However, his experience last night on the walk home and the very real flutes he was staring at in front of him suggested that it was not nonsense at all. There was an internal battle raging inside Jackson head. He couldn't reconcile what he was experiencing with the rational, tangible world that he had grown up in. Further to this, if he were dealing with some sort of godly being, why would it have any inclination to talk to or involve or even acknowledge a nobody like him in the first place?

The questions and doubts kept smashing around in his skull. At times they would bounce off each other and at other times join, provide links, and create a whole new set of questions Jackson knew he wouldn't be able to answer. Closing his notebook (nearly full now, he would have to get another soon) Jackson got up and walked over to his phone near the entrance of his apartment. He was quite old fashioned like that, keeping a landline at all but for what reason. He preferred the more real connection he felt through an old telephone line as opposed to the detached feeling he got from a cell phone. Jackson also remembered Alex had her own landline, a weird little something that they had in common. He dialled that number and waited for Alex to pick-up. It rang but there was no answer, so he assumed she must have already gone into work. He replaced the receiver in its cradle and checked the time on his watch; 09:15. If he hurried, he could probably pop into the police station before his shift started. With his mind made up, he hurried off to the shower and got ready to leave.

An hour later he was downstairs waiting in the reception area. He had asked for Detective Levi who was just finishing up on another call. Instead of coming down to pick him up, Detective Levi called the officer at the front desk and asked her to send Jackson up. It was starting to feel like he was visiting a close friend rather than a formal interview. Jackson made his way up the stairs and found himself in front of a tired looking detective.

"Sorry for making you wait, been a busy day." Without any other formalities the detective continued straight on. "I'm glad you came Jackson, I wanted to update you on the Fred Harver case. It just keeps getting weirder… oh yes, please keep this to yourself, I'm not officially supposed to be working this as it a closed case." Not waiting for acknowledgment from Jackson, Detective Levi continued. "I tracked down and spoke with both Miles and Phillip. At first, they had no idea what I was talking about, and in Phillip's case, he couldn't even remember who Fred Harver was. It was only as I recounted some of the things that Fred had told me that they start agreeing with me. It was like me telling them what happened, made it so in their minds. They started telling me of little things that happened over the period, small little details that made it more real and real by the minute. It was exactly how it went when we interviewed Freddie. I just wanted to tell you that because, well, I don't understand it and I don't have any inclination to tell anyone else in case they think I'm going senile or something." Detective Levi threw up his hands and put them behind his head as he leaned back in his chair.

"Nothing about any of this makes much sense Detective."

"John," Detective Levi cut in.

"John then. That's only the half it. Some weird stuff is going down. By the way, do you have any leads on the Linda Gerard case yet?" Jackson asked.

"Um, what's that got to do with Fred? What your interest in that? Most importantly, how did you know it was Linda Gerard?" Detective Levi was leaning forward, squinting at him in suspicion.

"Oh no real connection, just being nosey I suppose, I think I saw something on the news this morning.' Jackson desperately hoped it was true. Detective Levi wrote something in his notebook but didn't question Jackson's motive any longer.

"I suppose if it's already out there no point in hiding it. It was Linda Gerard. She had been tortured before dying from heart failure, loss of blood I believe… and before you ask me, no leads as yet, and nothing I should tell you regardless." Jackson and the detective chatted briefly for a while longer but with nothing much more to discuss, Jackson left with a thanks. He was on his way downstairs when Ben caught him on his way up.

"Hey Jackson… got a sec?" Jackson didn't but it was always usually him chasing Ben for information, so he was intrigued. He could be a few minutes late at the bar.

"Sure," he replied. "What's up?"

Ben looked around and said, "Let's find one of those cubicles upstairs and chat there." Jackson followed his friend back up from where he had just come from. Luckily, Detective Levi had left his desk and didn't see Jackson return. He and ben sat down in the confined but private space of the cubicle. Blue grey carpeted dividers blocked everyone else from view.

"Jackson, you know that crime scene I gave you the address of the other day?" Ben saw Jackson nod and he continued, "Well something strange I wanted to tell you. I know that you have some, uh, experience, in uncovering things… um unusual… so I wanted to see if you could help?" Jackson could see Ben was uncomfortable, he had never questioned Jackson on his abilities and never wanted to. Ben preferred not to question things of this nature when the result from such engagements with Jackson generally were positive or at least assisted in whatever investigation they were working on. "You know it was Linda Gerard, right? Yes, OK so the scene was an absolute mess. I can't tell you how awful but it's not what I want to tell you. Have you ever seen something like this?" He showed Jackson a picture of a silver ring lying in a puddle of blood. The ring had something written on it, but it was legible. Jackson didn't need to see what it said because he had already seen it in his Dream. "For such a gruesome murder scene, we have absolutely no clues as to why it happened, why Linda Gerard, what motive. It almost looks like a spur of the moment murder, but it can't have been given the location of the scene of the crime. It was in a deserted area, out of view of potential passers-by and completely out of earshot. So, some sort of premeditation took place. It's the randomness of the scene that has got the whole PD up in knots, they have no direction to follow on this apart from this ring. Do you know anything about it, is there anything you can tell me?" Ben asked imploringly. Jackson pretended to study the ring a little longer and then shook his head.

"No, I'm sorry I can't help you one this. There appears to be something written on the ring, could you make it out?" Jackson feigned interest and watched for Ben's reply.

"No, it seems to have faded with age. All we could make out was 'vocar'... but that it." Ben shook his head resignedly. Jackson said if he came across anything or had any other 'insights' he would call Ben straight away. Ben thanked him and Jackson left back down the stairs. On his way to the bar, Jackson decided he needed to visit that gym again, there were more questions he needed to ask the manager, Robert. He hadn't realised the ring was a real thing. Usually in his Dream objects like the ring were intended as platforms for messages, not as real objects. Now he had a lead to follow up and he would have to do it quickly because it would take the police too long to find out about the gym. When he got to the bar, twenty minutes late, he had to contend with a foot-tapping Randall at the entrance, looks like his day was about to get a bit spicier.

"You're late!" was all he said as he disappeared back into the bar.

The Tasselled Bookmark was doing some good business today, Alex thought as she watched Susan put a couple of books into a plastic bag and hand the customer that and some change. She was back in the little office behind the counter and could see Susan's back through the open door. She had been sitting watching her interact with customers all day while trying to complete all the back-office admin that went with running the small bookstore, but as her heart wasn't in it. Her mind was running in all directions and she was finding it hard to concentrate on any one thing. Susan popped her head around the doorframe and scowled and Alex.

"Why don't you go see your brother and your folks Al, you really aren't getting too much done here anyways?" The scowl was friendly banter, but Alex realised Susan was right. She was just wasting time. Some part of her was afraid to go see Freddie, to look into those haunted eyes of his and not know how to help him. It wasn't just that, the more she thought of Freddie the more she started to believe that she was missing something vital, something she should be seeing... it was alarming and frustrating. "Hey, are you going to answer me or just sit there frowning at me?" Susan said with a smile.

"Sorry Suzie, I can't seem to concentrate today. You know what, you're right. I'm going to pack up. You OK to close?" Alex asked picking up her things.

"What do you think I have been doing the last few weeks here?" Susan joked. "Speaking of which, I think a raise might be in order...?" Alex narrowed her eyes at Susan on her way past before replying.

"What's that? I can't hear you; you need to speak up." She ran for the exit and climbed into her car before Susan could answer back. She was laughing to herself as she drove away seeing Susan shaking her head while laughing as well. Alex whistled a tune to herself on the way home and shortly pulled up into her folks' driveway. Remembering to knock this time, she waited for her mother to answer the door. When she did, they greeted, and Alex immediately made for her brother's room upstairs.

"He isn't there dear; he's sitting in the living room watching the news." Well that can only be an improvement, Alex thought as she changed direction and headed for the living room.

She found Fred sitting cross legged on the floor about a metre away from the flatscreen. He had the remote in his hand and was changing between all the different news channels furiously.

"Hi Freddie." Alex said as she walked over to him. Fred didn't turn his head but did say Hi back to her. He continued flicking through the channels. "Is there something you are looking for?" Alex took a seat across the room from Fred on the floor. From there she could see the TV and Fred at the same time.

"I'm not sure. Just a face I remember. It must have been from the last couple weeks while I was away." Alex noticed how Freddie looked down at the floor and grimaced when he said, 'while I was away,' it looked like it really bothered him. "The face I want to find, it's important but I don't know why. I just… I just… I just feel like something terrible is going to happen and that face is important! I need to stop the dreams, need to find the face," Fred continued. He kept up the steady cadence of switching between news channels.

"Why the news Fred?" Alex asked leaning forward.

"Dunno, just a feeling," Fred said, his eyes never looking away from the screen. Click, Click, Click. Alex didn't know what to say. Freddie was clearly ill at ease and Alex thought it best just to let the story play out. Click, click, click... Alex looked up. Fred had dropped the remote and was staring wide eyed at a picture on the TV. He was blinking and he started to shake all over. "That's it, that's the face!" he whispered. Tears were running in streams down his cheeks. Alarmed Alex moved over to Fred's side and looked at the TV. She suddenly found her world tilting at an alarming angle and had to grab onto Fred from falling over. The shock of seeing Linda Gerard's smiling face had almost made her faint. When she had recovered somewhat, she roughly turned Fred's face away from the TV to look into her own.

"Freddie, how do you know her, what do you know about her?" The intensity of the questions didn't help Fred's fragile state of mind, but he didn't look away.

"She's in trouble Al, something terrible is going to happen to her! You must help her Alex, you must... to... to do something. Please help me. Please." Fred collapsed into her arms. Both of them kneeling holding onto each other as the silent TV switched between other pictures of Linda. Linda at school, Linda the cheerleader, Linda with friends at a rock concert. Fred was still sobbing in her arms. He obviously had not been reading the headlines on the TV (so intent had he been on finding the face) and hadn't yet realised that Linda was already dead. Putting off all the questions she wanted to ask Fred until later, Alex called her mom and together they helped Fred up the stairs and into his bed. He fell asleep immediately, his tear-stained cheeks highlighting how young and vulnerable he was. Alex's heart broke for him. Alex and her mother retreated downstairs quietly.

"What happened Alex?" her mom asked. Alex could see the concern on her face. "He was doing well... I thought he was starting to get back to his normal self," she continued. Alex told her about him recognising the face of the murdered girl on the TV. "How can that be? I saw the news this morning. She was found at an office block here in town. Fred was off on tour with his band friends." Alex looked at her mom and realised how desperately her mom wanted that to be true, even though she probably didn't believe it herself.

"I don't, Mom, maybe Fred met her before he went away," Alex shrugged and shook her head. She needed to get back to Jackson, he would know what to do with this and she didn't want to stick around and upset her mom anymore.

"Mom, are you going to be OK here? I need to go. When is Dad home?"

Mrs Harver composed herself and told Alex that she was a grown woman and could look after herself, but she hugged Alex and said, "Dad is home in an hour." Alex hugged her back and left. She would go to the bar. The time was now 16:30, Jackson would still be working, and she could use a drink.

Jackson could tell that Alex wanted to talk but before she could say anything, he seated her at a booth and brought her something to drink.

"Take a breath and relax. I can see you have are itching to tell me something and boy do I have a story to tell you," Jackson kissed her on the cheek. "But I have got to keep these people here hydrated or else Randall will have my ass. He already isn't happy with me being late this morning." Jackson reached over to another table and propped the menu in front of Alex to read. "I can recommend the Chicken Parm," he said.

"Sounds great, do you think you could get another of these?" she replied holding up her glass.

"My pleasure my lady," Jackson laughed and went and placed the order with the kitchen. The rest of his shift passed without incident. Alex had finished her meal earlier and was now up in his apartment watching TV. He had been happy when she asked him for his keys holding a carry all she had retrieved from her car. He was worried he wasn't going to have too much time to catch up with her on account how busy the bar was. Alex must have figured that might be the case and prepared in advance. Once he handed the official on-duty cloth over to a smirking Shelley he made his way upstairs, eager to get to Alex.

"Don't do anything I wouldn't do!" Shelley shouted at him. Jackson smiled at her over his shoulder before reaching the top of the staircase, turning left into a narrow corridor that led to his place and two other apartments. One was empty and the other was inhabited by a man named Tyler who worked some or other job, night shift. Jackson didn't see him that often, something he didn't really mind. In a first, Jackson knocked on the door to his own place.

"Who's there, can I help you?" came Alex's voice from inside.

"It's me," he replied. The door open and Alex appeared in the soft light wearing one of his t-shirts. Everything he wanted to talk to her about left his head as he swooped on her and gathered her in his arms. He kissed her then.

"Whoa there tiger!" Alex said smiling while trying to break away.

"I missed you," Jackson said. Once again, Alex took a moment to see if he was serious.

When she convinced herself of what she saw, she put her hands on either side of his head and said, "I missed you too. Now come inside before someone sees me wearing only this." Her hand held the bottom corner of the t-shirt and she pulled at it enticingly. Jackson walked inside, closed the door behind him, emptied his pockets on the nightstand and followed Alex into the TV/Dining room. She curled up on the couch and nursed a tumbler of whiskey. "I hope you don't mind, I brought this with me from home. There is a distinct lack of alcohol in your place," she said smirking. She lost the smile and suddenly asked, "It doesn't bother you, me drinking, I mean, it's not hard for you or anything."

"Nah it doesn't bother me and truthfully, if it brings you over more often and will start (**sticking**) the place up," Jackson said as he collapsed next to her. "So, who should go first, who has the better story?" he asked.

"I think since I have been waiting patiently on you, I should have the honours," Alex said before taking a sip of her drink.

"The floor is yours," Jackson said theatrically. Alex recounted the episode with her brother in as much detail as she could. When she had finished, Jackson brought out his notebook.

"So somehow Freddie recognised Linda Gerard's face but nothing else. He was supposed to have been on a tour across the country for the last two weeks or so when Linda was found murdered her, in New York, in an abandoned office building. When, where did he see her?" Jackson mused out loud.

"There was no prior contact between the two of them," Alex said. "Freddie told me everything and he never mentioned any girl. Also, my mother didn't recognise Linda either, so she probably wasn't a close friend of Freddie's or anything." Alex was just about to finish off before she remembered, "Oh Jackson, not sure if it's relevant but Freddie doesn't know that Linda is dead. He must not have read the headlines on the TV; he was kind of excited at seeing the face he was searching and probably ignored everything else. He just kept shouting at me to help her, that I must do something. Then oddly, he said, "save me." I am really worried about his mental state, I think Mom should take him to get checked out. I only mention it because if you speak with him, best not to mention Linda's current state, not sure how he will process that," Jackson said he wouldn't and made a notation in his book. Jackson recounted his own experience at the police station, the discovery of the ring and his idea to re-question the gym manager, Robert. He found he couldn't quite bring himself to talk about the experience on the misty street on his walk home last night. It felt extremely personal and he was terrified what Alex would think of him if he told her. To be fair, he wasn't sure he had seen or heard anything. As more time passed, it had the effect of making it seem incredibly unreal, a figment of his imagination. Jackson was still musing over this when he noticed that the room was very silent. He looked up and saw Alex staring at him intensely, a look that left him as to no doubt what she wanted from him. All thoughts of investigation left his mind in a rush as he leaned over Alex and kissed her. After a while he got up, picked Alex up in his arms and carried her to his bedroom.

The next morning, they got up early and found a coffee shop for a quick breakfast. On the way there, Alex called Susan to tell her she would be late. Jackson had the day off but would have to come in for the night shift. They had agreed to drive back up to the gym to see what they could discover further. The drive was uneventful but soon they found themselves in the same nearly deserted parking lot, in front of the gaudy gym. The neon JYM sign, on even during the day, beckoned them inside. The gym hadn't changed much in the few days since they had last visited which left Jackson strangely confused, but for no possible reason. Janey, the receptionist, looked up as the door tinkled open. The blaring music unable to mask the tone of the little doorbell hanging over frame.

"Hi there. Is Robert in today? I have a few more questions for him if he is still willing?" Jackson asked with his most friendly smile. Janey didn't seem impressed by the smile and stared at him a bit before answering.

"Robert is in but is on a call if you want to wait," she said flatly.

"No problem. Do you mind if we look around, maybe we could go visit that little tiki bar?" Jackson persevered with the smile.

"Sure, whatever floats your boat man," she waved them away.

"Smooth," Alex chirped beside him as they walked around the reception and into the gym proper. Looking around, seeing nothing of interest, they eventually seated themselves at the little juice bar. The man working there looked like he had just come from a workout himself. He had short, brown hair cut close the scalp with a little patch at the front pushed up, a bit like Tin-Tin. The rest of his body was covered in multi-coloured spandex ending in shockingly white trainers.

"Smoothie? We got only the basics today, apple and oat, banana and peanut butter and a Jyms favourite, orange, yogurt and smores." Jackson figured you could blend anything these days.

"No thank you," he said and looked over to Alex who also declined with a small shake of her head. "I was wondering if you have ever seen these people before." Jackson held out the pictures of Linda and Freddie for the barman… juice man to look at.

"Oh, that's Linda Gerard, poor thing. I saw on the news she had been murdered. Old man Joe must be wrecked." Jackson had not expected that at all, it was only a whim that he had even brought the picture with him, having already asked the manager these questions before.

"Who is Joe?" Jackson asked as he pocketed the pictures.

"Joe is Linda's old man; he would come here every week. He was so proud of his girl that he would show anybody who was near the little picture of her he kept in his wallet," the juice man told him.

"Why was Joe here every week, did he do any work for the gym?" Jackson asked.

"Not for the gym exactly, he worked for the company that supplies fruit to juice bars all over the state. He would often say we were a small client but the one he enjoyed coming to most often. Maybe it's all the women in tight clothes?" The juice man winked. It was amazing how quickly he recovered from the sad news of old Joe's little girl's passing, Jackson thought to himself. He pulled out the picture again but before he could ask a question, he got a strange feeling of being watched. He looked up and to his right. The little office block was on a level above the gym, it took up the entire mezzanine. The blinds were pulled closed but were swaying like someone had just moved back from them. The juice man noticed his

124

gaze and said, "Ah the office of our great leader, he can see everything from up there." Jackson brushed off the uneasy feeling and showed the juice man a picture ofFreddie. He just shook his head and said, no.

"Last thing, does the gym give out rings to their members…?" Jackson wasn't able to finish as the juice man interrupted him.

"Oh yeah, those. Vocare ad regnum. Quite cheesy but the members love them. It gets given out to all people that sign on for a multiple year contract upfront. Something to do with reminding them of their commitment or something, like a motivator of sorts. Jackson thought that when it got out that such a ring was found at a murder scene, they wouldn't be so popular any more. He thanked Juice Man for his time and made his way back to reception with Alex. Before he could say anything, Janey beat him to it.

"I'm sorry, the boss says he is going to be stuck in his conference call for a while and won't be able to see you. He said to leave me your number and he'll call you back when he is free." Jackson frowned but left her his number. On the way-out Jackson looked over his shoulder and saw the same sort of blinds, closed and gently swaying. Alex had also seen it.

When they got into the car she said, "That was creepy." Jackson couldn't have agreed more.

Alex was driving while Jackson was going over his notes. He frowned at something, circled it and then closed the book.

"Ok so we have a possibility of a connection between Fred and Linda. I know the barman didn't recognise Fred but there is a strong possibility Fred could've been there when Joe, Linda's dad, was and going on what we just heard, Joe could easily have shown Freddie a picture of his daughter," Jackson theorised out loud.

"Yup, it's a possibility but it doesn't explain how Freddie knew that Linda was in danger. What else are we missing here?" Alex said back to Jackson. Jackson was rubbing his eyes; the headache was slowing taking root again. This confused him as it shouldn't be happening.

Linda was dead, he was to late already, he wasn't able to stop the killer and he wasn't able to save Linda. A sudden thought came to him.

"I think the killer is going to strike again. I think the person who killed Linda is most likely the same person who is going to kill those campers in my dream… that's the only thing that explains why my headache is coming back," Jackson said to Alex. She in turn glanced at him quickly and then looked back at the road. She wore a worried expression.

"I really hope not Jackson, it would be quite an escalation if it was. Going from a single abduction and murder to mass murder is quite the step up. What would be next if that was the case?" Jackson didn't answer her, he didn't need to, he was feeling the same way. They were both quiet for a while, thinking things through on their own. Jackson spoke up as they reached the Seven Eleven near his apartment.

"Do you think that Fred would be up to some questions? Maybe we can understand from him why he went all the out to that gym in the first place?" Alex thought about it and then continued driving past Jackson's place and onto her parents' house.

"Jackson, we can't push him, we can try but we mustn't force it. I am really worried where his mind is at the moment." Jackson agreed and said he would be as gentle as possible.

"I want to tell you something Alex because I know you probably haven't thought about it yet. I am not saying this to scare you but rather to prepare you." Alex pulled that face that brought that dimple out on the side of her mouth, she said nothing. She waited for Jackson to continue. "We are ahead of the game here; the Dreams have given me an advantage over the police but they will catch up." Jackson stopped to see if Alex was following his train of thought. She said nothing and continued looking at the road ahead while she was waiting for Jackson to continue. Jackson noted her concern and really didn't want to upset her. "At some point they are going to figure out Freddie's apparent involvement with Linda Gerard. They will trace the ring to the gym, they will question the manager or the Juice Man, they will find out about Freddie!" Jackson finished. Alex hit the indictor and pulled over to the side of the road.

"What are you saying Jackson, that Freddie had something to do with Linda's death, that he was involved somehow?" Alex was practically shouting at Jackson but he let her continue. "How could you believe that, how could you even think that?" Alex's eyes blazed with fury. "I am not saying that at all. I know you and I think I have an idea of Freddie through you.

I don't think he is the sort of person that could be involved in this at all. What I am saying is that without too much to go on, the police will start thinking along those lines... the evidence will point them in that direction. What I am saying is that you need to prepare yourself for that eventuality, yourself and your family." Jackson had grabbed both of Alex's hands in his own and was talking to her passionately, trying to make her see. "I am trying to tell you that we need to figure this whole thing out soon, to clear Fred before the police get the bit between their teeth." Jackson said finally. The heat leaked out of Alex's eyes and had the effect of softening her entire body. Alex could feel her loosen up in his hands and watched as she backed off from her fighting pose.

"We? Are you going to help me figure this out? You don't have to you know, you don't owe me or my family anything?" Alex's eyes filled with tears and she looked on at Jackson hopefully.

"I am already part of this Alex and even if I wasn't, I would do it for you anyways. I will do anything for you." Alex searched his face again for something (he was getting used to this by now) but eventually accepted his answer.

"Thank you Jackson, it means the world, having you here with me. I don't think I could've done anything like what we are doing by myself." Before Jackson could reply she leaned in, grabbed his face and kissed him hard. He could feel the tears from her eyes on his cheeks. She pulled back, straightened her blonde hair and redid her ponytail. Composed again, she checked her blind spot and returned into the traffic, making her way to the house where Fred was. They didn't speak too much over the next ten minutes, but they were very aware of each other. They had become partners, an un-worded commitment to see this thing through to then end, regardless where that end might be.

The man with the clunky shoes was enjoying himself, the story was unfolding deliciously. The bread crumbs were positioned and the mice were following. He rubbed his hands together with real hunger and excitement at the thought of all the confusion, the sudden light-bulb moment of insight, the dread, the hope and even the love. It was all weaving into a masterpiece, some of his finest work. Bob, as he now thought of himself, was pacing up and down a suburb not too far from where Alex's parent lived. He loved the sound his footfalls made on the concrete sidewalk. He was unseen by all, but seeing of all. Runner and dog walkers would serve out of his way without seeing him. They would all later remark to their families of the sudden gooseflesh and mild panic they experienced on the afternoon exercise but it would soon be forgotten. Bob only allowed himself to be seen when he wanted to be.

Last night was just one such occasion. The man Jackson had intrigued him and he couldn't help but lean in for a closer look. He was not always in control of the environment around him when he intruded on the perception of mortals, but the fog and the flickering lights were a real nice touch he thought. He remembers savouring the growing terror and burgeoning panic in the man as he fully forced himself into the reality of that plane. He recalled the man Jackson looking around and thinking of running, his fear and confusion were mouth-watering. It had come as quite a shock to Bob when all those emotions he could feel pulsing from the man were suddenly cut off. It was not often that Bob would feel shocked and he had taken a moment to try and understand the sensation. Jackson was not the first person he had encountered with the ability to Dream Stalk, but he was certainly the first person he had come across that was so proficient at the Mind Split. The fact that he could do it in different realities was even more impressive. However, it was doubtless the man Jackson even knew what was he was doing. That encounter with Jackson had been quite informative. It added a new dimension to the story he had woven and that thrilled him to know the end. It was unexpected and welcome and worth watching further. The little flute gift was something Bob allowed himself. It was a mark to his achievement, a herald of his mastery of the story. It was a vanity he couldn't resist. It also served as a rather bold breadcrumb and link, something unmissable, something open doors on questions that would never have been considered before. He loved the flute. It took him back to a time of great stories and epic adventures and his seemingly small role in each. Although he was the creator, he liked to involve himself in his creations to get the maximum effect of the emotion it produced. It was what sustained him. Not recognition, not worship, not belief in him. Experience. Experience and emotion are what filled him. The man continued with his clunky walk down the street and came upon the Harver household. The next chapter of this tale was about to unfold and for the first time in memory, he wasn't entirely sure what was going to happen. The introduction of the Dream Stalker was an unintended ingredient that was making this meal all the better. Bob stared at the house across the street and saw Fred looking down at him with wide eyes. He removed his hat and waved back at him before making himself unseen yet again. That was a lapse of concentration, he shouldn't have let it happen. As always though, the fearful recognition from Fred was delightful. The man in the clunky shoes kept on circling the block, he liked to keep moving and observing. He knew he wouldn't miss it; he knew he would find himself right outside the house he was watching exactly when he needed to be. He pulled out a flute and started playing. Birds and other small animals scurried out of his way at the tune. Unwitting passer-by's shivered in sudden fright for no reason. The man walked on.

Chapter 5 – Stepping Through the Window

Fred blinked. He had uneasy sensation in his belly left by a wave of fear that had disappeared as swiftly as it had arrived. He could have sworn he had seen a man walking, there across the road. He had even stopped at waved at him. He stuck his head further out the window to look down each side of the street but he was gone. It wasn't just the man and his disappearance that was disturbing him, it was that Fred had recognised him. He recognised him, but not with familiarity of a friend or even a colleague; he recognised him with a sense of dread and helpless that could not be placed. Fred hurriedly closed the window and returned to his bed. He had never felt so conflicted and torn in his entire life. Nothing was making any sense to him. He was really battling to distinguish between what was real and what was imagined, what was dream and what was awake. He could see the memories of the last few weeks as clearly in his mind as if they happened just yesterday. There was absolutely no doubt that these had happened. He could remember smells, conversations with people, laughing at jokes, drinking eating, dancing, showering. All of it! It was as real as any of his other memories. But it didn't happen. It was physical thing. It was his body that was rejecting what his mind was telling him. All the evidence said it had happened but it was not the truth. He felt split in two, living in somebody else mind. He knew where he was physically, he knew this body was his but he didn't trust is own mind anymore, it was lying to him. At least the compulsion to seek Linda Gerard had faded. That had been exhausting, but was now a fading memory, like a bad taste in the mouth. As had become normal over the last few days, Fred curled up into a ball on the bed, hugging a pillow between his legs and rocking slightly on his side. There was nothing for it but to just sit there and wait it out, wait until the sense of 'two,' of real and unreal, as they untangled themselves so he could just be one Freddie again. He couldn't stop looking out the window. With an icy certainty, he understood that he must not go out there. Out there, out of the house, was a place where the real an unreal tangled even more. He understood that nothing good would come of him leaving the house, more than that, something bad would happen! But he couldn't stop staring out the window. Something he was trying very hard to suppress, to hide away from himself was the pull, the desire to do exactly what he knew he shouldn't do, to go outside. He had no idea why but the outside was calling him. It was promising not more tangled identity, but it's opposite, clarity! Outside called him as fish was to a hooked morsel floating in front of him. Fred screamed into his pillow and turned around to look at the door of his room. It only took a few minutes before he rolled back over as was looking at the window again, listening to its silent sweet promise of normality, no, of purpose, of identity. Fred got up and went back to the window, opening it to let in the evening air again and repeated a cycle he had maintained the whole day, between the bed and the window. The man with the hat hadn't returned and Fred found himself disappointed, despite how the sight of the man had made him feel. It was just an ordinary evening once again, although Fred thought he heard a hint of tune on the wind. Someone out there, he thought, was playing a flute.

Alex and Jackson arrived shortly after Fred had fallen asleep. Her mother had them both in the kitchen drinking coffee with her.

"I tell you Alex, I think he is slowly getting better. He hasn't left his room at all but I can hear him moving around up there, so at least he is just not sleeping all the time like he was in the beginning," Mrs Harver said. Jackson wasn't sure it was delusion or hopeful optimism that had her thinking this, but he didn't say anything. Alex was still dwelling on their conversation in the car on the way over and it was etched all over her face.

"Mom, I know I have asked you this before, but can you think of any connection Freddie might have had with Linda Gerard? Did she ever come over, did Freddie ever mention her name?" she asked, frowning. Mrs Harver didn't take any time to think it over before responding.

"Linda Gerard, the murdered girl? No hun, I have thought on this myself but Freddie never mentioned her before yesterday. I think he must have heard her name on the TV from his room and it just got stuck with him or something. He hasn't mentioned her since you left yesterday... and I'm glad for it. He was in an awful state before that," she answered.

"Mrs Harver, I know this whole thing is very upsetting and completely abnormal but has anything from Fred's behaviour struck you as odd...I mean apart from the obvious?" Jackson asked. Mrs Harver stared and Jackson before locking her eyes on her daughter.

"What are you two up to, why are you so interested in in Freddie? He's a good boy and he is home now, can't we just leave it at that," Mrs Harver said this all in a fluster.

"We are just confused and trying to help Fred is all," Jackson said. The concern and anxiety that she had tried to hide was coming out in a rush. She left the table and went to pour them all more coffee. She fiddled in a drawer below the coffee machine and pulled out a well-worn, pack of cigarettes and, without turning around to face them, lit up.

"Oh don't look at me like that Alex, I think I deserve one of these after the last few weeks," she said waving smoke that had gathered in front of her face away. Alex said nothing but stared at her impassively. Jackson doubted this was her first cigarette, he had noticed the stains on her middle and index fingers of her right hand when she handed him his coffee. For a while Mrs Harver stood leaning with her back against the kitchen counter smoking her cigarette, watching them while she thought. "Alex, do you remember the incident with Tigger, the cat?" Alex at first look confused but then went pale. She started fidgeting with her jacket zipper.

"Yes, I see you do but for Jackson's benefit, lets fill him in," Mrs Harver said.

"Mom, I don't see what that has to do with anything..." Alex started to protest but Mrs Harver went on over her, looking at Jackson.

"It was quite a few years ago. Freddie could only have been about six and that would have made Alex... 17. Our neighbour's cat went missing and they were sticking up posters of their missing Tigger on street poles and going door to door handing them out. Dorothy, the neighbour on that side"—Mrs Harver gestured with her head to the left—"was at our door with the poster, clearly upset but I obviously hadn't seen the cat and was telling her just that."

"When I closed the door, I noticed these two," she said looking at Alex, "disappear at the top of the stairs. They were so obviously spying and so obviously trying to hide that I immediately became suspicious. When I confronted the two of them, it didn't take Freddie long to confess. We went out back and Freddie pointed to a mound carefully hidden behind recently raked up leaves." Mrs Harver took a deep drag of her cigarette with her eyes closed before she continued, "Anyways, without going into too much detail, it was Dorothy's cat, missing its head and tail, just a mess of black and white fur and blood... so much blood." Alex got up and started pacing but said nothing. "Needless to say, I was horrified. Alex would say nothing and just stared at me stoically, but Freddie was another matter, he was completely panicked and clearly upset. Turns out Alex here had convinced him to do it. To catch and kill the cat, to mutilate the cat." Mrs Harver was crying now. "I will never forget that day. It broke my heart that my two babies could have done something like that. Anyway," she waved away the memory, "I couldn't tell Dorothy what had happened but I made the two of them bury the cat and swore them to secrecy. I think I grounded them for the remainder of their childhood," Mrs Harver finished off, waiting for Alex to say something.

"Mom, we were stupid kids, I still don't know why he did that but it long over. Besides, like I told you, Freddie made the part about me up, I caught him in the act and he tried to shift the blame. Why bring it up now?" Alex said eventually.

"Because," Mrs Harver said with a pause, "Freddie is acting the exact same way now. That sort of panic-stricken shock, looking at all directions at the same time. That's the only way I can describe what going on with him." Jackson absorbed all of this while watching Alex. She had lost all the bravery and self-assurance she had displayed until now. He always knew she was hurting and scared underneath it all, but he had never seen is so thoroughly exposed until now. Jackson could see that the conversation was pretty much ended at this point and he suggested to Alex to go and check on her brother. While she was away, Jackson looked at Mrs Harver.

"Why that story, I can see it upset you both?" he asked. Mrs Harver sobbed before answering.

"Like I said, it feels exactly like that. Nothing else comes close to it. One minute my little angels are the perfect little children and then the next they are mutilating and murdering a defenceless pet. There was a never an incident like that before then and there was never one like that after... doesn't mean I could ever forget it happened though." She finished speaking and crushed her cigarette in her empty coffee mug. She then chucked away the bud and rinsed it before putting all their cups into the dishwasher. Alex returned a little while after that and said Fred was still asleep. She moved over to her mom and hugged her fiercely, trying to ease the wound that had just been opened. Mrs Harver hugged her back with just as much intensity. When they broke apart, Alex and Jackson said their goodbyes and walked out. They needed to talk and Jackson could sense she was uncomfortable. They agreed to go to her place for that night and said nothing at all to each other on their way the way home.

Alex remained withdrawn and kept to herself when they got to her apartment. She hardly noticed when Jackson ordered in a pizza and didn't even acknowledge the doorbell when it rang. Jackson opened the door for the delivery man and paid for the food. She only looked up at him when he put a plate in her hand and laid the pizza box on the coffee table in front of the TV.

"I hadn't thought of that since it actually happened." Jackson knew she was referring to the story her mother had told earlier. He kept quiet and waited for her to continue. "She still blames me you know, she never ever let it go. I was the one who made Freddie do that... according to her. I caught him doing it you know? Mom was away and I heard this godawful scream coming from the back yard. I went out through the kitchen and saw him standing there, bent over a log we used to sit and play on. He was holding that poor cat down, there were scratches all over his arms..." Alex paused to swallow a sob and took a moment to compose herself. Jackson said nothing but passed her the napkin he had been holding. She took it gratefully with a smile and wiped her eyes. "Jackson, it was something no kid should ever see. He was pressing down on that poor creature's back so hard to stop it from squirming away, its legs were all splayed to the sides. He was... he was sawing at its neck with the little pocket knife he kept on him. The cat's blood was mixing with his own from the scratches and then suddenly, the cat stopped screeching and stopped moving all together. Freddie just went right on sawing and sawing until the head came away." Alex was crying properly now. He was grunting with the effort it had taken, like an animal.

When he looked around and noticed me he didn't seem surprised and said, "Almost done Alex!" It was so bizarre it pushed me out of my frozen shock. I asked him what he was doing but he just gave me this confused little look, like what he was doing was expected, or normal. I was too scared to even go near him, full of scratches and blood as he was. I thought he must be crazy. He bent down again and slowly sawed of the cat's tail. I managed to finally find the courage that had been absent until then and moved over to him, to make him stop. I remember slapping him hard and grabbing the knife from his hands. It had the desired effect because he seemed to come back to himself and then burst into tears. I stood there holding him for a bit, trying to get a grip on my own fear and shock as well. I told him he needed to hide it and he agreed and took the cat and its parts to a little compost heap we kept in the corner of the yard. I took him to the bathroom and cleaned him up as best I could. We agreed to keep this a secret from our parents. Anyway, you know the rest of the story. Funny thing is, you would think it would be hard to forget something like that but I swear to you, I hadn't given it even one thought since we were caught on that day. It just left me. Even my mother was fine after the initial shock. She treated me differently for a while after that day, like I said, she blamed me for it. Then we all just forgot and it was business as usual. It was only today, when she looked at while she was speaking, did I remember how my mom seemed to hate me. I could see it in her eyes again! "Oh my god why are so many bad things all happening at once?" She broke down and Jackson moved across to comfort her. Eventually she pushed him away and said, "Pizza is getting cold." Jackson looked at her quickly and saw that she was done with this story.

"That's the way I like it, don't know why they just don't serve it like this," he said as he took a large bite from the recently remembered slice in his hand. He was trying and failing to lighten the mood but Alex smiled in appreciation of his effort. She took a bite of her own slice and a bit of marinara splattered the top of her hand, looking so much like blood.

"You know what, I'm not that hungry anymore,' she said suddenly as she threw the slice back into the box. Wiping her hands clean on a napkin, she stood up and pulled Jackson along with her. 'I think we first need to work up and appetite," she said as she led him to her bedroom. Jackson followed without hesitation.

Jackson was lying on his back in Alex's bed listening to her breaths becoming deeper, waiting while they got deeper and more consistent. Glancing at her in the darkness, he drank in her shape. She was lying on her side with her back to him. She had one hand under curled under her head with her open palm cupping her cheek, on top of the pillow and the other hand was wrapped around the duvet. Both her legs were pulled up to her chest. He noticed how narrow her waist was, how her lines curved over her hips and then down to her knees and eventually ending at her toes. The silhouette of her clearly visible under the thin blanket. Jackson looked away guiltily, as if she had just woken up and scolded him for being a creep. He smiled in the darkness. He had never felt anything like this for anyone before, in fact, he had never felt anything for anyone before. Alex had dropped into his life and turned his stable and solid emotional reality into a whirlwind of new sensory delights, so foreign to him, so welcome.

He started to understand what he had missed in his life until then. He had purposefully cut himself off, denied himself even the smallest of intimacies between himself and others and he was coming to realise that he was regretful of a potentiality he missed. Jackson shook his head, what he had done in his thirty odd years was necessary. The violence he carried and had to live with always affected others, no matter how hard he tried to avoid it. At times he hated himself for it. He almost drank himself to death because of it before he caught grip of his life again. Alex was different though; he knew with total certainty that he would not able to push her away like the others. She was woven into his story as tight as a drum. He had accepted it, gratefully, however much it concerned him. He hadn't realised that the smile had slipped from his face being replaced with a frown. He was indeed worried for Alex; they were neck deep into something that couldn't possibly end well. Even for Jackson, the level of weirdness of the latest event left him confused. He hadn't even given thought yet to his encounter with that thing in the mist. He pushed that thought away, he knew he couldn't answer the millions of questions that came to over that incident. He was lying in the still of the night lost deep in thought and memory when he remembered the army days and he was still thinking about that when he finally fell into a deep asleep.

Jackson looked around. He was not in The Dream, there was no fear or panic but rather a sense of familiarity. He was able to walk around, he wasn't closed in. Once he determined he didn't have too much to worry about, he set about exploring with greater confidence. He was in some sort of desert town. Every single building around him was either half broken down or completely demolished. Most of the multistoried brick buildings were either missing a roof or an entire floor. He saw a group of five soldiers in dessert fatigues pressed tightly against a wall, two on each side of a doorway and a third getting ready with a battering ram. There was dust swirling around them in the wind and the air had a dry almost oily scent to it. The moment Jackson focused on the squad and immediately his vision zoomed in allowing him to see the individual features of the soldiers. This gave him a bit of a shock and left him feeling quite disorientated. The soldiers in front of him had frozen and weren't moving. Jackson looked down at himself and saw that he wasn't there. He had no body. It was like he was sitting behind a monitor changing the perspective of the camera for better view. That thought gave him an idea and with no small amount of excitement, he moved ahead with an experiment. He looked away from the frozen soldiers and focused on the Humvee they had disembarked from. With a sudden pull, he was there, looking at the vehicle from the front right hand side passenger door. He tried to move his view to the other side of the Humvee but wasn't able to. Ok, so there are some limitations to his control here he thought to himself.

That made him pause. He zoomed back to the group of soldiers and focused on the first one to the left of the doorway. It was him, a young Jackson Brandt, Private First Class. With an increasing sense of déjà vu and detachment, Jackson quickly scanned his surroundings once more. He was in a memory of his own, a memory of a sweep they were conducting in the neighbourhood of some small village or town whose name he couldn't remember. Jackson refocused his attention on the dream-memory. He pushed the boundaries of his perception point and after a while, released.

He could only do so within the limits of what the live Jackson had done, what he had observed while in the act. Refocusing on the soldier, Jackson mentally pressed the play button and the dream-memory became alive. The soldier with the battering ram broke down the door and the dream-Jackson lobbed a flash bang through the open doorway. Not even a second after the bang announced detonation, the soldiers entered one after the other with shouts of "clear" and scanned the room before them. Jackson focused again and his perception shifted into the eyes of dream-Jackson. The smoke made it difficult to see but the squad had strong intel and instructions to end whatever was moving inside the building. Jackson looked on through dream-Jackson's eyes. He remembered, always knowing precisely where his squad members were around him and he shot down any movement where they were not. They continued like this until the building was cleared. Jackson must have pulled the trigger on at least five occasions before it all suddenly ended. He heard his name being called by the squad sergeant.

"Jackson! Get your ass up her private." He hurried up the stairs to the roof. Sergeant Ben Hasset watched as Jackson made his way to the roof of the building. The walls were crumbling all around the edges and in some places, had disappeared altogether, along with the floor. The desert sun was bright and Jackson squinted in its glare. Behind the sergeant were a group of four turbaned prisoners, on their knees with their hands on their heads. "Do your thing Private," the sergeant said as Jackson moved passed. Suddenly Jackson remembered what was being shown to him. He remembered this memory and he wanted out. He pushed his perception away but every angle he tried to escape to still

offered a view of what was about to happen. Jackson watched on as dream-Jackson moved before each of the kneeling men. He paused before each of them and looked at their faces. At the third man, dream-Jackson recognised something and without wasting another moment circled to the back of the man, removed his knife from its holster and slit the man's throat. Jackson watched on in horror at what he had just done. He focused on the soldiers around him and saw the same disgust the he had just felt. He saw all of them look away and pretended Jackson wasn't even there. The killing stroke was so swift that the other prisoners only noticed something was wrong when their colleague collapsed next to them, gurgling in his blood. They all started screaming and wild-eyed tried to run. The sergeant was ready for this, this wasn't his first rodeo. The soldiers standing behind the prisoners raised their guns and bashed each prisoner on the head with the butt. They were also well-practiced at this. Each prisoner was knocked out cold, their screams cut off suddenly. Jackson knew that these prisoners would, 'disappear' before anyone could question them again. Jackson froze the dream memory and looked at himself. Dream-Jackson was calm and assured and not at all disturbed by what he had done. He was in his element. Jackson knew that the strong intelligence they had received came from him. In fact, this whole squad was dedicated to maximising on his ability. This was a hit squad, a squad poised to land pre-emptive strikes. In this particular case, Jackson had dreamed of this location. He had seem a dummy man, with a scar running down the whole left side of his face, ambush a unit of patrolling marines. He saw him organise and plan with his colleague as they fired grenade launchers and small arms down from a roof top onto a unit of patrolling marines, fired from roof tops on both sides of the street. The man Jackson had killed had hopefully put end to that particular scene from playing out. Jackson pressed play on the dream again and watched as the prisoners were bound and hoisted onto backs and carried away downstairs. He also noticed how no one came too close to dream-Jackson. Like a magnetic repulsion, they swerved before they got too close to him and never looked him in the eye. Sergeant Hasset was different; he had noticed the unique advantage Jackson gave his squad and was proud of it. He didn't care how this advantage came about, it had saved his men before and he was thankful for Jackson. He showed this by treating Jackson as a normal person, like everyone else.

Jackson woke up in bed next to Alex. He was surprising himself with how his ability was evolving, but it also scared him. He had never been able to control a dream before; usually he would be aware of it and in most cases he had to just go along with whatever the dream had in store for him. His army days coming back to him suddenly reminded him intensively of the need to act on the dreams. He had never felt as fulfilled or as full as purpose as he had during his tour to Afghanistan. It was the one place he could imagine in the world that he could let the violent consequences of his dream to run unchecked. When he first touched down in the desert, he didn't give too much away to his squad members. Jackson believed that because of the nature of the combat zones of war, his Dreams started to occur much more frequently. At one stage he was having he dream every three days. The difference between the army and civilian life, he reflected, was that he could act on the Dream with far less restriction than he could as a civilian. In the beginning, his team thought it was just good instinct or intuition but Jackson's 'nose' always had them placed right where they needed to be at exactly the right time. However, their military successes were becoming hard to ignore by the top brass and with a few questions to the squad as a whole, the big boys called Jackson in. Jackson didn't tell them about the Dream but he did tell them he could sense what was coming, so to speak. After hours of interrogation, Jackson left behind some very frustrated officers but he never let on exactly how he was able to do what he had been doing. Hoping that had been the end of it, Jackson was disheartened to find he had been summoned back again. However when got to the tent, there was only once officer present along with Sergeant Hasset. The officer didn't display any rank and didn't offer any after Jackson saluted and entered. It wasn't an interrogation this time. He was merely told that a special unit would be formed around him with special dispensation to act pre-emptively where required, without the other usual authorisation that standard operating procedure required. The unit itself would be called simply, Point Unit and Sergeant Hasset would be lead it. Jackson would be the one to provide necessary intel and would form part of the team (executing against it). Jackson himself then went on to kill many people; he tried not to count how many. The unit itself was responsible for hundreds more. They quickly gained notoriety within the greater army on the grounds of their successes but for the same reason, didn't get the chance to mix very much. To be fair, no one wanted anything to do with them. This was Jackson's life for nearly three years before it had become too much. He had started drinking to the point of blacking out. It was the only way he knew how to not dream. With the special dispensation the squad was afforded, Jackson always had access to whatever he needed, including alcohol. It didn't make a difference what alcohol it was, so long as it did the job. Eventually though, the drinking caught up with him. He was still drunk the morning of a raid and he had nearly killed a civilian and his family. Actually, it was because he was drunk that he had missed. He pulled the trigger and nearly blew some little girl's head off. Jackson was later court martialled leading to his eventual dishonourable discharge, despite Sergeant Hasset having stood up for him at his hearing. For Jackson though, it was a blessing in disguise. He needed to get a grip on his life and he wasn't doing himself any favours in the army. Also, he hated and thoroughly despised himself for almost killing a child and being a marine reminded him of that every day. As soon as he got back to the States, he checked himself into a rehabilitation centre and had never taken another drink since then. It was the rehab centre where he first learnt to control his emotions, where he took the first tentative steps to partitioning his mind. He used to take all his craving and desires for a drink and put them at the back of his mind to forget about. It was really hard going at first but he eventually started mastering it. It evolved from hiding cravings, to hiding fear, to hiding happiness. Jackson was eventually able to lock away whatever he wanted into that box. He thought it was simple thing until he tried it in the Dream. The Dream must have sensed his state of mind during his recovery and for the most part stayed away. However, they didn't completely disappear. On one such occasion when the Dream came and its panic and fear assaulted him, he tried to box them up. He failed miserably and had to suffer the full Dream experience. However, over time he mastered this too and he slowly built this ability into a shield of sorts, allowing him the mental space to do what he needed to do. Alex was stirring next to him and with a start, Jackson saw that the sun had come up. He was just about to lean into kiss her good morning when the phone in the hallway trilled suddenly. Jackson checked his watch, 05:45 – that was early for anyone to be calling. I suppose, due to the nature of the last week, the time didn't bother Alex at all. In a flash, she was up and running barefoot (and bare-bummed Jackson noticed with a smile) to pick up the phone.

"Hello?" she said enquiringly.

"Alex! Please come quick. Freddie is gone!" Alex listened on for a little while longer before telling her mom to calm down.

"We'll be there in 40 minutes. See you now!" Alex hung up. "Jackson, Freddie has disappeared again. I know its lot, but can you come with me to see Mom?" she asked while pulling on a pair of jeans.

In his mind, Jackson thought Randall would have a heart attack with him missing another of day but out loud said, "Of course, I'm in this as much as you are."

Alex drove with mad speed born of anxiety. Jackson was thankful that it was still quite early and there wasn't too much traffic yet. It actually took him a while to realise it was Saturday. It had been such an eventful week he had difficulty remembering what day it was. With a screech of tires, Alex pulled her Tesla to a dead stop in the driveway. They both got out and went into the house via the front door that had been left ajar from them. Alex's mom was in the kitchen being consoled by Mr Harver.

"Alex, I don't know what to do. This can't happening again!" she wailed at them as they appeared in the kitchen entrance. Alex ran over to her mother and hugged her. Mr Harver looked over at Jackson sternly. "Not sure why you are here again son, I don't think this has anything to do with you. This is a Harver family issue," he said. Jackson only ever remembered seeing Mr Harver once, when Fred had initially returned.

"Oh come on Dad, Jackson has been very good helping me through this. Besides, I have officially adopted him as my new boyfriend as of last night. I want him here for this. Leave it be." Alex smiled softly at Jackson (which he returned). Mr Harver just grunted and looked away, as if it didn't really matter to him anyway.

"Mr and Mrs Harver, do you mind if I take a look in Freddie's room, perhaps he left us a clue as to where he could be going?" Jackson asked.

"You won't find anything there but go ahead if it pleases you. I already have done so and found nothing of what that damned boy was planning," Mr Harver said gruffly. Jackson could see he was deeply upset, so he nodded to him and moved out of the kitchen and up the stairs to Fred's room. The first thing he noticed was the open window so he moved straight over to it. There was scuff mark on the window sill, Fred obviously left the house this way. He turned around on the spot and gave the room a once over. It was a mess, clothes lying all over the place, cupboard doors open. The whole place felt cramped with the disorderly mess and there was a strong smell of stale sweat in the air. Nothing jumped out at Jackson straight away so he moved throughout the room and searched in detail in smaller squares. Working around the room in circles until he had covered the entire floor revealed nothing. Not wanting to leave without something, Jackson turned over the bed and found more piles of clothes along with food wrappers and a torn magazine, pages hanging on for dear life to a frayed and broken spine. A rotten banana had taken up mouldy residence there as well. Jackson was pawing through the clothes when his hands grabbed hold something of a coarser texture. He closed his fingers and pulled it out from the bottom of the pile. It took him a while to register what he had in his hands but when it did, he felt the familiar light sabre of pain behind his eyes. It was intense, so much so that he blacked out for a bit. When he came to he was lying on top of the pile of clothes where the bed used to be. Right next to his nose was the source of the pain. He was looking at a beanie. It was grey and made of rough woven wool. It had tassels attached to the side, the kind that cover your ears when you wear it.

"Alex! Alex we need to go! We need to go now!" Jackson screamed as he bounded back down the stairs. He had obviously startled the Harvers and slid to halt in the kitchen. He took a moment to catch his breath before going on. 'I can't explain it all right now Mr and Mrs "Harver, but Alex and I need to go!" he said. Alex looked at him and instantly made up her mind.

"Ok let's go," was all she said.

"Now wait just minute…" a red-faced and very angry Mr Harver shouted. "You can't just go bounding about like headless chickens without explaining anything. Alex, look at your mom, she needs us all here!"

Alex did stop gathering her things but instead of answering her dad, she looked at her mom and said, "Mom, I can't tell you everything right now and I don't know if I could explain it even if I had the whole day. I can say this though," she said pointing to Jackson, "he can help and I trust him. In fact I trust him with my life. If he says we need to go, and that it's urgent, then I need to go. I believe he can help with Fred," she said as she looked over at Jackson again who nodded back. "I'm going to go and do what I can." Alex let go of her mom's shoulders, which she had been holding tightly and had creased the bathrobe. His mom blinked away a few tears and nodded back at Alex.

"Go then, find Fred!" was all she said.

"No, stay right where you are, you are needed here…" Jackson didn't let Mr Harver finish. He moved in front of him blocking his way towards his daughter.

"Sir, I will have Alex back in no time, please don't worry about her. We need to move quickly if we are to help Fred. Please, let her go. Your wife needs you now." Mr Harver looked from Jackson to his wife and slumped back in resignation. He was suddenly a very tired looking old man as he went to his wife's side. He took her hands in his and sat down with her at the table.

"You come back with Alex soon as you possibly can Jackson. When you do, we are going to have a chat you and me. We have lots to talk about," he said this with his back to him and Alex. They didn't say goodbye to the Harver's but shared a look and left together. As Alex was getting into the car she looked questioningly at Jackson.

"You had better have a good explanation as to why we just ran out of there. I hope to God we didn't leave them worse than they were we got here for no reason." Alex was battling to hide her anger but her curiosity was always going to be stronger. "What did you find up there?" she asked. Jackson said nothing but held up the beanie he had found. Alex looked at it without recognition. Jackson pulled out his notebook and showed her his sketch from the Dream. For a while, Alex stared at both the beanie and picture without comprehension.

Jackson waited, he needed her to see it. Alex's eyes widened and she slowly brought her hands up to cover her mouth. She started shaking her head and repeated, "No, no, no, no…" over and over. "No, it not right. The Dream was wrong, it can't be, it just can't be!" she kept saying to no one. Jackson tried to reach out and touch her shoulder for comfort but she pulled away. "You are wrong Jackson. You are so wrong." Jackson pulled his hand back and said nothing, he just waited. Sucking in deep breaths, Alex calmed down and redid her ponytail. "Let's go find Freddie, Jackson, let's go find him so I can prove to you that you are wrong." She put the car into reverse and pulled out of the driveway. When she was in the road, she put the car into drive and said, "So where are we going?"

Jackson thought for a bit, "My place. I want to go over my notes with you, see if we missed anything." Alex nodded and without argument, drove to the bar.

Jackson was fighting an internal battle. He knew without doubt, that Freddie was Linda's killer. He also knew, without doubt, that the campsite massacre would happen exactly as he had seen it his Dream, and that Freddie would be the one, the one hacking with machetes. He had too much experience with the Dream to ever have reason to doubt it. It always played out in reality exactly like he saw it. He believed that Alex knew this as well, deep down. It must be difficult to reconcile the fact that her sweet baby brother was a murderer, a murderer about to act again. At this moment, she refused to see it and Jackson couldn't blame her. She would come to terms with it soon enough. Jackson right now found himself in a difficult position, hence his internal conflict. He knew she should alert the police. Detective Levi would require a lot of convincing, without any evidence apart from a beanie and Jackson's Dreams.

However, he knew that his old Sergeant, Ben Hasset, would act without question and this is what was bothering him. He needed the resources of the police to initiate a state wide manhunt for Freddie before the campfire massacre came to be. If Jackson did this though, he might destroy any trust he had with Alex and any future relationship he was hoping to have. Alex, as of right now, was only searching for her lost, disturbed brother. She was not on the hunt of a killer. If Jackson went to the police, Alex would never forgive him and he couldn't live with that. It has only been a week with her but he had felt more alive in those seven days than had his entire live before that. Jackson suddenly understood that he needed Alex in his life, the police could wait for a bit, he would do all he could until the last minute. It was a risk, but a risk a relatively manageable one, for now. Alex parked the car and made her way to the fire escape entrance at his apartment from the alley of the building. Jackson had given her the keys. He would go through the bar as he had to tell Randall he would be missing work again. It was still too early for the bar to be open but Jackson had the right keys and opened the red door to the bar. He closed behind him and locked it again, worried that the day drinkers would spot an opening and dash inside. Saturday was a good day to start a little earlier for some. He made his way to the back of the bar and used the phone in the little office before the kitchen. As expected it wasn't a pleasant conversation. In the end though, Jackson managed to secure a full week off, but at a cost. He would have many double shifts when he was back and he would have to make it up to Randall as well as Shelley who would be covering him. Jackson also agreed that he would split all his tips with Shelley for a week after his return. Jackson hung up. It was a small price to pay for a full week off he knew but it still hurt a little. He walked to the stairs and made his way up to his apartment. Alex had left the door open for him so he walked straight in. She was in the kitchen making coffee and not the couch where he expected her to be. He helped her finish up and took their mugs to the nook. They both sipped quietly before Alex spoke up.

"I am not going to argue with you because I can see by the look in your eyes that you don't believe me. Freddie didn't do it; we are going to find him and sort all of this out." The passion in her voice was noticeable. Jackson merely nodded. The primary goal was to find Fred as soon as possible. They both agreed on that. He took the beanie he was still holding and dropped it in between the two of them on the table. They both stared at it. Tentatively, Alex reached out to touch it. When she did, Jackson noticed how her eyes widened in surprise before quickly being replaced by wary impassivity.

"Did something come to you, did you remember something?" Jackson asked straight away.

"No, nothing. Nothing that's useful," Alex replied, clearly not telling the whole truth.

Jackson laid his hand on top of her, the one touching the beanie.

"Alex, it's me. Think of all the ridiculous stories I have told you. Nothing to me will seem weirder than my own life. Tell me." She looked away before replying but she didn't move her hand.

"It came to me like a picture. I saw the campsite Jackson, how weird is that? It wasn't a vison, it was memory. I have been there before… with Freddie." Jackson immediately went into business mode.

"When was this, where was this, was it near, was it in state?" he asked, pen ready to take notes.

"I'm not sure," she said and closing her eyes and rubbing her temples as if trying to massage the memory into being. Something about the gesture struck Jackson as familiar but he dismissed in light of the urgency of the questions he needed to find answers to. "It's very strange, I usually have such good recall but with this I am battling. It's like my mind is full of fog, it parts every now and then to show a piece of the memory, but I can't see the complete picture," she said. Jackson shared her frustration but pushed on.

"Did you visit this place recently, is there anything else you can remember?"

"No, that's it. I'm not even sure it was a real memory any more. It's like a feeling… and if I had to go with that, it's a feeling that says it was recent," she said with growing conviction.

"Ok that's good Alex. When last did you go camping or when last did you have a reason to visit a park?" Jackson asked relentlessly.

"No, I don't camp, neither does Freddie. If we visited a park in the last year or so I can't remember it." Jackson stood and paced while he thought. He moved over to the little bookshelf he kept in the hallway next to the table with the phone on it, and pulled out a crumpled map of the state. It had been wedged between the pages of a novel he had forgotten he was reading. He returned to the table and open the map out for both of them. With a pen he circled three camp grounds about an hour's drive away. He noted them in his book; Beaver Pond State Park, Heckscher State Park and Clarence Fahnestock State Park.

"Ok, we can start with these. We should be able to reach them during the course of the day. It's a long shot but at least it's a start. From there, if we have no luck, we can extend our search out towards the ones further away." Jackson slipped the pen into the notebook and closed it. Alex nodded and got up. '

"May I use your shower quickly? I feel dirty for some reason and if we are going to be in the car all day I don't think I'll get another chance," she asked. Jackson went and fetched a fresh towel from the linen closet and while she was getting cleaned up, packed a cooler bag with bottles of water and some snacks he had lying around. It wasn't much but he figuredthat he could get more on the road. Alex returned from the shower looking slightly pink from a vigorous scrub, he assumed. Her hair was still wet but bound in its familiar ponytail. Even though she was still wearing the same clothes as yesterday, she seemed in better spirits. "Let's go," she said.

Detective Levi was fiddling with an evidence packet while lost in thought. Within the packet, was a ring with some inscription that had worn away. It was similar in look to those college rings some schools gave out, but somehow cheaper looking. For such a high-profile case, in terms of media coverage, the police had next to nothing to go on. The Linda

Gerber crime scene hinted at an act of impulse, at least in how the body seemed gruesomely but randomly mutilated. However, the location and the set-up where they found the body tied to chair in the middle of a dark room with a single, battery powered spotlight shining down on it, was without question premediated. Rope and chairs and battery powered spotlights didn't just appear when you needed them. The contrast of the actual murder versus the scene almost would have you believing there were two separate people involved. One planning ahead and one committing the act. It spoke of a very confused mind or a very disturbed mind. One way of the other though, there were no clues to be found, other than this ring, this one single signpost in a desert of confusion and blood. Breaking the news to the Gerard family had been difficult for John Levi. He had been in the force for over 30 years and had been considering early retirement only last year. Informing families of their murdered children was always hard but this on really had punched him the gut. He only had empty words of condolence to pass on. He could give them no facts about who did this or why. He had absolutely nothing to go on and deep down he didn't know what to do. Once again, his mind started to drift off to thoughts of retirement. Detective Levi shook his head and repeated a mantra of his own to help refocus.

"You can't understand what you don't know, work on what you do know." He returned his attention to the ring before picking up the phone, "Ben, don't you want to come across to my desk for a moment. I want to run something by you." Ben Hasset was an excellent officer, only recently made detective. In John's opinion, he should have made detective much earlier than last year but for whatever reason, Ben waited until only recently to write the exam, which he subsequently passed with flying colours. John was intrigued by the former military man. A strict disciplinarian who had the look of someone who would get any job asked of him, done. His demeanour was the sort that brooked no argument but if one went looking for fight, Ben was not shy to dish it out. So far as John knew, Ben had never missed a day of work. His clothes were always smart and neatly pressed and his standard black tie always tightly and impressively knotted at the nape of his neck. Ben wasn't the sort to back down from a fight or to step aside if asked. These might be some of the reasons that didn't endear him to his colleagues, but if any of them had been asked who they would take to war with them, Ben would be first on each of their lists. Detective Levi watched as Ben strode towards his desk, straight backed and serious.

"You asked to see me John?" he said in clipped tones. Although of the same rank, John was the more experienced and had the overriding respect of the whole precinct. Nearly everyone deferred to him as of higher rank.

"Take a seat Ben, loosen your tie. I just want to ask for your help on the Gerard case." Ben did take a seat but didn't loosen his tie. John knew he wouldn't. He suddenly felt a bit embarrassed at his own shoddy dress. He hadn't done up the top button of his shirt for the last 15 years and the tie always hung lose, at a slight angle. His white shirt was nearing see-though grey with age and his grey suit jacket, with brown reinforcing on the elbows, hung over the back of his chair. In fact, recently it lived there more than on his shoulders. "Ben, this ring we found, do you have any idea what we can do with it?" Ben took the ring and turned it over a few times.

"I have already briefed a couple of informants with a picture but nothing has come back as yet," he said smartly, but politely.

"Would Jackson Brandt have been one of those informants?" John asked slyly. He watched as Ben coloured slightly on his neck and cheeks before his natural control reasserted itself.

"You know I don't give up the name of my informants John." was his reply.

"Yes I am aware of that and I would never expect you to Ben. I know how well your network has helped in the past. However, this is a little different. You see, Jackson came in with his girlfriend the other day you know, Alex Harver, the one whose missing brother recently returned." Ben nodded and John continued, "Well, he slipped up and I think he knew it. He asked me about the Linda Gerard case before it became public knowledge. Yes it went on the news the same day but Jackson was several hours ahead of them. How do you think that happened?" Ben stared impassively at John before making up his mind and answering.

"I showed Jackson the picture of the ring to see if he could help but I didn't mention any names. Also, I gave him the heads up on the murder scene when it was discovered," Ben said without the slightest trace of guilt.

"Why would you do that Ben? That wasn't not information that should be public knowledge," John asked more out of interest than actually flagging a breach of protocol. For the first time Ben looked a little uncomfortable.

"It's hard to explain. Jackson is a bit different. He, kind of, well he see's things. My past experiences with him, both here at the police and before in the army, has given me complete trust in his ability. I have never had reason to doubt any of Jackson's insights and he has more often than not helped me on cases where conventional methods would and were failing." Ben had once again regained full composure and was confidently telling his story, regardless of what John might think of it. John himself was impressed. He was impressed with the surety Ben put behind his assessment of Jackson, even if it was absurd.

"So you knew Jackson in the army?" he asked.

"Yes, I led the specialised squad Jackson was in on tour in Afghanistan. I was his Sergeant. In fact, Jackson still refers to my rank when he is lost in though sometimes," Ben said smiling.

"Specialist Squad?" Jon asked.

"I can't tell you anymore about that John, even if I wanted to. It was classified then and remains so. What I can tell you is this, The Marine Corp trusted Jackson's insight impeccably. Because of his actions, many American lives were saved." This really got John's attention but he knew better than to press any further.

"Do you trust him Ben?" was all he asked.

"With my life then and with my life now," Ben said with fervour. "I will also tell you this because you will undoubtedly find out yourself with a bit of digging; Jackson was court martialled and dishonourably discharged before his tour was up. Don't read too much into his character from that. There is way more to the story that what was recorded," Ben said. John wondered what Jackson must have done to earn such admiration and loyalty.

"Thanks for being honest with me Ben, even with the limitations you are under," John told him with sincerity. Ben merely nodded back. For whatever reason, the conversation with Ben had eased an unknown worry about Jackson he had been harbouring. "Ok, but back to the present, I need your help with the Gerard case. As of right we have nothing. Can you dig up some info on this ring for me? I think the best place we need to start is where it was made. I know that there must be a million places that inscribe rings, but maybe there are fewer that make custom jobs like this. It isn't the sort of ring you see in the shops you know." Ben took the ring and said he would look into it.

As he got up, he hesitated before saying, "John, I can vouch for Jackson. If you need help, pull him in. I never questioned how he does it and truthfully I don't want to know, but he gets results." Ben turned and walked away without waiting for a response. Detective Levi chewed the end of his pencil, replaying the conversation in his head.

Detective Levi had already spoken with and taken statements from both Miles and Phillip from the Fred Harver case. He thought it would be worthwhile updating the parents that Fred's story did indeed check out. He remembered the day their son had come home and how anxious everyone was after Fred told his story. It was as good an excuse to speak to that boy as anything. He was still extremely bothered by that whole episode and wanted to see if there were any updates to the yarn that Fred how spouted. His gut had told him there was more to this and he had learned to trust his gut a long time ago. This whole thing was all wrong. He just knew this and from what Ben had told him, Jackson seemed a pretty good judge of evidence. Truthfully, he also hoped he would see Jackson at the house as he had a few things he wanted to ask him too. It was a long shot but he had moved on much less before, sometimes you just needed to trust the little you had. He was just about to knock on the door of the Harver house when it opened suddenly.

"Oh Detective, do you have news already? Where's Fred?" Mrs Harver had grabbed the front of his jacket, she had a wild, crazed look to her.

"Joan! Joan let the detective go," Mr Harver shouted from the hall where he was watching the exchange. Mrs Harver let go of his jacket, a little embarrassed, and tried to smoothe his clothes before stepping away. The detective didn't try and enter the house. He spoke from the landing '

"Is Fred missing again?" he asked with genuine confusion.

"Yes, yes he disappeared last night. Alex and Jackson went off after him… I thought that they must have told you." She burst into tears again and Mr Harver put his arm around her shoulders.

"No, I haven't yet heard from Alex or Jackson. You said Fred left last night. Did he leave a note or anything?" he asked.

"Nothing, nothing at all. Just left in the middle of the night, though his window," Mr Harver answered this time. "If not for Fred, why are you here detective?"

"Nothing special, although it was about Fred. I just wanted to tell you that I had checked in with Miles and Phillip. Fred's story checked out. I was here to tell you that you had nothing to worry about." He looked at both Mr and Mrs Harver in turn. "I'm sure you still don't have anything to worry about!" he said hurriedly, noticing the concern on their faces. "Did Alex and Jackson say where they were going?" he asked them.

"No, but that Jackson was pretty adamant that they move fast. He grabbed Alex and they bolted in a rush," Mr Harver said. This interested the detective greatly but he didn't show it. Instead, he chatted with the Harvers for a few more minutes but nothing worthwhile came from it. He thanked them both and left. On the road back to the PD he reminded himself to look up Alex's number. Something was very, very wrong and he was going to find out just what the fuck was going on. Alex would be his first call.

Fred had finally given into the urging from the outside. It had all happened without conscious thought. One moment, he had been lying in bed staring out of the window, then the next moment, backpack strapped on, he was out the window on the house roof and then eventually, scaling down the trellis covered in ivy. He was just about to take off before he was noticed when an impulse pushed him towards to the shed. Luckily the moon was hidden behind some clouds and it was inky dark as he crept through the back garden. He needn't have worried about being spotted, his mom and dad were asleep and were dead to the world. No doubt, with thanks to their worry over Freddie. It had been an exhausting period since he had returned home. He kept being asked if he was OK, what had happened, can they get anything for him... and on and on. Fred didn't have the answers they were looking for; he wished he had. If it were so he wouldn't feel so different to other people, like being operated by remote control. The conflict within him was constant, never ending. It bordered on psychical pain at times and to cope, Fred would shut himself off from everyone. He had to hide in his own house. After many tears and angered shouting (mostly from his dad on that score) his parents had decided to leave him alone and allow him the space to come to them when he was ready. Fred somehow knew that he would never be ready. The decision to leave must have been made at some point when Fred had given over to complete hopelessness. He had given up trying to understand, he had given up worrying over it and he had given up caring. He just wanted it all to end. That was when the longing to move must have taken control. Fred had been really surprised to find himself outside at first as he couldn't remember even getting out of bed. However, now that he was moving, at least one part of him seemed renewed with purpose. Like a man dying of thirst, Fred reached out gladly at any hope of salvation. Standing still in the darkness before the shed, Fred waited for the count of ten and then hearing nothing, slowly pushed open the door. He didn't know what he was looking for until his hands found it as he slid them over the work table in the middle of the shed. As a kid, Fred had always been fascinated by the shed. It was filled with tools he didn't understand, all exotic and full of potential only a child could imagine. It was the smell of fresh sawdust and cut grass, everything that he associated with summer. During his early school years, he would sit on a little bench his father had made for him and watch while his dad made little bits and pieces furniture that the house behind them was filled with. Fred's dad was no master craftsman but in his eyes, his dad looked like a giant wearing his tool belt and wielding saws and hammers and the like. They were some of Fred's fondest memories and he had to stop suddenly to release a brief sob. That Fred was no longer around, someone new had grown out of him, someone Fred didn't know or understand. It terrified him to no end but he had accepted his new path and would walk it as best he could. He had to know what it was he had become, or was becoming. With his hands on the cold metal of the object he was touching, he came to from his reverie and lifted the long, sword like an object closer to his face to better see it. It was a machete, recently sharpened. He remembered his dad saying that all the fancy equipment you could buy these days came nowhere close to whacking weeds, bushes and hedges as expertly as the machete did. Fred gripped the machete with both hands on the handle and mimicked a sword fight just as he did when he was much younger. This time however, there was no one to catch him in the act and to hand out a hiding. Fred mused on this for a while – he knew now that his dad was trying to make him understand that is was a very dangerous weapon and that he could badly inure himself in an accident. But then it had seemed like a great injustice to a small nine-year-old. Fred strapped his sword to the lacings in his backpack and was just about to leave when he spotted a matching machete mounted on the wall. This must have been a replacement his dad had bought for the older one that Fred had already appropriated. It took a few more seconds to retrieve this as well. It now sat laced next to the older machete on his back. Kind of like his favourite ninja turtle, Leonardo. Pushing such childish thought away, Fred took one last look at the shed before leaving. One of his favourite places in the world, so full of happy memories.

He knew that he would probably never see it again but couldn't explain why. Closing the door quietly behind him, Fred looked at the house in front of him. Still no lights, no sounds. He tiptoed around the side and made his way into the street. He had no idea where he wanted to go but moving felt good, so he didn't stop. The road was empty and nothing moved around him. He checked his watch, 01:45. Fred was smiling without realising it, just being out of the house doing something felt so right, so purposeful. Forty-five minute later Fred was outside the bus stop and even though it remained open all night, there were no busses in the lot. A sleepy clerk at the counter and was startled into full wakefulness when Fred quietly spoke from the other side of the counter.

"Hi, can you tell me when the next bus will be coming through?" Fred asked politely, now that he had the clerk's attention.

"Ah where to?" he said. "We have quite a few long distance, inter-state ones coming through in the next two hours. Nothing local though. They only start running from about 06:00." Fred stood awhile staring between the clerk and the departures board behind him. He hadn't even heard the man speak as his eyes focused on one line and wouldn't move away.

"Could I please get a ticket to Harriman State Park," said Fred. It just seemed right to him. It was the name that triggered some sort of pleasant memory of the place and with desperate certainty, Fred knew that was where needed to go.

"Sure thing. The first bus only comes in at 08:00 on that route, it stops off on the way outstate so you need to remember your stop." The clerk seemed quite bored and Fred thought it was natural given the time and monotony of the work. Fred paid and accepted his ticket.

"Um, those things on your back... I'm not sure that you are allowed to carry weapons on the bus," the clerk said. He had woken up fully now and was clearly interested in what Fred was carrying.

"These aren't weapons, they're garden tools but I am taking them for the hike. If I remember clearly, Beaver Pond

165

Camp group had some pretty overgrown trails around it given the fact that it primarily served as a party spot for kids." Fred smiled disarmingly.

"Well maybe work at covering them up. You don't want to scare the other passengers." Fred agreed, thanked the man and walked off. He found a row of empty benches in the nearly deserted station. There were a few people clearly asleep in their seats. As he worked to cover the blades on his backpack with a towel he had packed, someone across from him spoke up. It was no more than a whisper but Fred could clearly hear every word that was said.

"You going off hiking? That's some serious equipment you carrying," the man said. Fred looked up into a face staring at him from a row of empty blue seat across from him. Later Fred would not remember any features or even that he had spoken to anyone, but what he saw then was faded black grey jeans, a tight-fitting overcoat and a wide brimmed black hat, like a dark cowboy he thought.

"Ah, you know how it is, rather be prepared. Would hate to get stuck out in the sticks without them. They help clear a path through overgrown trails and stuff," Fred head himself say. The man just continued to stare at him for a while. The brim of his hat covered his eyes mostly but Fred could clearly see the smile spreading on his face. He still didn't reply.

"Well I don't want to disturb your wait Mister. I'm going to move across there," he said as he pointed vaguely away, "Hopefully I can get some sleep. Enjoy the evening." Fred hurriedly picked up his backpack, now secured with a towel and covering the machetes and moved as far away from the smiling man as he could. He was badly shaken and disturbed by the man and didn't want to be anywhere near him. Finally alone and out of direct eyesight of the man, Fred propped his bag on his lap and rested his head against it. He was exhausted again and would try and catch a bit of sleep before the bus arrived.

Bob watched as Fred scurried away from him, drinking in all the sudden alarm and fear pulsing out from him. He didn't need to present himself in such a way but he found it hard to resist. He loved the look of unwitting recognition that was quickly overlaid by blanketing panic. This story was developing nicely, all the moving parts in play. There were countless other stories he had in motion but for some reason, this particular one, on this particular plane and time had really captured his attention and he found himself watching closer than the others. Not that it was more important or anything, because they all served the same purpose, but just that it seemed to have more of an element of uncertainty about it. Thinking on that for a bit, the man who thought of himself as Bob also thought it was because of the Dream Stalker. That man Jackson was only starting to come into his gift and was such a wild card in this story that Bob couldn't see how the end of it was going to play out... and it was delicious. It truly didn't matter what happened, but some endings were so much more nourishing than other and he couldn't wait for this final meal to be served up. The Dream Stalker already seemed to know the price his gift extoled from him but did he really understand it purpose, it's true mission – Bob didn't think so, at least not yet. The way this Dream Stalker was progressing in his evolution was frightfully fast and exciting and Bob was loving it. He had not come across many like Jackson and he was going to make sure he squeezed every little drop out of the experience. Looking back at the boy, his puppet, Bob hoped that his mind wouldn't break again. The episode with the Gerard girl had almost ended the story before it could properly be told and Bob had to do some serious damage control to keep the plot rolling on. The kid was trying to sleep but Bob knew he wouldn't be able to. He knew that the boy was feeling a sense of anticipation and anxiety but without any foundation to base it on, would only remained excitedly confused. Feeling rather happy about it, Bob drank in the confusion and pulled out his flute. When things were going well he liked to play. He found it relaxing and that it added greatly to his experience of events. At that moment Fred felt a jolt of panic and immediately stared at where the man he had spoken to earlier had been sitting. There was just an empty row of seats. Rubbing his eyes with the back of his hand he looked again, the man had disappeared into thin air. All that remained to Fred's senses was a faint hint of a tune, possibly from a flute or some such. Fred shook himself as if from a dream and returned his head to the top of his bag. He tried to sleep, but he couldn't. He just lay there with his eyes closed, tightly holding onto his bag and waiting. If anybody had noticed him all they would have seen was lonely, tired backpacker waiting for his ride, like a million others before him.

Chapter 6 – Campfire Songs

Jackson was wide awake. Alex was asleep, fully clothed, on top of the covers on the bed. The small TV was on, playing something softly in the background. There were containers with the left-over take-out scattered about the small table Jackson was working on. 'He must have missed something!' he thought with frustration He kept going over his notes, the pages of the book starting to look really ragged. The whole day had bene a complete waste. They had only managed to visit two of the three parks they had initially planned. The first one they came to, Hecksher State Park, was definitely not the one they were looking for. Most of the camp sites in the park that they checked out were on the lake. Jackson had seen no hint of a lake in his Dream. It was the same for Alex, she had absolutely no memory of the place. The other park had taken an additional two hours to reach. The Clarence Fahnestock Park was closed to all visitors and no reason for the close or the opening date was shown on the sign on the fence.

Apart from having nothing but a list of parks to visit and a used beanie, Jackson had no other clues to follow up on. He kept thinking of the timing of the whole thing. If Freddie was the murderer and was about to commit a crime on an even greater scale, why bother even coming home? Why the break in between the events? Jackson knew and trusted his ability but even with his past experience and knowledge of what he could do, he wasn't sure. Freddie was not the sort of person who could do the things he saw happening. It might have been because of his feelings for Alex that were clouding his judgement but he had to admit, part of him agreed with her. Despite Freddie's apparent confusion and possible mental issues, he didn't seem like the sort of person that could plan and pull off these things off without some help. Freddie struck Jackson as the guy going along with the plan, not making it. In this way, he and Alex were so different. Alex displayed a wily sort of street smarts and came across as very capable. Freddie on the other hand seemed more of the molly-coddled type, always looked after, always forgiven for any indiscretion. He was without doubt very smart, as the college replies to his applications he received indicated. But it was more book smart. It was one of the reasons Jackson had completely discounted the story that Freddie had told, he didn't believe Freddie could go that long without support, or even calling his parents. The fact that he had disappeared again had completely blindsided Jackson, despite his Dreams foretelling it. He pushed his chair back with his legs as stood up. He needed some air, he needed to think. He moved over to the bed and gently manoeuvre Alex under the covers. He stood staring at her for a bit while she slept but then moved away, feeling guilty at how creepy it might come across to the person sleeping. He turned the TV off before opening the motel door and stepping outside. It wasn't anything special, the motel. It was two parallel rows of identical rooms running for the span of half a block. The doors and tin roof were painted green while the walls were off-white. Apart from the rooms at the edge of the rows, all the rooms shared dividing walls and you could more often than not hear the conversation of your neighbours.

The one row was slightly above the other as it is built on a slope and you could look down on the roof of the row below from the front door, which was where Jackson was now. He was in a room near the middle, 14C, two rooms away from the staircase that cut the two rows into four separate blocks. Jackson headed to that short stairway, walked down it and headed towards the office where the vending machine just outside the main door. He inserted a few coins and a Pepsi dropped down with a clang into the slot at the bottom. He picked up the can and sat down on a bench next to the machine. He sipped the drink as he watched the empty road across the parking lot. The time must have been around 02:00 but he knew he wouldn't be able to sleep that night. He was worried, the headache was constant now and he felt the drawstrings of the conclusion pulling closer together. The road in front of him was dark but interrupted by regular little pools of light around the poles supporting the street lights, each pole joined by telephone lines. Jackson took another sip and looked again. Where before the road was completely deserted, a man with a wide brimmed hat now stood. The pool of light did little to reveal much more than a silhouette but it was the presence of the man that had Jackson taking notice. It seemed like he was drawing the darkness towards him, through where his feet met the road. It had the effect of making the pool of light around him seem even brighter, but hiding more than revealing. Jackson heard a strange flute-like sound and immediately felt a wave a panic engulfs him. Without thinking he partitioned his mind and the emotion ceased to exist. He looked back at the man in the road, his drink forgotten and falling from his dead fingers. The man across the street stood straight up suddenly, as if caught off guard. They both stood like that, staring across a parking lot and the hip-high chain link fence in a silent staring duel.

"Hey buddy. Hey, watchya doin? Aw c'mon man look at that mess." Jackson immediately came back to himself. He saw the Pepsi can leaning on its side spilling its dark liquid at his feet. He quickly looked up across the road again but the man was gone, as was the panic. The night clerk of the motel was still pointing from the floor to him and getting red in the face.

Jackson apologised for the mess, picked up the can and quickly returned to his room before the man's face turned purple and he passed out. Jackson was extremely anxious as he quietly opened the door to his room and slipped inside. It was the sense of familiarity with the man across the road that had him on edge. Where had he seen him before? His thoughts were interrupted when looked down at Alex. She must have got up and looked at her cell phone while he was away, as the screen was still glowing blue when on the bedside table.

It wasn't here before; it must have been in her bag. It turned off before he could see anymore but he would have felt weird snooping anyways. It was just strange as Alex didn't seem to have too much time for cell phones. Much like him, he had never seen her use it so it was strange that she had now. He thought it must be to check in on her parents, check if there was any news or something like that. He would ask her about it when they woke up. He got undressed down to his boxers and slipped into bed beside Alex. The time was 03:15 when he finally felt tired, at least enough to sleep.

Alex was up before Jackson the next morning and gently shook him awake. When he finally opened his eyes he looked around in confusion. At first he didn't know where he was but it came to him eventually. The motel, they were at the motel. He looked up at Alex lying in bed next to him, rubbing her eyes. She looked equally as disorientated and confused. Jackson tried to remember what had happened last night but it wasn't clear, in fact it was clear as mud. Both he and Alex took a moment to let their brains engage first gear; they were sat up in bed, leaning back against the headboard. After a moment, Jackson stretched across to the side table to his watch, he could never sleep with it on. He got the shock of his life when he looked at the time.

"Jesus, its 16:00 Alex, we've been asleep the whole day!" Alex heard the alarm in his voice but couldn't make sense of it as she was till hazy with a sleep hangover. When it hit home, her eyes widened and she scrambled for her cell phone. She was out of bed in a second digging through her bag. "It's there on the bedside," Jackson pointed.

"Oh, OK, that's weird!" was all she said. She confirmed the time on the phone display. "What the hell, how could we have slept the whole day?" she said. Jackson just shrugged his shoulders and made for the shower. He desperately needed to wake up and focus on what was going on. He turned on the tap and was letting the water run to get hot when Alex slipped past him naked and into the shower ahead of him. "Ladies first!" was all she said. Despite his newest worry about losing a whole day, Jackson smiled and contented himself with brushing his teeth while he waited his turn. When they were both showered and dressed, they quickly discussed their plan of action. They would drive immediately to Beaver Pond

State Park, although it was late, they had chosen a motel close enough to get there before dark. Jackson went down to reception to pay for the extra day he had unwittingly stayed, while Alex took her bag to the car.

"Thanks for the extra day. We didn't realise how tired we were," Jackson told the man at reception.

"No problem. When I came to inform you that you were past check out time you kind of made it very clear you wanted another day!" the man said inquisitively. "In fact, you kinda screamed at me to go away!" he followed on saying. Jackson hated that he had been rude but was more concerned that he didn't remember any of it.

"I must apologise, that's not normally like me. I think with the week I have had I was just exhausted." Jackson had tried to sound sincere but he heard the worried tone in his own voice. By the way the man behind the counter looked at him, Jackson realised he wasn't going to ever be friends with this person. He thanked him, picked up his bag and walked towards the car. The time was now 16:45 and they still had a 20-minute drive to the park. The moment Jackson was buckled in, Alex drove off.

"Any ideas as to what happened last night? Have you ever slept an entire day away before?" Alex asked worriedly. Even in Jackson's experience of the weird, this had never happened and he told her so. They both understood that there were no answers to be found discussing this so they just listed to navigation software giving them directions, lost in their own heads. What he didn't want to say was how scared he felt. His headache was bearable but couldn't be ignored any longer. It was a drum beat behind his eyes that made him squint in the late afternoon sunlight. More than this though was the inexplicable feeling that he was being manipulated, someone somewhere had already plotted his next steps and was guiding him along the way unseen. It came to him suddenly, the memory of the man across the street last. 'How had he forgotten that,' he thought to himself? He was about to tell Alex of it when she spoke up.

"We're here Jackson," she said so quietly that he almost missed it. She was looking at the sign before the entrance and was shaking slightly. "This is it! This is the park where we'll find Freddie!" Her face had lost all its colour, she looked pale as a corpse. "I remember this place Jackson. Nothing about it really, but I remember being here before. I can't really explain it but this is it!" Jackson took a moment to study her face. "Do you believe me?" she asked.

"Yes Alex, I do. I have asked you to take many a leap of faith before and I think it only fair I do the same for you." Jackson replied while placing his hand on top of hers, which where clasped together in her lap. It seemed to break the spell that Alex was in. She turned her head towards him, smiled and leaned into kiss him. They drove into the entrance of the park. Jackson could feel that this was right, he was in the right spot. He hadn't yet recognised anything familiar about the place but he knew he would. The drawstrings were pulling tighter in his mind.

With the fading light of day, Jackson managed to secure them a little cabin for the evening. For once the stars were aligning for them, there had been a last-minute cancellation and Jackson eagerly took the booking. They had both realised that they couldn't search the area properly this late and decided to begin hunting at first light. They drove out to the little wood cabin and while Alex stayed behind to unpack,

Jackson drove off to get some supplies for the evening. They had driven past several stores outside the park on the way in so it wouldn't take too long. He had other reasons to go though, the pain in his head was becoming unbearable which needed some serious painkillers, and he had to make a call. They needed help on this. Even though they both agreed they were in the right vicinity, a quick look at the park map revealed a large search area, too much for just two people. The clock was ticking and Jackson wanted to call in the reinforcements. Once he was outside the park, he headed straight from the drug store where he bought the strongest non-prescription drugs he could find. He also stocked up on waters and a bottle of wine for Alex. Then he made his way to the mini mart across the road and stocked up on dinner supplies. He knew he should have made the call by now but he couldn't help putting it off. If Alex found out he didn't know how she would handle it. He had no doubt that word like betrayal would feature in their conversation. He was in the car thinking of all the reasons he shouldn't make the call when the cell phone in his hand rang. He got such a fright he dropped it to the floor of the car under the steering wheel. It took him a few frustrated moments to reach it but he eventually did. This phone never rang, he had only given the number to a couple of people, one of them Alex.

The other... "Hi Ben, speak of the devil," he said without looking at the phone display. "Hey Jack, what the hell have you gotten yourself into? I have had John Levi all over me, wringing me dry on information on you." Ben said, straight to the point as always.

"I promise I will explain later Ben, but right now I need your help. I'm working a job," Jackson told him. Ben was quiet for a bit. 'Working a job' was a phrase Jackson used when he was following up on one of his more supernatural leads. "Ok, I can't give you all the details now Sarg and I don't have any real physical evidence to back it up, but there is going to be an event, either tonight or the next judging by my headache. It's going to be bad Sarg, at least 5 kids hacked to death by machete." He let that sink in before continuing. "I have traced the event to a park up state, Beaver Pond State Park. I have booked a cabin for the night and will start searching properly tomorrow. It's going to happen here no doubt. Do you think you can rustle up the cavalry to help comb the area?" Jackson finished. As always, Ben Hasset digested all the information calmly before responding.

"Jack, are you with Alex Harver?" Jackson said he was. "What else do I need to know Jackson; I will be putting my head on the block here? It will take more than my hunch to send the police over in force," Ben asked. Jackson considered his words carefully but realised he had no real choice in the matter.

"The bad guy here Ben… it's Freddie Harver!"

Ben didn't waste time "Alex's brother? Does she know you are telling me this?" Jackson shook his head and realised that Ben wouldn't be able to see that. "No," was all he simply answered.

"There is something else Ben. Freddie is also the person who murdered Linda Gerard." He heard a sharp intake of breath through the phone.

"Ok, you and I will be having a very long chat when this over. I will see what I can do about getting some officers over to your area. Last thing Jack, you can trust Detective Levi, he knows about you. Not sure he believes any of it but he knows what I know. I know it wasn't for me to tell him but the reality of the situation is that it was unavoidable. I tell you this because it sounds like you might need as many friends in this as possible. You have really rolled yourself into the thick of things. Keep this phone on you at all times!" Ben hung up, not one for waiting on formalities. Jackson considered Ben's words. Detective Levi was in the loop now, could he trust him? Jackson was still thinking of his conversation with Ben as he drove back towards the park. It was dark now, approaching 19:30. He popped a few painkillers in his mouth and chewed them down as he drove.

Detective Levi hadn't slept all day. Like Alex and Jackson, he was following up on a few leads on the Linda Gerard case. Things were starting to get really weird. Ben had managed to dig up a few places that made custom designed rings, of the specialised sort that had been found at the crime scene. He had hit pay dirt on only the third call of the day, at a small jewellery store about thirty minutes from the PD. It was the type of place probably making more money from flipping trade-ins than actual new sales. The owner of the store had only taken a quick glance at the ring before telling him that he had made good on an order of 100 of the rings.

"I don't make many more these days, more of a reseller you understand. I remember that ring clearly. I have a sign up front saying I do custom work but I had never before been asked to do anything on that scale, so I was surprised to say the least." The man had a bit of a greasy demeanour. Balding, with black hair only present in an arch around the ears and the back of his head and he constantly wiped sweat way from the smooth dome on top with hanky. It wasn't all that hot inside but Detective Levi thought it must have been an ingrained habit for the man by now. "Anyways, I took that order about two years ago, I might still have the receipt if you would like to see." Detective Levi said that he would certainly like to see it while the man went around into a small office behind the counter to search.

Detective Levi asked, "Do you remember what you inscribed on the rings?"

A detached voice answered from behind the wall, "Not exactly, it was something in Latin... hold on, here's the receipt." The man propped a pair of reading glasses onto the end of his nose from where they had been hanging from a cord around his neck. He returned into view, reading the small piece of paper held at a distance from him in order to read it better. "'*vocare ad regnum*' is what I inscribed. After doing a hundred off them I can't believe I had forgotten that." The man smiled and asked if he should make a copy. Detective Levi graciously accepted the offer.

When the man disappeared around the corner he asked him, "Any idea of what it means?"

"Yup, *call to fight or call to kingdom,* or some such thing." the man said as he returned to the front and handed over the duplicate of the receipt. John read the client's name and address. 'Jyms', it was only a few minutes away from here. "So detective, can you tell me what case you are working? It's not every day cops come here asking for my help, you see?" Detective Levi pocketed the copy of the receipt before replying.

"Nothing too exciting I can assure you. Just trying to find someone, hopefully this will help." Detective Levi shook the man's hand and thanked him before walking out on the street. After a quick consultation of the map he had in the car,

Detective Levi drove to Jyms. The lot seemed mostly deserted when he arrived but Jyms was unmistakable. It was so garishly bright it was impossible to avoid. Detective Levi's was the only car present as he parked in front of the gym. He got out of the car and walked to the entrance. The doors were closed and he had to cup his hands to look through the glass. It looked clean and tidy inside but there was nothing else to notice. Stepping back from the glass doors he noticed a piece of paper stuck to his shoe so he bent down to pick it up. *Jyms is sad to announce that it has officially closed!* It was unadorned and printed simply in bold letters as a heading. It must have been stuck to the doors and blown off. There was a number at the bottom with other details about recouping subscription fees and such. Detective Levi tried the number on his cell phone but it just kept ringing, no answering machine. Cursing his luck, he folded up the closed sign and pocketed it. He was right alongside his car door when a voice suddenly spoke up.

"Strangest thing, closed just a couple of days ago. No warning at all. Very strange, one minute they were straining at the seams with members and the next, BOOM, closed. I tell you there were some very pissed off members here yesterday," the wheezy voice giggled and took a sip of something from a bottle wrapped in a brown paper bag. Detective Levi admonished himself for not noticing the man before. He was a vagrant, the sort that always managed to find run down shopping centres like this. He was dressed in a shoddy back overcoat that covered most of him. A hat had been pulled over his face, hiding his features. His was sitting on a piece of cardboard and leaning against the window of a deserted pool care shop.

Detective Levi approached him, the strong smell of raw spirits, piss and sweat forcing him to keep a good few metres apart.

"You hang around here often?" he asked the man.

"Ole Robbie here calls this lot his own. Although I might have to move soon seeing everybody is now gone," he said sadly.

"Any idea of why they closed down?" Detective Levi asked.

"Nope, a great mystery!" Robbie replied and giggled at his own joke before taking another sip from his bottle. Detective Levi couldn't think of what else to ask the man, so he reached into his wallet and dropped a couple of dollar notes into the man's hand. Robbie nodded his thanks and then returned all his attention to his bottle. Detective Levi was about to climb into his car when Robbie spoke from behind him. "You'll figure it out soon Detective Levi," the voice giggled. Detective Levi stopped and turned around.

"How did you know my… name?" he asked, but the man had gone. He walked right over to where the man had been but not a trace remained, even the smell was gone. He was stumped. Did he really just have an imaginary conversation? Confused and quietly worried about himself, he drove back to the PD.

Jackson bought take-out from the first joint he saw on the way back to the cabin. They were both too lazy and on edge to cook, so he and Alex nestled themselves onto the couch in the small but neat cabin, eating their noodles with chopsticks. Alex had the bottle of wine open on the table in front of them. There was no TV, only an empty fireplace to look at. It was a solid log cabin, a single combination room consisting of a kitchen, small round table, double bed, couch and fireplace all taking up their allotted posts in the rectangular space. It was cosy and on any other occasion, Jackson would have enjoyed it. Tonight it was different through. There was anxiety in the air leading to a sort of mental static electricity. Both he and Alex could feel it but didn't acknowledge it. Conversation had been limited to the plan of action for tomorrow, the route of different camping grounds across the park. Once that was done and the food was finished, they both sat in contemplative silence. Without any urging, Alex curled her legs under her and cradled the glass of wine against her chest, leaning into Jackson. He put his arm around her without a word. Jackson believed Alex felt the same way about him as he did for her but he was worried, no, he was terrified that what was happening would somehow pull them apart. He made a quiet promise to himself not to let her go, no matter the circumstances. It was selfish, he knew that. He couldn't force her to feel anything for him regardless of the situation. He knew only that he wanted her close enough to never let go.

Alex sensed the intensity of Jackson thoughts as he squeezed her with his arm.

"Jackson, I haven't thanked you properly for all your help in this. I know what you're going to say…,'the Dream makes it impossible to avoid'… but I wanted to thank you anyway, having you here makes it… bearable." She chewed her lower lip in thought. "No that's also not right but I'm a bit ashamed to say it. I know my brother is missing and more than likely in some sort of trouble, so it's hard to admit that times like this, on this couch tonight, that I am actually happier than I could imagine. It's you Jackson, you make me happy. I wanted to tell you this because the way things have been going, I'm not sure it has been properly acknowledged." Jackson looked down on her curled up against him.

"I feel the same, regardless of everything. I would rather be no place else but next to you." He leaned down and kissed as best he knew how. They had been siting there comfortably for the at least half an hour, Alex sipping her wine and Jackson his Pepsi, when the first scream broke the silence. Immediately Jackson and Alex were on their feet, nerves on edge, waiting. A second scream echoed out of the darkness; this time joined with other sounds of movement. Jackson ran outside onto the little porch and peered into the darkness. It didn't sound like the noise was too far away but without more to go on, he had no idea from which direction to look. Alex was next to him, holding his arm with both hands, squeezing.

They both waited. Screams and shouts from several people hit them suddenly from the front left of the darkness. As Jackson's eyes turned in that direction, he saw a column of sparks shoot straight up, as if something had been dropped on top a bonfire.

"There!" Jackson said and pointed. "Alex, do you have your flashlight on you?" She nodded. "Good, let's go!" he said. There was no point in trying to ask Alex to remain behind, she wouldn't have done it and he knew it. The dirt path ran from their cabin to a narrow road where the car was parked. Hand in hand they ran down it. The cries and scuffling noises were more regular now but fading. They were still on the road when another piecing scream halted them. "There!" Jackson said pointing to a narrow path leading away from the road that was illuminated by the beam of his flashlight. They sprinted down it, hardly aware of the branches and bushes scraping their face as they rushed past. The five-minute run down that windy narrow path led them deeper into woods, further away from the main road and any sort of civilisation. In the darkness the sounds of a struggle ahead of them were amplified and quite terrible. Jackson skidded to a halt just as a light appeared ahead of them over the horizon of a line of bushes. Alex nearly tripped over as he pulled her to a stop with him. "Careful!" Jackson whispered while putting his index finger up to his mouth to indicate silence. The flashlight in his hands was already turned off. Alex's face, pale in the moonlight, nodded back at him. Jackson let go of her hand and motioned her behind him while they crouched over and moved silently to the edge of the bushes. Parting the leaves in front of him, Jackson straightened up as much as he could without revealing himself, to look over them. What greeted him was a scene from hell. The large fire, set in a ring of stone was turning into a genuine bonfire as camp chairs that had been tipped over in haste, were burning brightly. It illuminated everything around it in a trippy strobe light effect. There was a body of a young girl, the top half of her in the fire, just her head visible from Jackson side. She was clearly dead; her neck having been hacked open by something. The sightless eyes shimmered in the heat haze and the blood splattered on her face was boiling, burning. Jackson heard a squeak from next to him as Alex saw what he was seeing. He quickly grabbed her and put his hand over her mouth to stop any further sound from escaping. He stared intently into her eyes trying, by force of will to make her understand. She stopped squirming, as he continued looking into her eyes, her breathing evened out and she became calmer. He let her go and looked back at the fire. The screams had stopped and there wasn't too much movement.

There were other bodies scattered about, Jackson counted four that he could see. Pools of blood on the ground reflected the flames. There was a dismembered arm that had come to rest against the base of a tree. It was the Dream come to life. A scrapping sound and sob came from the darkness directly behind the fire, out of sight. Jackson broke from the bushes he was hiding in and sprinted towards it. He knew what he was going to see before he did. There was girl on her stomach, bleeding badly from multiple slash wounds. She was shuffling away on her belly with one leg, her knee, pushing up and down. A bloody trail behind her revealed her attempt to get away. A man was slowly walking towards her, with a machete in each hand. As Jackson watched on in horror, the man threw away on of the weapons and sat down roughly on top of the girl's back. Jackson was only about ten metres away but he knew he wouldn't get there in time. The man looked over his shoulder and smiled at Jackson, then savagely pulled the girls head back and slit her throat with his remaining blade.

"Noooo!" Alex had seen what had happened, she had clearly seen Freddie murder the girl. Jackson was nearly on top of Freddie before he jumped up and, with surprising nimbleness, bolted into the darkness. Jackson quickly reached down to help the girl but he knew nothing could be done for her. He had to get Freddie. He straightened up, left her squirming in the dirt and ran in the direction Freddie had disappeared. There, a narrow trail, a game rail, no wider than the span of his forearm. He turned on the flashlight and ran. He could hear movement in front of him but it was rapidly fading away. He had to hurry on but it was difficult running in the thick bush with only his little light guiding his way. How could Freddie be moving so fast in the darkness?

Jackson became aware of his own panting and realised he couldn't hear any movement in front of him anymore. He was disoriented from the mad dash down the twists and turns of the path. He stopped suddenly, knowing he was just running in circles and could easily be running in opposite direction than he needed to be going. It was hopeless, Freddie had gotten away.

"Tell Alex I did it, tell her how good I was!" Freddie's mad, high-pitched voice echoed out from somewhere. Then it was gone. Jackson, hands on knees, was trying to catch his breath. He had failed again, just like with Linda.

A few minutes later, after a bit of 'Marco-Polo', Jackson eventually made his way back to the campsite. Alex was responding to and answering questions, but she didn't seem to want to look Jackson in the eye. Her face was a mask of apathy, emotionless. When Jackson came into the clearing, she was sitting on the ground hugging her knees in amongst all the corpses. She had already checked, everyone was dead. Jackson went over to the last girl he had seen alive, she was also gone, her dead face in a puddle of her own blood. He moved over to Alex and draped his jacket over her shoulders but she didn't respond, she just kept staring straight ahead.

"I need to call the police Alex. This is a murder scene and we shouldn't be here stuck in the middle of it." Jackson checked Alex's face, still no hint of reaction. "I need to let them know about Freddie; they have to find him before he does something like this again."

Alex finally moved and looked at him. "I can't believe it. I know what I saw Jackson but I still can't believe that was him!" She broke down into silent tears with her head hanging between her knees. Part of Jackson was relieved that she was finally showing some emotion but her anguish was hard to have to witness. He squeezed her shoulder in support and then moved away a bit to make a call on his cell phone. He had to fiddle a bit to unlock it but he eventually managed to and called Ben on his personal number.

"Jackson, all good?" said the simple, straight to point voice on the other end of the line.

Ben didn't like to waste time and wasn't concerned about the late hour. He knew that if Jackson had called him, it would be for a good reason. He was not wrong.

"We were too late Ben, its happened. You need to get everyone over to the campsite I told you about earlier. There are six dead kids Ben!" Jackson's voice almost broke at the end. "It was Fred, I saw him and chased after him but he got away. You need to get here soon as possible."

There was a brief silence on the other end of the line and Jackson could imagine the million questions Ben probably had, but ever the efficient professional, Ben simply said, "Don't touch anything, don't move. We'll be there in forty, fifty minutes max. Keep your phone on you." Just like that, the call ended. Jackson shook his head and walked over to sit down in front of Alex. With their knees touching, he took his and in his own and pulled them towards his lap.

"Alex, look at me. Look at me!" Alex did after his second request. "We need to talk before the cops get here. We only have about half an hour and we need to make sure we are on the same page. As of now, we are probably going to be the prime suspects and there are a few things I need to understand." The urgency in Jackson voice had the desired effect as she looked at him and nodded, fully aware. "First thing, do you have your phone on you? Last night at the motel,

187

I saw you had either called someone or sent a message to someone, do you recall?" Alex was genuinely confused.

"I don't have my phone on me, it's at the cabin, but I didn't call anybody. When we get back there I'll double check but I honestly don't remember anything like that," Alex said with sincerity.

"Good," Jackson said. He believed her. "Next, and this is hard but I need to hear you say it. Did you see Freddie tonight? Do you now believe that he is indeed the killer?" Jackson asked her sternly. He had let go of her hands and was holding her shoulders as they sat before each other.

"Yes!" she sobbed and tried to look away. Jackson needed her full attention and moved his hands to her face so she was forced to look directly at him.

"Alex, when I was chasing Freddie he told me something, something that doesn't make sense but I need to ask you. He said, '*Tell Alex I did it. Tell her how good I was.*' Why would he say that Alex, does it mean anything to you?" A strange thing happened then. Jackson could swear he saw something register in her eyes, a shift in her features. It was so quick that had Jackson not been examining her so closely, he would have missed it. It was so quick though, that he immediately doubted he had seen anything at all. In that split second Alex immediately came back to herself.

"No… no! Why would he say that? I don't understand any of this Jackson. Is he proud of what he did, does he want me to be proud of him?" Alex said the last part with no small measure of disgust and revulsion. Jackson believed her, believed that she believed, so to speak.

"OK, I don't think we need to mention that last part to the police. What we do need to do is to have a story on we found

188

ourselves here. Dreams and memories aren't going to cut-it. We need something solid backed by evidence and we need to be aligned on it." Jackson was in work mode now; he had gotten up and was pacing before Alex while she watched on with big eyes. "Ok, so your folks called us and we found out that Fred was missing. Yes? Good.

Ok, when we got to the house we found a beanie that had been left behind as Fred packed up before leaving. His backpack was gone, along with some clothes and his wallet." Alex was listening, nodding her agreement and acknowledgement where she was required to. "When I told you his backpack was gone and that I had found this by the window, you immediately remembered some trail or campsite you had visited with him, although you couldn't remember exactly which one. He liked to have this beanie when camping. Yes?" Alex nodded again, she was more than surprised at how readily Jackson had come up with this and was quite happy for him to be taking control. She herself was a mess of conflicting emotions that made it difficult to think straight. Primarily amongst all those emotions was disbelief. She had seen Fred with her own eyes but was still battling to believe it. Then there was anger, confusion, horror and just now, shame. She was so ashamed at what had happened. All these kids dead because of Freddie. She suddenly realised that Jackson had resumed talking so she tried to focus "So we drew up a map and decided to scout as many of these parks as possible. We got lucky, so to speak, when we got here. Alex, did you get all that, can you remember it and repeat it back to me," Jackson asked. Alex thought for a while and then repeated the story. It was a surreal experience, reciting the story while sitting in the woods surrounded by hacked-up corpses. Jackson listened intently. He added a few small, but significant, details here and there to make it more believable and then made her repeat the story again. Once Jackson was fully satisfied they both had it. He slumped down next her on the ground and hugged her close to him. There was nothing more to say. They sat there, in the middle of the campsite littered with bodies, waiting for the police to arrive. It didn't take too long. They heard the sirens before anything else. Jackson's phone rang and he guided Ben to where they were sitting. The conversation was clipped and short. Jackson looked down at Alex and said, "Are you ready?" She didn't respond while Jackson stared at her anxiously. Just before Ben and several officers came into view through the bushes, she nodded at him. They stood up, he holding her face to his chest, and confronted the coming storm together.

The crime scene was secured in record time, at least to a watchful Jackson. The yellow chevron tape cordoned off the immediate area around the campfire and an external perimetre beyond was put in place to cut off any really early morning spectators. The area was swarming with police. There were forensics in their hazmat-looking suits placing little spikes with yellow flags on them here and there, a circle of detectives in conference and many uniformed officers obviously on guard. There were also several ambulances and paramedics in attendance as well. Jackson and Alex had been ushered beyond the chevron tape and were currently under the guard of a stony-faced officer who refused any attempt at conversation.

Someone had given Alex a blanket which she wore over her shoulders. Detective Hasset and Detective Levi were part of the little gathering of detectives. Ben had come to them when everyone had first arrived at the scene but did not stop and chat, just directed them to where they were standing now, waiting. Jackson checked his watch, 01:45. It was too early and too remote an area to attract any spectators but they would come, just like the reporters monitoring police chatter on radios. In fact, Jackson was surprised none were already there. He hadn't spoken a word to Alex while the officer stood watch over them and in truth they didn't have too much to say to each other that hadn't already been said. Jackson was quite proud of how she seemed to be coping, her jaw was thrust forward into the night as if daring anyone to challenge her. He couldn't imagine what might be going through her head. It was an evening from the twilight zone for him. The dark night alive with the colours of flashing red and blue lights, the crackling of radios and mumbled conversation. Someone had removed the chairs from the fire and all that remained were the burning coals. It was no longer needed for light as mobile spot lights had been set up highlighting the whole area in fluorescent detail. Jackson and Alex had been completely ignored up until now, although it was very clear they couldn't leave even if they had wanted to. Every time Jackson shifted on his feet, stony-face would look over his shoulder and glare at him until he stopped moving, clearly ready to chase should Jackson try to walk or run away. Jackson had given up trying to smile back at him, to put him at ease, it wouldn't make a difference. Eventually he saw Ben walking over to him alongside Detective Levi. Jackson waited impassively for them to approach. Out of the corner of his eye, he saw Alex straighten and thrust her jaw out further.

"Jackson, Miss Harver," Ben nodded to both of them in greeting, "Thanks for calling this in. I'm sure you have a lot to tell us and I can tell you we have a lot of questions for the both of you. However, we need to let the chaps here do their job without interference and this is not the time or the hour for long chats." Ben motioned with his hand and a uniformed officer appeared next to him. He had hand-cuffs at the ready. "On the basis of the initial evidence, I have to arrest you both on the charge of murder." The uniformed cop came forward and proceeded to cuff them both. Alex was about to protest but Jackson forestalled her.

"Its formal procedure Alex, let them do their job. We'll have this sorted soon," he said with little confidence.

"Officer Marlow here will read you your rights and escort you back to the holding cells." Ben said and walked away. There was no room here for any friendly interaction, this needed to be done by the book. Ben's association with Jackson could jeopardise his involvement in this case and he wasn't going to allow that to happen.

"Miss Harver, I'm sure we'll have this cleared up shortly." Detective Levi smiled at Alex sadly. She said nothing back, the tilt of her jaw was not so prominent anymore. They were led away to separate police cars and placed in the back. The cars were parked next to each other and Jackson could see the manacled form of Alex in the other car. She looked up and caught his gaze as he tried to smile and convey some sort of comfort with a look. She seemed to understand and smiled back but could not stop a small tear from escaping her one eye though. It would be a while before they would be able to talk to each other again.

Bob now dressed as a police officer, was smiling inside. He was standing guard at one of the points around the chevron per metre. He had a good view of the bodies, post immediate examination and photographs, being zipped up into bags and being carried away on gurneys toward the waiting ambulances. He shivered with pleasure at the memory of the horror and terror that was just recently experienced by the deceased. It had been a feast! He had only remained to watch on out of interest. There was not too much sustenance to be had from a crime scene, all the good stuff already gone, replaced by cold, hard focus. Even in this slaughter house, the officers were professional and apathetic. This age and time had acclimatised people to such things, robbing Bob of the emotional experience he would have swallowed up gleefully. These people had seen too much of a similar thing, it was now just a job to them. Bob refocused his attention to his right, beyond the yellow tape. He could see Alex and Jackson standing under attentive guard. He watched as they were cuffed and bundled into separate cars. This story was really building to something, Bob could imagine the climax of it and he shivered involuntarily again. He realised why he was still standing here even though he had nothing to gain from it. It was Jackson and his remarkable abilities he wanted to watch and understand more. He could taste the confidence emanating from the man. It wasn't pure, it was mixed with worry and concern, not for himself but for the girl in the other car. Although the confidence wasn't pure it was strong, bolstered by a drive and motivation Bob knew was only partly unique to him. Some people possessed this internal drive, it wasn't uncommon but it what made it special was its degree. It towered over everyone else around him, like a stack of pancakes looking down on bowls of cereal. Jackson was so certain of himself but Bob doubted even Jackson knew of how powerful this trait in him was. He had taken it for granted due to the way his life had panned out, the experiences he had had. There was a new element to Jackson's pulsing, aromatic personality, one that was acting as a catalyst for exponential enhancement of what he already possessed. It was love. In its purest form, it was almost as sustaining as terror was to Bob. Jackson was in love with Alex, Bob could see that, even if the couple weren't completely aware of it themselves yet.

Bob the officer rubbed his hands together in gleeful anticipation. Love, terror, horror... this story was really forming up beautifully. He had to leave here now, there was more to be done with other stories, in other places, other times, other planes. His hunger was insatiable and had to be fed constantly. Even as it was sated, it grew ever more. No one was watching as officer Bob seemed to shimmer and then disappear entirely. He wasn't gone at all; he had just become indifferent to the perception of everyone. Bob never truly disappeared despite what the sheep thought. He had his shepherds crook and was slowly guiding each of them to slaughter. The more unaware the sheep was at the time of slaughter, the tastier the meat.

Fred became suddenly aware. He looked around and seemed to be a small cottage or cabin of sorts. He stood up to go outside to gather his bearings. He opened the door to move outside but realised he couldn't pass through. There was nothing there blocking his way but his body just wouldn't respond to commands. He stood there for several minutes, huffing and puffing and willing himself forward, but nothing happened. It was too close to how he felt staring out of the window of his room earlier so he gave up. He decided to look around. It was a cottage, a bedroom with an en-suite bathroom attached to a lounge cum kitchenette. It was a no-frills and totally utilitarian space. The only consideration to comfort being a large cushy, two-seater sofa placed in front of a large flat screen TV with a remote balanced on the arm of the couch. Moving to the kitchenette, Fred started pulling open drawers and cupboards. The place was very well stocked. Fred judged he had enough provisions to last him a couple of months at least. Someone had gone to extraordinary lengths to keep him comfortable without him ever having to leave. Moving to bathroom, Fred opened the little storage space beneath the sink and found every medicine he could imagine to treat accidents or whatever might suddenly ail him. He was so confused, who had done this to him, why couldn't he leave? He moved over to a window to look outside. There was a short perimetre, maybe a couple of metres deep, of lawn that seemed to run around the circumference of the house. The grass ended in a wall of densely packed trees which Fred couldn't see through. He turned his attention back inside the cottage and the open doorway. He again tried to walk through but couldn't. Strangely, he realised he had no desire to leave, it was more an experiment to see if could. He gave up for the second time and closed the door. He wasn't sure what was going on. He felt as if stuck in dream, but one he couldn't wake up from. It was useless trying to figure out something that couldn't be figured out so he went to the sofa, sat down and turned on the TV. He was starting to feel that horrible sensation of being two people again, that internal conflict of real and unreal coming on thick and fast and he needed a distraction. All the channels he flicked through were news channels, nothing else was on offer. He randomly settled on one and watched on indifferently. The picture showed some early morning view of a line a police officer's blocking access to the woods behind them. The information bar below the picture highlighted; '*Multiple murders reported! Victims believed to be high school kids, no survivors. More information to follow shortly.* Fred quickly turned the TV off. He had no reason to but he started to feel cold, feverish and sick to the stomach. It was the Linda Gerard episode all over again. He instinctively knew he was involved in this mess somehow but couldn't bring himself to learn more. He wanted to run away from everything. He didn't know what day it was; he didn't know where he was and he didn't know what to do. In his mind he was being split apart, he no longer had any sense of self left and was raging against nothing and everything. He made his way to the bedroom and lay down on the single bed. He rolled over on his side and stared out of the window, trying his hardest to ignore thinking about anything, trying hard to suppress the sense of two, the sense of conflict in his own mind.

Chapter 7 – Conversations with Gods

Jackson and Alex spent the remainder of the dark morning in separate holding cells. Jackson figured that it might still be a while before one of the detectives would be able to leave the campfire scene to talk him, or interrogate him seeing he was now suspect number one. He was pleasantly surprised then when a uniform rattled some keys and escorted Jackson out of his cell to a little windowless room. The room was four blank walls, one with a mirror, two-way no doubt so mysterious figures could listen in on conversations, a small metal table and two metal chairs bolted to the floor. The uniform ushered him into a seat and then cuffed him to the table in front of him. He closed the door then proceeded to set up shop in a corner, not a word was said to Jackson. It wasn't long before the door opened and to let in a dishevelled and clearly tired detective Levi. He took one look at Jackson and told the uniform to un-cuff him. "Sorry about that Jackson, the guys are just following protocol," Detective Levi said. "Please can you go and rustle up two coffees son?" he asked the uniform. Clearly uncomfortable, the uniform hesitated. "Don't worry son, if anything should happen I will take full responsibility. Now, hurry on! Don't forget the sugar and cream." The officer nodded once and hurried out the room. "The new ones these days, so formal and strict." Detective Levi laughed to himself before sitting down and frowning across the table at Jackson. "Ok, before we start, I want to let you know that Detective Hasset is in the other room having a similar conversation with your girlfriend. So, if you were thinking of leaving anything out of your statement, or dare I say it, thinking of lying, we will cross reference everything you say with that conversation."

Jackson offered an innocent smile and nodded. "Of course detective. I have nothing to hide," he answered. In his head, Jackson partitioned his mind (he could do so without conscious effort now), as he needed to focus on getting this right, he couldn't afford to let any emotion cloud his mind. Without knowing it, detective Levi was now talking to what was effectively a robot, intelligent, but not hampered by feeling.

"Let's start with how you came to the scene of the murders?" Detective Levi asked.

Jackson mentally checked his notes and then started telling the detective about how they had heard Fred was missing from his parents and then about the trail they deduced and followed until they got to the scene. He went on to explain about hearing the screams in the dark, the discovery of the campsite fire and the mad chase through the woods after Fred. He didn't mention what Fred had told him, as per his agreement with Alex. Detective Levi watched Jackson closely as he spoke, taking numerous notes while he did. "It seems like quite a leap of faith, lucky or otherwise, that you ended up where you did wouldn't you say?" he asked. Jackson nodded.

"That's the way it would seem detective but it's the truth," he replied. "You seem exceptionally calm Mr Brandt, for someone who just witnessed what effectively was a massacre last night. Jackson noted the 'Mr Brandt' without letting anything reflect on his face. It was only natural that the experienced detective would be suspicious, the story required a certain level of imagination to accept at face value."

"I have seen worse in the army detective. Also, I am exhausted, maybe in shock, I don't know. I haven't slept since yesterday," Jackson said as he rubbed his eyes for effect.

Detective Levi started at him hard. "Would you have more to tell of this if you were speaking to your friend Ben?" he asked. Jackson looked back just as hard before replying.

"Maybe detective, but the story and what I presented to you would be fundamentally the same. I have left nothing out that I believe would help you find Freddie," he said. "My," Jackson hesitated before going on, "*visions*, may have given me a little more of a push in the right direction but the details of it wouldn't help in any case." There was a long period of silence after Jackson mentioned his visions. Both he and detective Levi were caught in a bit of staring contest. It was only broken when the door opened to the returning officer holding two paper cups of coffee before him. It managed to break thc intense spell both he and detective Levi were under.

"Ah thanks Steve!" Detective Levi said as he took the coffees from him and handed one Jackson. He took a grateful sip of the offered warm drink. He hadn't realised how thirsty he was.

"Ok Jackson, I think now would be the time to fill you in on what happened after you were escorted here. You will be happy to know that your story does check out. Preliminary investigations indicate a third party was present. Footprints and such," he said vaguely. "We also tracked the path you described in your chase of Fred. Turns out it was a game path that you were on. It must have been scouted beforehand as it was quite hard to notice." To Jackson, he realised now how Fred had managed to outpace him during the chase. He must have studied the path beforehand, possibly even traced its route over and over. Jackson looked up, emotionless, detective Levi had started speaking again. "The path was littered with blood splatters on the foliage and dirt. It was quite clear once we had the necessary light on the area. Anyway, the path led to a concealed car. Skid marks indicated a hurried exit.

Some of the boys managed to track his path until it hit one of the concrete roads in the park. Not too sure which direction the car went after that. We have already put a perimetre in place, ten miles in every direction, we'll catch him!" Detective Levi said confidently, "he can't get too far away!" Jackson doubted it would be that easy but he didn't say it out loud. He knew there was more at play here than just Fred randomly killing a bunch of teenagers. There was some major prep work that precipitated him doing this and he doubted Fred had not planned for a proper escape. He also deduced that the detective thought the same, regardless of what he had said. "We also found a couple of machetes on the scene... murder weapons?" the question was asked offhand, just for confirmation of what they already knew. Jackson nodded. "Ok, we will run prints on them, pretty sure it will confirm Fred's presence at the scene as well as confirm him as prime suspect." Detective Levi looked askance at Jackson.

He just nodded again, nothing further needed to be said on that. "That brings me to this," the detective said holding a plastic zip lock bag in front of Jackson so he could see. "Any idea of what it could mean, does it have any relevance?" Jackson inwardly thanked his own preparation in partitioning his mind because what he was looking at was another flute, just like the three he already had in his possession. Had he not been mentally prepared, he would've fallen off his chair.

"No idea detective, it's a flute of some kind? Perhaps one of the kids was playing it?" Jackson guessed for the detective's sake.

"No I don't think so Jackson, it's quite a unique piece, not something you can get from Walmart. It has the feel of a calling card don't you think?" asked Detective Levi.

"You would know better than me detective. Must say though, weird thing to find at a murder scene." Jackson told him. Detective Levi mumbled something to himself that sounded suspiciously close to agreement.

"Well we have no compelling evidence to hold you any longer Mr Brandt. I need to inform you though that you are still a part of this investigation and that you cannot be allowed to leave the state or country. You may be required to come back later to answer some more questions, do you understand?" Jackson said that he did. They both stood up together. Detective Levi escorted him back to the administration block where he collected all the things that were confiscated from him during his short incarceration. "Keep close Jackson, we will be in touch!" Detective Levi shook his hand and walked away. Jackson walked back to the reception area to wait for Alex. Turns out she was already there waiting for him. She jumped up and hugged him as soon as she saw him.

"All good?" he asked her when she broke away.

"As good as can be," she replied. She looked exhausted, he imagined that he did as well. At that thought, he opened the box to his mind and became whole again. She picked up the bag from the seat next to her then they both walked out onto the street. Jackson hailed down a cab and directed the driver to his apartment. He took a deep breath and leaned back in the seat. It felt like the end of something but he knew that this whole thing had only got into first gear. More was ahead of them. He had to wake Alex up after the short drive back to his place.

"Come, let's get something to eat upstairs and then go to bed. We can shower after we get some rest," he told her as the exited the cab.

"No, shower first," Alex said, "I feel filthy, I need to wash last night off me." Jackson couldn't argue with that. They walked through the bar, past a clearly inquisitive Shelley and upstairs. A shower actually sounded wonderful to Jackson as well.

Jackson was back at the campsite but this time the party was still alive. You wouldn't have known it. They were alive, as everything was stuck, frozen in time, like a photograph. The flames of the campfire illuminated a space around the kids like a puddle, light stretching further in some places than others. The sudden capture of the moment in time, with the fire flickering, had the weird effect of throwing features of the scene into half-light, no light and full light. Obviously Jackson knew exactly where he was but the fright, the fear, the terror was strangely missing. Perhaps, with the constant practice of partitioning his mind, he had managed to build a sort of mental muscle memory of how to do it. That thought reminded him so he checked inside… yes the box was there, all that was him, apart from basic awareness, was safely locked away. He didn't remember falling asleep but now that he was here in the Dream, he thought to experiment a little more, maybe learn a bit more of what went done last night. Jackson pictured a rewind, pause, play and forward symbol in his mind, like the controls on a YouTube video and set about his experiment. He mentally pushed rewind and the scene he was standing in remained. Nothing happened. He looked around and spotted Dream Jackson hiding in bushes. Of course, he couldn't move behind the point of his own awareness in what happened in the real world. He next pressed play. The scene silently became alive around him. He saw the flames licking around the dead girl lying half in the ring of stones around the bonfire with the chairs also burning. The arm of another victim was dripping blood from the shorn end, into the ground at the base of the tree. Jackson shifted his perception and came to view Freddie from the side and as he slowly walked towards another girl trying to crawl away. Jackson pressed paused, then zoomed into the side of Freddie's face to get a closer look. He wished he could have seen straight on, but the Dream Jackson point of view wouldn't allow it. Freddie was smiling. It was an awful thing to see, not because it was so out of place for what he was doing but rather because of the dead look to his eyes. There was nothing there. Fred wasn't in there. Jackson was looking at glossy doll's eyes, puppet eyes.

"Remarkable isn't it?" said a voice suddenly. Jackson spun around and saw a man dressed in shadows thrown by a

wide rimmed black hat. He was idly poking the dismembered arm against the tree with the toe of his boot.

"Who the hell are you? Where did you come from? How come you are moving?" The control Jackson had over the tightly secured box had wavered and broken open at the sight of the intruder to his Dream. He sucked in a mental breath, and pushed the box closed again, reinforcing its locks. He thought he might need the extra locks to face whatever it is he was facing.

"That's another remarkable thing Jackson, what you just did there. I have never come across another like you. Another so quick to grasp his talent, such strong a strong sense of intuition. It is remarkable but I digress. I said this is remarkable," the man made a sweeping gesture around him, "is it not?" The man was suddenly standing before Jackson, just a moment ago he had been by the tree kicking the arm. In Jackson's current state of control, he had more time to process the experience, rational explanation wasn't needed, he just processed and adapted.

"What's remarkable? This murder scene? I don't think anything about it is remarkable. I think it's awful, deranged, disturbed... that's what I think." Jackson replied without any real feeling. "Bahahaha no, no you misunderstand me Dream Stalker. Not the scene, this world, being here, what you can do." The man laughed at Jackson, incomprehension of the initial question. Jackson looked around and a part of him did acknowledge the fact but he didn't say so. Instead he asked the man again, "Who are you? How did you get here? This is my memory." The man ignored his question. He was suddenly behind Jackson looking at the girl lying on her stomach with *her throat slit. Not to be out done, Jackson imagined himself on the other side of the girl and suddenly he was there.*

"Very good Dream Stalker, such excellent grasp of the basics for one so new to this," The man said with seemingly real sincerity.

"I asked you a question," Jackson went on, "Who are you and how did you come to be in my memory?"

"Memory, Jackson, you think this is a mere memory? Bahahaha!" the man laughed and walked around in a little circle. "No Dream Stalker this is no mere memory, this a whole other world. You think you are Dreaming? Bahahaha, no it's not as simple as that young one!" the man continued to laugh, lost in his own private joke. Jackson acknowledged that he would have found this annoying had his little box not been so secure, but as it was, he patiently waited for the man to get over his laughing fit. The man eventually came back to himself, "Ok my inconsequential little friend, let me give a dummies guide to the universes, in a way that you can comprehend." As he talked, the man would disappear and reappear at different spots around the campfire. Jackson was battling to keep track of him. "As I mentioned earlier, you are in a new world. This does not just exist inside your head as memory, regardless of what you may think. Let me ask you this Dream Stal... Jackson... If you hadn't secured your true self away, what would you be feeling? Fear, anxiety, doubt, terror, confusion... yes? Yes." The man didn't wait for an answer but answered his own question.

Jackson was surprised but he stared on impassively, waiting for the man to continue. "These feelings, these emotions, they are born from perception and experience, the truest of the truest of building blocks of human conscience...

of life. You following?" He didn't wait for a reply again but forged on right ahead. Jackson watched at how animated the mysterious figure before had become. "These emotions, these feelings, these experiences aren't bound by the standard prescripts of reality, they transcend worlds. What you feel here Jackson, is just as real as what you feel in the other place, your waking world, is it not? Do you think the people here, lying around frozen before you are not real, do you not think they FEEL the same as you? What makes this reality any less real than the reality you live in hmmmm?" This time it appeared he did want an answer from Jackson.

"This is not real… whoever you are! In what reality can I manipulate the environment like I have? I can only do this because it's my memory, me re-looking at what I have already seen." Jackson responded.

"Ah you are thinking like a person trapped by their own lack of imagination Dream Stalker. Answer me this, if this is your memory, how am I here, how are we having this conversation?" the man asked as he suddenly appeared right in front of Jackson's face. Even this close it was hard to determine any of the man's features.

"I, I don't know…" Jackson stammered.

"I said you were unique at your quicker than usual grasp of your talent, but I didn't say you were unique in this universe Jackson. I have encountered your kind before… your ilk would go by names such as prophet, shaman, witch doctor, seer… I can go on and on. This memory, as you would believe it to be, is in fact another whole reality. These people before you are frozen at your command," the man waved his hand and everyone came alive and the scene was moving again. He waved again and it froze. "But they are ALIVE, they are just manipulated by you without any comprehension it is happening to them. You, shaman, can control them like your puppets for your own gain. However, whatever you do does leave a trace. You affect improbabilities in their reality… déjà vu, a glitch in the matrix, things like that. Are you still following?" Jackson nodded although it felt like he was drowning. "Hmm you are, are you? Regardless, I will go on. Your abilities do extend into your born reality Dream Stalker, but you are only just beginning to see that, you are only scratching at the surface. I, however, am not your teacher. You are too far below me for me to give you more attention that I already have. You will figure it out on your own. Your other Dreams, Jackson, the ones where you see terrible things happening, are those not real too?" The sudden switch from lecture to question caught Jackson off guard and the mention of his Dreams almost had the 'emotion-box' he had built exploding apart.

"How could you possibly know about those…?" the man didn't let him finish.

"I know countless things you couldn't even imagine Dream Stalker, but let me leave it at this. I said you weren't unique remember; I have encountered your like before. Anyway, your Dreams are much like this dream, this reality, and this world. They are just forward looking instead of backward looking. You ever wonder why certain details seem indistinct, like certain things like faces and places are hidden. Let me guess, you see puppet-like pictures doing these awful things?" Once again the man didn't wait for answer that he already knew. "It's because this forward view reality isn't yet fully formed in your perception because they haven't yet happened in your reality. You can only build on clues you *might have already perceived without even knowing. I can tell you this though, the forward dream is as much real as this dream and as your born reality. In that forward Dream, people are real, their features and surroundings are as clear to them as your world. The fact that it hasn't happened in your world doesn't mean it isn't happening for them right at that time. The consequences of your interference in your world could lead to multiple outcomes in that future world, countless other outcomes, countless other realities, countless other worlds!" Jackson's head was truly spinning now and he was having trouble maintaining his equilibrium. The man was so alien to his understanding of everything that it was becoming harder and harder to follow what he was saying.*

"You still haven't answered my question, but I don't think you will." Jackson was buying time to regain his balance. "Me being here, I am able to manipulate this backward view world because I have already experienced it. So by that assumption, I can't manipulate the forward world because I have no control over what I haven't yet already perceived." Jackson sensed the man smiling at him as he talked so he continued. "Are you of my world? Are you manipulating events in my reality?" Jackson finished in a rush. Part of him knew the answer anyways but he wanted confirmation.

"Yes, yes, yes you got it Dream Stalker, such a good student! We are having so much fun in this current story, are we not? But I am not of your world, I am of all worlds, all realities. I whisper in ears, I pull strings... I feed on experience, emotion, the food of the gods. Is it not fit, is it not the right of the gods to be fed on what builds and drives everything?" The man was growing larger in front of Jackson

208

eyes as he spoke, like an inflating balloon. He was already towering over Jackson, twice his original height. "Your Dreams Jackson, are not just views of the future or the past, they are portals to other worlds." He was still growing, his blackness starting to fill up Jackson's entire view. "You have already taken up too much of my time, but like I said earlier, you intrigue me. I will leave you with this one last titbit, your headaches Jackson are not a curse, and they are signs; signs of when the different worlds align or come into contact with each other. Heed them!" The world around Jackson was now entirely black, dark, nothing. Jackson's little box inside his head exploded. Jackson sat up in bed, heart racing. He sat like that for several minutes. He wasn't awake or aware, he just was. Without a word or a blink of an eye. He lay down and went back to sleep.*

Alex left first thing in the morning. She wanted to be with her parents when they found out the news about Freddie, but truthfully, she needed some time to think. It was Friday, her mad adventure over the past week had sped up time, she felt like she had lived a full year in the space of those seven days. The moment she had woken up she had rolled over to see Jackson still fast asleep. He was frowning and there was a fine, delicate sheen of sweat across his face. She knew that he had been dreaming but she didn't think she could deal with any more crazy, at least not today. She had leaned over and kissed his cheek. When he opened his eyes, still groggy, she told him she need to go see her parents and that he should not to get up. He needed to get some decent rest. He had smiled at her then, and for some reason her heart nearly broke. He gratefully accepted her offer and closed his eyes, almost immediately asleep. She was thinking things through on the drive to her parent house. The full shock of seeing Freddie with the bloody machetes in his hands, had not yet worn off. The sight the dead and dying of that night had been seared into her brain, she thought she might never forget it. Worst of all had been seeing Freddie run off with Jackson in pursuit. It was a complex set of emotions she had been dealing with since then. There were the two men she loved most in the world, running away, away from where she was. She wasn't sure how to process that. Part of her had desperately wanted Jackson to catch Freddie, catch him before he could hurt anyone else. That other part of her wanted Freddie to get away. She didn't want to see him caught and possibly hurt, that part of her had willed him on, faster and faster away. Watching him run away had been a confusing mixture of exhilaration and dread, hope and fear. Driving in her Tesla, she still had no idea which emotion had won over the others. All she knew was when she woke up, she had to get away and sort her head out before chatting with Jackson. It was also what Freddie had told Jackson, to tell her. It was absolutely horrifying that he seemed to seek her approval. It twisted her up inside to such a degree that she thought she might never be able to eat again. What would make him say something like that, why, why, why? She realised she was hitting her steering wheel and forced herself to calm down. Once again she had to be honest with herself. She was pleased that Freddie had sought her approval. That galled her! She pushed that thought to the trash can of her mind. It wasn't true, it was just the emotional state of her mind throwing her off balance. She had arrived outside her parent's house without remembering half the drive there. She wasn't the only one visiting today. There was an unmarked police car (little red siren attached to the roof on the driver's side) parked ahead of her. She should have figured out they would be here by now. She closed the car door behind her and made her way to the front of the house. She was greeted by a uniformed officer sitting at the entrance. He greeted her with a nod of the head and then went back to staring down the hall. Alex reciprocated the greeting and went to find her parents. As was usually the case, they were sitting next to each other, he holding her, she crying. Detective Levi was sitting across from them the sipping a cup of coffee. Alex went to her mother's side and gave her a hug. Her mom barely noticed.

"Hi detective, nice to see you again so soon," Alex said sarcastically. Detective Levi never batted an eye.

"Yes, you to. Was just filling your parents in on… the latest developments." Alex heard a wail from her mom next to her. "Anyway, Officer Bradley will remain behind, in case Freddie does show up again and for any other support the family might need. Alex, will you walk me out?" The detective stood up and waited for her to follow. Mr Harver also got up, but only to shake Detective Levi's hand.

"If you hear anything, any, about Freddie, please let us know." He started intensely and waited for Detective Levi to nod, then went back to console his wife. Alex was waiting for detective Levi in the hall.

"How can I help you, Detective Levi? I thought that we covered everything yesterday. Am I still a suspect?" she asked.

"No, nothing like that. It just that something weird happened while I was chatting," he nodded to the kitchen. "Your mom seemed to think you might have something to do with Freddie actions. She seems to think you could be involved somehow. Now before you get all angry and stuff, your dad immediately came to your defence. He explained that your mom was just extremely emotional... um... fragile at the moment. Why would she say that Alex, why would your own mother try and implicate you, her own daughter in this mess?" Alex was too shocked to respond straight away. She was suddenly a teenager again dealing with her mom, Fred and the dead cat. It all came smashing into her, an avalanche of memory and feelings. Taking a deep breath, she explained the cat story to the detective again.

"She never got over that. Well I thought she had but clearly not," Alex eventually said. "That's quite such grudge if true Miss Harver. Anyway, if you and Jackson can think of anything else that might help, or come across anything new, don't do anything without calling me. Is that clear?" Detective Levi had never sounded so stern before.

"Yes, yes of course detective," Alex said as she ushered him out the house. Detective Levi gave her a meaningful stare before turning and leaving.

"Remember Alex, this is police work, leave it to us!" he said walking away. Alex stood in the doorway watching as he drove away. She couldn't yet deal going back into the kitchen, to face the person who tried to lump all the blame on her. Eventually she did get control and moved back towards where her parents were still sitting.

"I just came to be here, Mom, Dad, to help in any way. I know how much you love Freddie; I do to!" she said more stiffly than she had intended.

"Alex, don't be upset with your mother, I can see Detective Levi filled you in on our conversation. Your mother is dealing with this the best she can and she didn't mean any of it," Mr Harver said, trying to forestall any drama.

"I'm not angry, dad. I'm hurt, to even think that of me..." she trailed off, wiping tears from her eyes with her back to her parents. "Well, I am here if you need me and you have my numbers. Please call... for anything." She had to get out. As she started walking, her dad had moved quickly around the table and had her in a bear hug before she could react.

"I love you baby girl," was all that he said. Slowly she responded back with a hug of her own.

"Love you too dad!" then she broke away and left the house. Alex drove straight to the bookstore. She wasn't in the right space to talk with Jackson yet and her plans to spend the day with her parents was now a non-starter. All she wanted to do was run away. She felt like she had no one to turn to, like her family had cut her off. It was so grossly unfair that Alex found herself angry. How could she be blamed for this? That was how Susan found her as she walked through the glass doors into the store.

"Jesus Al, what happened?" Susan said as she rushed around the counter. Alex found she couldn't speak. It was all too much. She burst into tears as she let herself be guided around the back to the little office her and Susan shared. It took a while, but with a cup of warm tea in her hand and a 'closed' sign placed on the shop's door, Alex finally felt her emotions begin to settle. She started speaking. It all came out, everything from her brother's disappearance, to meeting Jackson, to the murders and finally to this morning, where her mother blamed her.

She must have spoken for about forty minutes straight. She didn't mention the supernatural aspect of it; that was for her and Jackson alone. She was on her second cup of tea when she stopped and looked at Susan. She had gone deathly pale. Alex having been at the centre of this nightmare for so long, was obviously acclimatised to the situation. Having dropped Susan in the middle of it, all in one go had, had a startling effect on her. "Jesus Alex... I don't know what to say... I thought you were just taking a break... just looking for your brother... Jesus!" Susan was more than just pale, she was frightened. "Alex, your brother knows me, am I safe here, should I be worried?" she asked. Alex couldn't blame her for being afraid, Alex was too.

"No Sue, the police are all over it. Freddie is in hiding now and it won't be long before they find him. Please remember, the public don't yet know about Freddie. They know about the murders, but not who did it yet. I'm sure it won't be long before they release his details, if they can't find him that is," she told Susan. This time, it was Alex who brought the cup of tea to Susan, she also made her sit down to drink it. Looking after someone else had an odd effect on Alex. She slowly started to find her own feet. Her confidence started to reassert itself, her natural optimism lifted her spirits. She reminded herself that she was a strong, independent woman. A successful business owner and someone she thought was admired by her friends, if not so much by her family anymore. She wasn't going to let this thing with Freddie define her life, it was just a part of it, not all of it. No matter what came her way, she could deal with it, just as she had dealt with all other obstacles that had appeared before her. It was with a smile that she let Susan take the day off. Once she was gone, Alex re-opened the store and set about having as normal a day as possible. She knew she needed to talk to

Jackson, to understand their next step, but for the rest of the day she was simply Alexandra Harver, successful owner/manager of the Tasselled Bookmark and she was going to act like it.

Jackson slept for most of the morning. When he eventually rolled out of bed he felt refreshed and energised, despite his overall worry and anxiety over Alex. He rushed through his breakfast and was out the door, laptop in hand not even forty minutes later. He made his way to the local coffee house, not too far away from the bar and set up shop near the window. His Dream conversation last night had him feeling more excited than he ever been previously.

The man had hinted of abilities (that he possessed) beyond what he had come to expect as normal. Several cups of coffee later, and lunch to boot, Jackson finally looked up from his laptop. It was mid-afternoon and Jackson's reserves of energy that he had woken up with, were nearly drained by the grinding research. For all his effort, Jackson now understood a great deal more of parallel universes, wormholes, time travel theory, astral travel, projection and meditative states, but nothing of this truly helped him better understand what he was trying to understand, about himself! He pulled out his notebook and started jotting down his thoughts. His Dreams were glimpses into future and past states of this world, worlds in their own right. He could control events in the past worlds (but not in the future world) by manipulating what he had perceived through his own presence there. He could partition his mind; he could lock what was essentially himself away for almost superhuman like focus. He could do this in past and future Dreams and, as recently discovered, his born world, the present Dream as he now thought of it. Without noticing, he had stopped writing and was doodling in the margin of his notebook. When he came to he saw he had drawn a little pan flute. It was very rough and by no means a work a work of art, but it was clearly recognisable. He quickly flipped back to his own notes and read up what he had previously learned about the god Pan. With his energy renewing, he returned to his laptop and researched further. Thought of as a lesser god within the pantheon of ancient gods, Pan didn't get as much of a mention as did the others. The other mythical beings were well characterised and most people could clearly summon an image of them in their minds. The bearded Zeus and his lightning bolt, Poseidon and his trident ruling over the seas, Ares, the god of war, evil Hades of the underworld and so on. These were fixed representations within the greater human conscience. They were as they were, never pretending to be anything else. Jackson tapped his pen on his notebook. Pan was a character theorised to be the inspiration for many characters throughout history and lore. The half-goat being appeared in different forms in many stories, recognisable by his horns, or hooves or his flute. He played many parts or at least inspired many parts. He wasn't as fixed as the other gods but with a little research, one could begin to see that he was possibly more prevalent in human events than all the others.

From all his research previously and this morning, Jackson was more than convinced (although he would never tell anyone else) that what he was dealing with something not human, closer to a god as described. From the way the man spoke in his Dream and from the encounter on the street, Jackson started to believe that, he was playing a dangerous game with Pan. He suddenly dropped his pen and ran his fingers through his hair, laughing quietly. Was he losing his mind? He reopened his book and continued on the line of thought he had been following. The flutes were obviously clues and hard to ignore. Everything pointed to this being Pan! Underlining powers in his notes, he re-read what he had written; *'Once upset, Pan was known to be able to let out an angry, blood-curdling shout which inspired a sudden sensation of fear and anxiety in everyone unfortunate enough to hear it. Pan could display excessive speed without getting tired or injured'* That would certainly explain his general sense when in his presence, in fact most of his Dreams had him feeling the same anxiety and fear… was it the Dream or Pan influence? Jackson wrote that down with several question marks. Back to his laptop he typed in; Flute + Pan and read the upper most result, *'The music of the syrinx was known to make people dance and lower their inhibitions'.*

Jackson roughly translated that into a form of manipulation which, at least in his own mind would explain the crazy events with Freddie. That thought ended his musings. He decided to call it a day and closed his book and laptop. He couldn't believe he had spent the whole day convincing himself that he was dealing with half man half goat being whose was manipulating their reality for his own pleasure. It was beyond insane but in the absence of any other evidence, it was all he had to go on. While walking back to his apartment, he thought of Alex and wondered how her day was going. Thinking of her brought back the reality of the situation. Freddie was still on the loose and by all accounts, was being assisted or manipulated by a godlike, supernatural being. That needed to be his focus! He couldn't fight the god head on but he would do everything in his power to frustrate his plans with Freddie. He couldn't let more innocent people die and he needed to get Freddie to a place where he could be treated, even if under lock and key. He knew his concern for Freddie was primarily because of his feelings for Alex, but so be it. Freddie needed to be caught for everyone's sake, not just for the sake of his relationship with Alex. He saw his regular boozy customer, Bob, leaning against the doorway to the bar as he approached. It seemed like an age since he had looked up to see Bob smiling at him with frightening intensity, so different to his normal watery gaze. That same intense stare was back on his face and it caused Jackson to stumble on his approach.

"Heya Bob, getting some fresh air?" Jackson asked him once he had recovered his balance, his arms were covered in gooseflesh. Bob said nothing and just continued on with that crazy stare. Jackson walked past him, suddenly frightened and wanting to get out of his way as soon as possible. What the hell! The feeling left as soon as the door to the bar closed behind him. Jackson hurried up the stairs before Shelley (or Randall, if he was there) could catch him. He had already forgotten about Bob by the time his was in his own apartment. The day had been strangely fulfilling, giving him an insight into something he still didn't understand fully and probably never would. However, *knowledge is power*, he chuckled to himself. He was looking forward to Alex getting home. He wanted to try something this evening, he wanted to see exactly what he was capable of with his Dreams. If he was right in his thinking, there was a whole new avenue of things to explore. Looking into his fridge he pulled out ingredients for dinner. There wasn't too much to work with; tomatoes, celery, onions and a few other veggies. He would make spaghetti. Smiling inside at his own sense of domestication, he set to work making the sauce. He couldn't remember when he had last made anyone a single meal. With Alex, he had already made several.

Bob remained outside the doorway to the bar, but he was no longer looking at the street. His head was tilted upwards, towards Jackson's apartment. He realised how creepy it might look to any passers-by, but he hoped that they would think nothing of the drunk Bob they had come to know. It would just be Bob being weird. He didn't remove himself from their perception, he was just playing the part and he was enjoying it thoroughly. If Jackson succeeded in his experiment this evening, the story he had in place would take on a completely new dimension. Drunk Bob rubbed his hands together in gleeful anticipation.

"Bob… Bob! You done out there? Your beer is getting warm," Shelly had opened the door and called to him. Bob assumed drunk Bob's watery gaze and retuned inside to his drink.

Jackson was just dishing up when Alex knocked on the door.

"It's open," he shouted from the kitchen. He heard the door open and close a few moments later.

"Hi," she said as she kissed him on the cheek. She seemed sad.

"Is everything all right? I mean, apart from the obvious," Jackson said as he finished plating up. He took the bowls to the living room, motioning Alex to follow.

"Nothing is right about this Jackson! As if it wasn't enough that I have a mass murderer for a brother, my mother now seems to think it is my fault. She even told Detective Levi that I made Freddie do it," Alex said it without emotion. She had spent the day getting over it and she was drained. She felt like she wouldn't be able to feel anything ever again.

"She really said that?" Jackson asked while blowing on a forkful of spaghetti.

"Yup, but let's not talk about that right now. It's been a long day. What did you get up to?" she asked him. Between mouthfuls of food, and without going into too much detail, Jackson told Alex about his day of research. Even though she didn't interrupt him, he could see the confusion on her face so he forestalled the question he knew was coming.

"Let me put these plates away and then we can move over to the couch. I need to tell you something so crazy it's almost impossible to believe." He scooped up the dirty dishes and moved over to the kitchen where he rinsed and stacked them into the dishwasher. He put some coffee onto brew before heading back to Alex to finish his story. She watched him come towards her and she made space for him next to her as he got nearer. "Ok, I am going to tell you something I don't quite believe but I can't explain away. Let me try get through it all before you ask any questions OK?" Jackson waited for her to respond before continuing. Once she nodded, he went on, "Remember that night we went out to dinner, you drove home afterwards, and I told you I wanted to walk…?" Jackson recounted the events of that evening as best he could. He then spoke about the flutes they both found and how he linked them up to Pan. He followed that with his research from today and his theories he developed from that. Alex remained quiet throughout the whole thing and when Jackson finished, she didn't rush into any questions like he thought she would.

She had a blank look on her face, "My murderer brother is on the lose Jackson, a murderer brother that my mother thinks I convinced to do all the awful things he did…" – she was now standing in front of him – "and you went out and spent the day playing fantasy games. Jackson, do you honestly expect me to believe anything you just told me. Really!" She was pacing around the little living room. Jackson held his tongue, he guessed that she needed to vent. He would have needed to vent to if someone had just told him that story. "The Dreams are one thing, Jackson, but even those I still don't fully understand, or even believe. What I do believe in, is you! And how you have helped me so well up to this point. Please don't ask me to believe this, I can't. Can you just let me trust you instead? I will follow your lead Jackson, but I can't believe any of what you just told me." Jackson waited again. After a while Alex stopped pacing and came to sit down next to him.

"I would never force anything on you Alex, the fact that you trust me is more than I could ever have asked for. I don't yet believe half the stuff I have told you, but I have a feeling that… that this stuff is going to help. I have something I want to try tonight; it involves you, and I wanted to give you context before I attempted it." Alex looked extremely doubtful. It worried Jackson when she looked at him with that expression, like he was losing his marbles. Maybe he was. She motioned for him to go on. "I think I want to… well I want to try and… well… I want try and jump into your dream." He quickly went on before she could protest. He knew it sounded crazy and it wasn't helping his case with his mental stability status, but he forged ahead. "I am not asking you to anything other sleep next to me tonight Alex, something I was hoping you were going to do anyway," Jackson rushed on with a smile. "I don't even know how I'm going to do it. I am just asking for your permission to attempt it?" he finished pleadingly. Alex shook her head from side to side.

"I don't know Jackson, even though I don't think it will work, it feels spooky and wrong…" she trailed off at a loss for words.

"I would never do anything to hurt you or put you in danger Alex. You are the only person I truly, truly care about in my life!" Jackson said with conviction. They both stared at each silently for a while.

Eventually Alex spoke with a weary sigh, "Why not Jackson, let's try it. It's no crazier than the rest of the things that have happened since I met you." Jackson moved closer to her and gave her a gentle, reassuring hug. He smiled at her but in his head, he was already planning what he needed to do to make this work. It wasn't just because Alex was the only person in his life that he could try this with, but also because he thought he could use her connection to Freddie to try and figure how to find him. Maybe tap into something forgotten, something subconscious. He felt this was the right thing to do, even if it also felt like he was grasping at straws. Both Alex and Jackson drank their coffee in silence before they cleaned up and got ready for bed.

As they were lying side by side, on their backs, Alex grabbed hold of Jackson's hand and whispered jokingly, "Don't mess around too much inside my head you Dream Stalker you!" Jackson's heart stopped when she called him that. He had only heard it once before then, "Ow, Jackson, my hand!" He released his grip; he had been squeezing her hand without realising it.

"I'm sorry Alex, must be nervous or something," he joked back at her and tried to hide his unease. "Goodnight Alex, sleep tight," he said.

"G'night Jackson, don't let the bed bugs bite," she finished.

Jackson concentrated on listening to Alex's breathing as he lay next to her. He had no idea what he was supposed to be doing but he reasoned he would figure it out as he continued along. Slowly, almost imperceptibly, her breathing deepened. He found concentrating like this, on her breathing, made him match her breaths, in, out, in, out. This wasn't working, she breathed too fast for him; he was nearly hyperventilating. He needed to try something else, to change his focus. So instead, he probed inwards and partitioned his mind, once again becoming that automaton, the emotionless observer. He was still amazed at how easily this now came to him. It barely took a thought, as easy and as well rehearsed as breathing. In this state, Jackson's observational powers were enhanced, there was no clouding of perception by emotion. What he could now do was observe, focus, with an absolute clarity, he now had access to the raw, unfiltered data of the world around him. In this state, Jackson returned his attention to the sleeping figure beside him. His intuition told him to wait, to observe, to be patient... so he did. After a while, he noticed that Alex had slipped into a deeper sleep, REM or something like that he had read about. Her eyes were moving below their closed lids, clearly dreaming. It was then that Jackson noticed something he had never observed before. A hum, or a slight tune, or maybe just a vibration coming from Alex. Listening to it more closely, he realised that her body had been vibrating/singing all the time. He had only noticed it now that

223

it had changed pitch as she fell into deeper sleep. He was still marvelling at this discovery when a sudden thought occurred to him – Alex probably wasn't unique, perhaps everyone was vibrating or singing a tune and he wondered if he could use this to identify others? Perhaps their tune was as unique as their fingerprints? Jackson brought his mind around to refocus on the task at hand. He listened to Alex's body, her vibration. Hearing it like this awakened something primal in him, like a long-forgotten sixth sense. Jackson also felt the pain of the headache flare up behind his eyes, but in this state, he was able to acknowledge it without feeling its physical effect. He took the headache as a good sign, a sort of acknowledgement that he was on the right path. Now that he had the tone of her, he doubted he would ever forget its uniqueness, it was the most fundamental part of Alex, her unique body fingerprint. Jackson let his attention remain attached to that vibration coming from Alex and while he did so, prepared himself to go to sleep. He took a few more regular breathes, always concentrating on Alex next to him, and slowly, minute by minute, drifted off to sleep. It wasn't long before they were both were transported away from the present Dream, destination unknown, for Jackson at least.

Jackson opened his eyes. He had no memory of the journey getting here, but he was here. One minute lying in bed next to Alex, listening, and the next here. It was a sunlit afternoon in the woods. There was a little cottage before him in a clearing surrounded by trees so densely packed together that he doubted anyone would be able to walk through them. The cottage itself was a small, seemingly a one room affair. Four white walls below a red tiled roof. There was a small

224

wooden patio that ran the length of the front of the building,
surrounded by a hip high balustrade. Jackson could hear the
wind as it moved through the canopy of tall trees around him.
He focused and suddenly he was on the porch, without having
walked there. He found a small rocking chair and sat down to
wait for whatever it was he was supposed to see. As he was
sat there waiting, laughter reached him from the other side of
the house. Instead of jumping there, Jackson chose to get up
and approach the sound the normal way, by walking. He
wasn't sure what or who he was going to see and more than
this, he wasn't sure if whoever he saw, would even notice him.
Jackson came around the edge of the house and saw two
people, one boy and one girl, sitting on a blanket with an open
notebook before them, the girl scribbling furiously as the boy
watched. Jackson moved in to take a closer look but it
obviously alerted the two people before him. So they could see
him.

"Uncle Joe, we didn't hear you coming," the girl said. She
stood up and closed the book before Jackson could see
anything. It was clearly a slightly younger Alex and her
brother, Fred. He also noticed how Fred tried to cover the
book up the corner of the blanket. Uncle Joe? Jackson looked
down at his hands. They weren't his. They were bony, the skin
stretched and pocked with age spots. With no small sense of
horror, Jackson brought his hands up to his face to feel a
beard and a completely bald dome, so smooth in comparison
to his own hands. Jackson quickly moved over to the house
and stared at his reflection in one of the windows. He was an
old man, wearing clothes he would never have worn. "Uncle
Joe is everything all right?" the concerned voice of the girl
behind asked. Jackson closed his eyes and sucked in a deep

breath to calm himself. He also used the opportunity to shore up his little mind-box, in case any other shocks should come to him. Jackson figured that here in this dream, he was Uncle Joe and he should play the part. "I'm alright Alex, just wanted to confirm that I was indeed old!" Jackson joked. It worked, the girl and boy both giggled and went back to their blanket. The book that they were working on was out of sight. "What are you guys working on?" he asked the pair. '

"Oh, nothing important," Alex said, "just messing around."

"Alex, Fred... I'm not sure if it's just age or if I bumped my head, but, where are we?" Jackson asked. They both looked at him quizzically, then at each other before Fred spoke up.

"Um, we're at your cabin Uncle Joe. You said it would be OK for us to come around whenever we felt like it. Are you sure you're feeling OK?" Jackson got the distinct feeling of suspicion wafting off the boy.

"Ah that makes sense Freddie, and of course you are welcome anytime. I think I just get confused sometimes." Jackson tried to brush it off, but the pair were now staring at him and a small part of him became alarmed. The box in his head was thrumming. Alex suddenly screamed. Fred was inflating and growing before their eyes. Jackson immediately moved in front of Alex, to block or protect her. He was standing in front of a Freddie that now was nearing ten feet tall and growing still. Alex was behind him, staring wide eyed with fright from around his shoulders.

"Who are you, what are you doing here?" the ever-expanding giant in front of him screamed with force. Freddie's body was now taking up most of Jackson's vision

but the horrors were only just beginning. Giant Freddie suddenly sprouted a tail that burst through the back of the shorts that he was wearing. As he watched, Freddie's face erupted in course black fur and whiskers pushed through the skin of his cheeks! "You see Alex, I told you I could do it!" Freddie screamed again. He had his own tail in one of his hands now and he started hacking at it with a knife that appeared in the other hand. He laughed savagely as he did it, spinning around in circles while he hacked. His maniacal laugher assaulting his and Alex's ears. Jackson felt warm blood hitting his face, his shoulders, and his chest. In short order, he was covered in the sticky red mess, just a pair of wide, white eyes staring up at the growing Freddie. Alex had left Jackson's shoulder and was now a few paces behind him. She was on her knees, covering her eyes wither hands, rocking. She continued to scream as Jackson backed away from Freddie and went to her.

"Alex! Alex! It's just a dream! You need to wake up now! Wake up!" Jackson screamed at her. Giant Freddie, now with his detached, bloody tail in his hand, had moved over to them. His foot was in the air, he was going to stomp on them like a bug. "Alex! ALEX! Wake up.

You need to wake up now!" Jackson pulled her hands away from her face forcefully. She stopped screaming when she saw the giant booted foot above them, it was coming down. Before she could scream again, she looked at Jackson and, for the briefest of instances, there was a sort of confused recognition. It was gone as soon as it arrived. "WAKE UP ALEX!" Jackson screamed again. The little box in his head had disintegrated, he was in full panic mode now and no sense of control existed any longer. He didn't want to die like an insect on the bottom of someone's shoe. Freddie's foot came down, Alex's scream cut off, and then there was nothing more.

Both Alex and Jackson woke at the same time and sat bolt upright. Alex was screaming, she had her hands up to her face, trying to hide from the horror. Jackson was no less frightened, unable to speak. It was several minutes before they both became aware of their surroundings. Alex has stopped screaming and was now crying. Shaking all over himself, Jackson moved to comfort her. They lay back down in each other's arms, not speaking, waiting for their hearts to stop beating so furiously and for their breathing to even out. They hadn't yet said a word to each other, the emotional strain of what they both just experienced was too much. Without planning to, their exhausted bodies drifted off to sleep. They slept like that, peacefully, no dreams, for the remainder of the night, in each other's arms. In the street below, Bob giggled to himself as he walked away. He pulled out his favourite little flute and played a tune in the darkness of the evening. The song faded with him and he walked further away from the bar and Jackson's apartment that sat atop it. To anyone that might have been watching, the flute-playing man seemed to slowly evaporate into the mist that had gathered around him. When he was completely gone, the mist slowly sank into the ground and after him, like it had never existed.

A few hours later, Alex was up. Jackson was breathing deeply. He was lost in a sleep so deep that her efforts to shake him awake had little effect. Concerned, but not overly worried about him, she left him to wake on his own. She wanted to be at the bookstore this morning but also wanted to make Jackson some breakfast. She jumped out the bed and hurriedly cleaned up before heading to the kitchen to light the stove. While she was preparing the eggs, she revisited her conversation with Jackson last night. Somehow, she had found herself living in the twilight zone, everything he had said sounded so ridiculous, so bizarre that she had had difficulty concentrating on the whole thing. Even though she was seriously beginning to wonder at Jackson's mental state, a small part of her resonated with what he said. This was possibly why she had reacted so angrily. Here she was a rational, successful, grounded adult entertaining a wild, impossible childish story. She was angry with that part of her that could believe what Jackson had theorised. Looking down, she realised she had burnt the eggs.

Cursing to herself, she scrapped the mess into the bin and cleaned the pan. She was cracking new eggs into a bowl when she heard Jackson stirring in the room. A few moments later, a bleary-eyed Jackson stood in the doorway of the kitchen.

"Mmmm, smells good!" he said.

Alex smiled, "Liar," she told him. "You look like you've been hit by a bus." Jackson nodded and wearily moved over to sit in the little kitchen nook.

"Feels like it to," he said as he rested his head on his hands on the table. "Honestly, Alex, if I knew you were having nightmares like that, I would have thought twice before peeking in." His forehead was still on his hands, so he didn't notice Alex's reaction. She had frozen, mid-pose, while beating the eggs. Until that very moment, she had completely forgotten about the nightmare. The moment Jackson had brought it up, she started shaking all over and had to put the bowl of partly beaten eggs down on the counter before her. Jackson finally noticed the quiet and sudden pause in activity.

He looked up and saw Alex shaking all over, like she was having a mini seizure. He quickly moved over to her and hugged her from behind. Stepping back a little, he rubbed her arms until her body seemed to be coming back under control, then guided her to the table where he had just been sitting.

She spoke up, "You saw that? It was the most wicked nightmare I can ever remember having. In fact, I hadn't remembered it until right now!" Alex crossed her arms under her breasts as she sought to hug herself. "I did see it Alex. Truth be told, I have never been so scared in my life, and I have had some serious disturbing dreams before that one. This was the first time that I wasn't just scared, I felt threatened, like I could have died there, died like a bug under the shoes of a massive cat man." Jackson was rubbing his temples at the memory but stopped as soon as he realised what he was doing. Instead he reached across the table and unclasped Alex's hands from each other then took them into his own.

"Did you recognise me; did you see me there?" Jackson asked conspiratorially, even though no one was near.

Alex shook her head, "No. It was only me and Freddie and Uncle Joe at his old cottage. How could you possibly have seen that Jackson? You weren't there, you couldn't be there… it's… it's impossible."

Jackson squeezed Alex's hands as he spoke, "I was there Alex, I was Uncle Joe! At least I was Uncle Joe in that Dream. I tell you Alex, seeing myself as another man was almost scarier that Freddie transforming into that giant cat." Alex looked up at Jackson with wide eyes, comprehension dawning on her face.

"You really did it! Just like you said. Jackson. This is beyond weird, what you are capable of, it scares me a little." She said the last part almost in a whisper.

"It scares me too Alex. It feels like I am learning new things about myself every day. However, what's important now is this; if this part of my theory is true, perhaps the rest of what we discussed last night isn't too far off. Are you starting to believe, even a little?" Jackson asked passionately. He needed her to think like he was thinking, he needed her to believe him. He needed a partner in this. If she could just be on par with him, it would be so much easier to deal with. If she believed him, she could maybe put to rest that nagging voice at the back of head telling he was going mad. Jackson watched Alex's face while she came to grips with this new reality.

She nodded, "Yes Jackson, I think I really do." Jackson let out a breath he hadn't realised he had been holding. His relief suddenly cascd a tension in him he hadn't noticed was there. He got up and walked around the table to hug her while she sat. When he was seated back on the other side of the table, they both looked at each other, smiled, then laughed.

"Here I was thinking I was going crazy," Jackson said, "but all along, I now find out we are both crazy!" They both laughed like they were indeed crazy for a while before sobering up. "Ok, supernatural aside, we have a lead Alex! Your Uncle Joe. Where is his cabin?" Jackson asked.

"Not far from Beaver Pond. But Jackson, don't get too excited, Uncle Joe has been dead for the past eight years, I doubt that little house even exists anymore!" Jackson was more than excited; he was convinced he would find Freddie there and the ache behind his eyes confirmed it.

"When last did you visit the cottage? In the dream you didn't look too much younger than you are today," Jackson asked.

"Really?" Alex answered with surprise. "I my dream I was hardly more than a child, early teens… Freddie must have been about eight or nine. We haven't been to that cottage in over ten years!" Jackson filed that information away for later. Apparently, perception is different amongst players in the dream.

"Ok, well it all we have to go on. Any idea of why the police wouldn't have found this cottage by now?" Jackson asked as an afterthought.

"It's quite easy to miss Jackson. Uncle Joe bought it for cash a few years before he died. I remember because my mom was very confused as to why he did that. It's very isolated, you can't get there directly by car. You have to park on the side of the road and then walk for about a mile to reach it. It is in this little clearing, like out of a fairy tale or something. I don't think Uncle Joe knew why he bought it either, he just told Mom that he felt at peace with himself there. I'm not even sure there is any record of ownership of the cottage. I was very young then so can't remember the details of it, but what I imagined at the time was Uncle Joe buying the little house like you would by a second-hand car, with no papers and such. Fred and I only went there twice as children, no one would remember the place," Alex finished talking. Jackson had been scribbling furiously.

"Can you get us there; do you remember the way?" Jackson asked without looking up from his notes.

"Maybe, I'm not sure, but I can certainly try Jackson. I don't know why he would be there but it's as good a place to look as any other I suppose." Alex answered him. The resolve in her voice seemed to come from a renewed sense of direction, of purpose. Jackson realised that he felt energised as well. They had something here, something they could do.

"I'm going to call Ben, Alex, we will need back up just in case. We need to include the police in this, even in a small way. Our position in this investigation doesn't allow us not to. Running off without them would undoubtedly seem suspicious." Alex agreed without a fight, there was sense in what he was saying. Jackson moved over to the phone in the hallway and punched-in Ben's number. He answered on the second ring. Jackson filled him in on the lead, leaving out the weirder stuff.

"Jackson, you and Alex are to sit tight. I am coming over to pick you up. I'll bring several of my boys along to help. Are you sure Alex can find this place?" Ben waited for confirmation before continuing. "Be ready in twenty minutes!" was all he said before hanging up. Jackson looked across to Alex who was still seated at the little table.

Looks like breakfast will have to wait, the cavalry is on the way. Thoughts of the bookstore and the bar and their jobs were the last things on their minds. Jackson moved to get ready. Alex moved to the bedroom to pack her stuff. The hunt was about to begin, again.

Freddie had been lying on the bed in the little cottage, staring blankly out the window… waiting. He was not motivated to do anything else. He drank when he was thirsty, he ate when he was hungry, and he used the bathroom when required. For the last couple of days, this had been his life. He was neither happy, nor sad. Neither excited nor bored, he just was. He waited and watched out the window. The scenery never changed. This morning he had woken up feeling a little different, the complete non-sensory, non-thinking apathy he had adopted was gone. There was a sense of anticipation, a sense of a finally reaching a destination. Freddie stared out of the window and waited, but this time with expectation. He didn't have to wait for too long. He noticed a slight movement amongst the trees, at the border of his available view. The movement coalesced suddenly into the shape of man. He was all shadows, all dark green, matching the surroundings. He wore a black hat that hid any features of his face. Instinctively, Freddie recognised him. He didn't know him, couldn't remember him, but he did recognise him. It was like smelling something and then being transported into a completely different emotional state. The sight of that man did this to Freddie. He was now excited but also extremely alarmed. It left him confused and anxious, but he watched on, and waited. The man's arm left the bulk of shadows and beckoned to him. He wanted to Fred to follow. There was never an instant of doubt. Fred knew he would follow that man regardless of what he really actually wanted to do. With that understanding, the small sense of excitement at this event started giving way to alarm, or something closer to panic. Freddie got up and left the bedroom, he paused briefly at the front door, remembering his previous inability to cross that threshold, but as he resumed his walk, he passed through without any resistance. It took only a few steps to walk around the house to the point in the trees where he had just seen the man. He was still there, waiting for Freddie. As soon as he saw Freddie had spotted him, he turned and disappeared into the trees.

"Wait!" Freddie shouted as he ran after him. He plunged into the trees and ran after hm, seemingly without direction.

He ran as fast as the brush around him allowed. In a moment, he was in a small round clearing, centred by a small fire surrounded by a ring of grey stones.

The featureless man in black was sitting cross legged on the ground, turning a small carcass (rat, squirrel?) roasting on a spit over the fire. Still panting from his run through the woods, Freddie joined him as he sat across from him in the clearing. He didn't say anything, he found he was too scared to. He didn't understand what was happening, but the fear was as real to him as anything else. The greater part of him knew he was not in control, so he waited for the man to speak. The little animal that was cooking above the fire was slowly turned by the man, on the improvised spit. Around and around, sizzling and spitting. The man suddenly spoke, softly, but it broke the hypnotic state Freddie was starting to fall into.

"So, we finally see each other Fred. I have been with you, watching you, guiding you, for large parts of your life. I have been your unseen influence Fred, your external intuition so to speak." The man seemed to find this funny and quietly giggled to himself. Freddie was frozen; the sound of the man's voice was so familiar; it was almost felt like an intimate part of him. It also filled him with horror.

"Who are you?" he asked when he could breathe again.

"I am the part of you that exists and drives you when you can't remember. I am Bob, I am the Green, and I am Pan. I have many other names and we don't have enough time to go through all of them. I reveal myself to you now so that you may choose your path, free of my… guidance." He giggled at his choice of words, finding humour in it that Freddie couldn't. The man stopped turning the spit and poked the meat with a long finger peeking out from black gloves. Seemingly satisfied, he pulled the spit from the fire blew on it, cooling it. Freddie watched on fascinated, entranced. After a few more blows, the man opened his mouth, just visible below the rim of his hat, revealing parallel rows of perfect white, small, sharp teeth. He took a tentative bite and sucked in a breath when heat hit his tongue. Then he started to chew, slowly, with his mouth open. Although Freddie couldn't see his eyes, he knew the man was staring at him, making him feel naked and uncomfortable. The sound of the chewing was nauseating, making him feel sick to his stomach. Freddie looked at the carcass and was horrified to see its eyes moving in the furless head, it was still alive, with-it skin roasted and split from the fire. It was implanted, alive but cooked, on the stick. Freddie watched on with sickening fascination. The man took another bite, Freddie could see the animal's eyes widen in pain but not a sound was made by it and all Freddie could hear was the awful sloppy chewing of the man. Juice was dripping from his open mouth onto his chin. "Do you know what you have done Freddie? Are you able to put the pieces together, have you filled in those blank spots in your mind?" the man asked as he slowly stood up, spit in hand. He was very tall, looming over the fire in the early morning sunlight. Freddie once again felt frozen, he could not bring himself to speak. In a heartbeat, the man was over him. He had dropped his meal and his greasy fingertips were pressed into Freddie's temples, staring straight into his eyes. Fred could smell his sickening breath, but it all happened so fast that he didn't even have time to be alarmed. "Let me show you then Fred, let me show you what you have been getting up too." The man whispered savagely. Freddie's world suddenly spun. There was brief moment of darkness, then he found himself in memory, his own memory.

He could still feel the man's greasy fingers pressing into the side of his head as he got lost in recall. He watched himself as he butchered the cat, he watched as he tortured several other smaller animals. Then he watched as he tortured and murdered Linda and finally he saw himself hacking at the kids at the campground. If he could have fainted, he would have. It was sensory overload and it hit him like a ton of bricks. He was a mass murderer; he was a killer! Everything he thought he knew about himself was a lie, a stupid, horrible lie. Everything he believed in was not true. His life had not been his own. His whole sense of identity was shattered in an instant. Whereas before he felt spilt inside, now he felt hollow, empty. The man let go of his head and returned to the other side of the fire. He picked up his dropped meal, brushed off some of the dirt and took another bite. The little animal's eyes widened again. What was keeping that poor thing alive? Freddie should have been crying, should have been scratching at his eyes, should have been a mess, but the shock of revelation had been too sudden, too intense. Fred couldn't feel anything, he wasn't Fred anymore: he was nothing now. Talking around a mouthful of food, the man spoke again, much calmer and more relaxed. "They are coming for you as we speak Fred, the police and your sister. You need to decide what to do. Are you going to run or meekly let yourself be taken in? Are you going to fight?" The man swallowed his food at waited on Freddie.

"I don't care anymore. I will just sit here and let whatever happens, happen," Freddie responded in a monotone. The man nodded his head as if expecting that.

"Well, for possibly the first time in your life Fred, you now know who you are. I also can promise you I won't be playing any more games with you, although I will watch. Now that you understand what's really going on, don't you think you should see what a real, unfiltered, un-doctored life feels like?"

Fred didn't even look up as he responded "No," was his simple, deadpan answer. There was a whisper of wind and Fred looked up. The fire was dead, and the half-eaten carcass was cold and lying in the dirt. Thankfully, it was also now dead, its eyes still in their lidless sockets. Of the man there was no sign, it was if he had never been. It didn't surprise Fred; he had a feeling he would never feel surprised again. He sat there a while longer thinking about nothing. After a while, he stood up and listlessly began his trek back through the woods to the cottage. Something of what the man said had stuck; who was he? Did he not deserve to at least know that? Having had his whole life manipulated and taken away from him, did he not deserve to live according to his own decisions? The hollow thing that was Fred, walked into the cottage and starting packing food and some meagre clothing into a backpack. He was wasn't going to wait around to be arrested. He didn't care about that anyway, if they caught him then so be it. What he wanted to do was live, even for just a little bit. He wanted to live according to his own rules, to do things of his own will. Perhaps he would find a way to feel again. Perhaps, in what he knew was limited time, he would come to know himself, he could only hope. He found a scrap of paper and wrote a brief note that he left on the floor just inside the door. Fred left the little cottage and walked into the trees without any planned direction. He never once looked behind him.

Jackson was in the lead car of a procession of police vehicles. Ben was as good as his word and had picked them up roughly thirty-five minutes after Jackson had ended the call. They were speeding up the highway in a trail of flashing lights and sirens. Under different circumstances, he would have enjoyed the sight of traffic parting for him, but today he was filled with a different sort of excitement. They were in the end game now, at least where Freddie was concerned. If they could catch him now, stop the carnage and the emotional turmoil they were being subjected to, they had a small chance at finding some semblance of normality. He was seated in the backseat and Alex was up front with Ben driving. When they neared their destination, she would be the one providing the directions. At the start, Ben had asked them some very pointed questions as to how they came to think of Freddie's possible location. There weren't any answers that would be real enough to suit him though and they settled on what was basically said to him on the phone earlier. Ben didn't press any further, and accepted that Jackson was the mysterious source. That was enough for him. It was one of the reasons Jackson really liked and trusted him. Ben knew nothing further could be gained from rational explanation so decided he had enough information to act that was all he needed. From Jackson's point of view, he hoped he was right. He hoped this would have some sort of tangible result. The rest of the drive was made in silence, each of the occupants of the car lost in thought, listening to the wail of the sirens with half an ear. When they reached the required exit, they turned and made their way to the park, back to the place of the latest murders. The day was mild and sunny, with a scattering of clouds that provided momentary shade as they passed in front of the sun.

At a certain point on the journey, Alex spoke up and directed Ben to a turn that led towards a different entrance into the park. Ben then spoke into his squad car radio and all the sirens and flashing lights turned off as the procession mimicked their turn towards to the park.

"Don't want to announce our presence." Ben said simply. They continued into the park and after several turns (Jackson decidedly lost by now) Alex directed Ben to a small parking lot, almost entirely overgrown with weeds. If Alex hadn't shown them the way, Jackson doubted anyone else could've found it. The other cars followed them and parked in the remaining spaces. There wasn't enough of those spaces however, some had to park half off the road. The cops all gathered in a huddle while they planned and discussed their approach. Alex and Jackson waited patiently just apart from them while weapons were checked and re-holstered. The point team, including Alex and Jackson, would walk, weapons at the ready.

Ben gave them some brief instructions and then held out official police bibs for them to put on. Ben shook his head a polite enquiry from Jackson.

"No Jackson, can't allow a civilian to carry a weapon. Even one as proficient as you, unfortunately. This is a police exercise now and you will follow my orders at all times, is that clear?" Jackson resisted an urge to stand to and salute, instead he nodded his head. Alex did the same. "Right! You all know your places and your jobs, let's move out!" Ben shouted to the larger group. To Alex, he inclined his head, "After you." Alex took a breath and with Jackson beside her, plunged forward onto the little walkway heading into the woods. Their gun toting entourage following them closely in single file. The whole thing was too close to a military exercise for Jackson and he had to supress some unpleasant memories at the thought. They walked on in the morning sunshine, like an incursion into enemy territory, which, Jackson supposed, it was. It was a short walk, but a difficult one. The path had not been walked on in ages and as a result they had to fight their way through the over-growth. After about ten minutes of silent struggling, Alex tapped Ben on his back, he was crouch-walking, in the lead. At her touch he held up a fist and the squad of police became immediately still as the message was repeated down the line. Crouched police officers pointed their weapons on each side of the file, clearly expecting attack at any moment.

Ben turned around and faced Alex whispering, "What's up?"

Alex copied his hushed tones, "You see the fork in the path ahead of you?" Ben nodded and she continued, "We need to go right for about another twenty or so paces. Then there should be a small breakaway path off that on the left, the house is only a couple of hops away from that if I remember correctly." Ben nodded and told them to hang tight for a moment. He moved back down the line and gathered men around him as he did so. He was clearly planning the assault of the house. He returned to them and motioned for them to crouch beside him.

"Ok, we got this from here. We are going to quietly approach the house and then surround it before moving in. If I need you, I will radio Roberto here to bring you to us." Roberto, looking like an excited kid, gave them a thumbs up. Jackson and Alex were both about to protest but Ben cut them off. "This is not a request nor a negotiation!" he said nothing more but waited calmly before them. Jackson reluctantly returned to his crouch and then sat down. Alex, clearly unhappy, sat down next to him.

"Please try to not hurt him," she pleaded with Ben.

"That's my intention Alex. If we can get away without any shots being fired then that's a win. I want this handled quickly and without fuss and if all goes according to plan, we will have Freddie safe and secure without anyone getting hurt, OK?" Alex looked at him and then after a little pause, thanked him gratefully. Roberto, stood guard over them just to their side. Ben and the other officers moved with practised steps and disappeared silently into the woods ahead of them. Without thinking, Jackson leaned over and put his arm around Alex and set to wait. She nuzzled her face into his chest.

"Do you think he really did it? Do you think we are about to catch a mass murderer? About to corner Fred the Freak?" Roberto spoke up beside them. Jackson looked up. The insensitivity of the question had caught him off guard, as did the nickname for Freddie. Did Roberto not know who he was talking to?

"Ah, officer, I don't think that an appropriate question and it is certainly not the appropriate time!" Jackson said sternly, before Alex could react. He had initially thought it was just youthful, inexperienced excitement that drove Roberto to ask the questions but when he caught sight of the officers' eyes, he was stunned into silence. There was an awful gleam in those eyes, eyes full of intense malice, they practically beamed out from his face like searchlights. Jackson almost recognised something in that stare, almost remembered something before it was gone and the normal Roberto seemed to return to himself. As if suddenly understanding what he had said, a horrified looked crossed his pale face. "Sorry miss, uh, ma'am. I don't know why I said that. I didn't mean to upset you or anything. It's just, like it's just my first raid is all." He stuttered off into silence. Alex and Jackson just looked on, watching. "Well, um, sorry." He finished off and moved off a little way to resume his silent guard. Feeling greatly uncomfortable at the strange exchange with the officer, Jackson looked to his side at Alex.

"You OK?" he asked.

"Not really Jackson, Sitting here doing nothing, waiting is killing me. I just want it to be over. I just want Freddie to be OK." Jackson didn't have any words that could comfort her so instead squeezed her tighter. Alex seemed to understand the silent message and attempted to smile up at Jackson. To Jackson, it was so obviously forced, clearly attempting to hide her fear and worry. They continued to sit there, waiting for Ben's signal. There were no gunshots, there were no raised voices, and it was just the sound of the forest all around them, eerie in light of the situation. Officer Roberto's radio suddenly crackled, startling everyone.

He held the radio to his face and pressed the button on the side of it. "Come in Officer Santiago," came through before he could speak. Ben's voice echoed around them.

"Santiago here sir."

"Please bring Jackson and Alex up to the house immediately!" Ben said and cut off. "Copy that," Officer Santiago replied. Jackson and Alex were both on their feet and followed the officer as he motioned for them to do so. Not even a minute later, they entered the clearing around the little cottage. There were officers posted regularly around the perimetre of the building, some were pushing into the trees at various spots, searching. The house itself was much like he had seen it in Alex's dream although it had none of the vibrancy he remembered. The red roof was faded, uneven colouring across its surface. The white walls desperately needed a coat of paint and in some places, the plaster was clearly visible where the paint had peeled off entirely. Jackson and Alex left the now quiet officer Santiago behind them and walked into the house. Fred was nowhere to be seen. Ben was poking a piece of paper on the floor with his pen. "Please don't touch anything you two!" Ben said without turning around to look at them. "I want you to take a look at this." Jackson and Alex crouched on next to him. It was a letter, hastily written.

I know now what I have done Alex. I am a murderer; I have done terrible things. I know what I have done but I don't know who I am, what I am. I want to figure that out in the short amount of time I think I have left. Sorry – F

To Alex, the note was so unlike Freddie, there was nothing behind the words. It was so emotionless it could have been written by a robot. Even the 'sorry' bit at the end seemed completely insincere. Her tears came before she realised that she was about to cry.

"Oh Freddie!" Jackson was there hugging her again.

"We must have only just missed him," Ben said. "The coals in the fireplace are still warm and all the lights are still on. The genny in the back is running. I have already called in additional reinforcements, he couldn't have gotten too far away on foot. We are going to have this place surrounded in a few moments. Any other mysterious clues you might have of where he could have gone?" Jackson shook his head; he had no idea. He was so sure this was it, the end, it was massively disappointing to not have caught Freddie. He had been so sure this was the moment. Ben acknowledged Jackson's shaking head. "This now an official crime scene and I need you both away from here. I will have an officer drive you home. Uh, don't plan any trips or anything, Jackson. We might need you and your unique... insights... at a moment's notice. Stay close, stay contactable! That goes for you too Alex." Ben made sure they both understood the seriousness of his statement before dismissing them and returning to his work. Jackson and Alex were greeted by a different officer who came in to fetch them.

They followed him all the way back to the car, where they climbed into the back. Alex had stopped sobbing but her silent tears continued. The officer attempted conversation on the drive out, but he gave up after a few toneless, uninterested responses from Jackson.

"Do you know officer Santiago, by the way? Roberto?" The question suddenly occurred to Jackson. The officer said he did not.

"He only transferred in a few days ago." Jackson didn't know why he asked, but that man had unsettled him quite a bit.

Chapter 8 – Notes from the Past

Despite what Detective Hasset had believed, they weren't able to apprehend Freddie. In one of the largest organised manhunts of the decade, the woods around Beaver Pond crawled with police officers and volunteers from all over the state. Freddie's face was plastered on every TV set, nationally, on all new channels. In fact, in the short while since the discovery at the cottage, Fred Harver had become a celebrity, a part of the national consciousness. The police were baffled, the public were concerned but Freddie had disappeared into thin air. The hotlines the police had set up produced nothing but the standard crazies calling in, either claiming to be Fred, or claiming Fred had been their neighbour for the last ten years. The police followed up on all these leads but to no avail. For Jackson and Alex, the two weeks since their return from the park had been fourteen days of anxious waiting. Waiting for some news from the cops, waiting on the hourly updates on the news. It had been draining, exhausting, both of them mentally timed out. It was also affecting their relationship, to the point that as a couple, the whole reason for them being together seemed to revolve around the hunt for Freddie. Alex had remained with Jackson at his little apartment for a few days but with no updates on the Fred situation, decided to return to her own apartment so she could be closer to her parents and closer to work. However, they were on the phone to each other constantly and more often than not, saw each other over dinner. Jackson returned to work and resumed where he had left off, Randall was grumpy as ever and Shelley kept looking at him with big eyes, drowning in sympathy. For the most part, Jackson ignored them and with manic focus, tending solely to the duties of serving his customers. Something else that was disturbing on its own was that boozy Bob had gone missing, well at least missing from the bar. He had become such a regular that Randall even reported his absence to the police, but with no other information apart from his description, they couldn't do anything. For his own part, Jackson was also really disturbed by the fact that his Dreams had not helped in any way whatsoever. He had spent night after night, focussing his mind while in bed. He would prepare himself to receive the Dream that never came. He hadn't even had a headache or a hint of anything that could help in the search of Freddie. There was nothing that could be done, he would just have to wait to see what happened as he had exhausted all his own leads. The police were not fairing any better. During one of their conversations on the phone, Alex had told him that the bookstore would be closing for a while. The media and the public had made the connection between Fred and Alex and had swamped the place, looking for comments and in some weird cases, autographs. This hadn't helped sales, rather it had chased most of her customers away. As a result, Alex thought it best for the Tasselled Bookmark to take a sabbatical, at least until the public interest in Fred wore off. Once closed, Alex had wanted to move in with parents for support, but it seemed the relationship with her mother was at an all-time low. That experiment only lasted a few days before she left, much to her father's dismay. With the extra time on her hands, Alex threw herself in to the search for her brother. With nothing else to go on, she started making lists. Lists of all the places she had visited with her brother, lists of all the places her brother had visited and lists of all the places her brother had told her that he would like to visit. It didn't help them much in the search, but at least it kept her mind occupied. It was what she was doing now, at the bar, waiting for Jackson to finish up his shift, she wouldn't have to wait to much longer. Lost in their own thoughts, as had become the norm these days, they walked side by side up the stairs back to his apartment.

"Wait up Alex!" Jackson whispered urgently as he dragged her behind him. Whereas Alex had been watching her feet as she walked, Jackson had been looking ahead. He had noticed something at his front door. "Give me sec, there is something on my door!" Jackson checked to make sure Alex had heard before moving closer to the door. There was a white envelope nailed to his door, on top of which was a cat's severed tail. There was a line of blood running down over the centre of the white paper, over it and then down in a single line over the door, to a little congealed puddle on the floor. It looked very fresh, like it had just been put there.

"Oh my god!" Alex whispered next to him. He hadn't noticed that she had followed him, completely ignoring his instructions.

"Let's not assume anything Alex. This could be some sort of awful prank!" With a rag he still had tucked into his belt from his shift at the bar, Jackson pulled at the nail and grabbed the tail and envelope before they fell to the floor. "Let's get inside before anyone notices this," he said. He unlocked the door with his one hand and ushered her inside. Once both were past the threshold, he hurriedly dropped the tail and envelope on the table next to the phone and the used the rag to roughly clean the trail of blood on the outside of the door.

When done, he looked up and down the hall to ensure no one had seen anything, then closed the door behind him. Jackson had never actually seen anyone in that hallway before but he wasn't about to take any unnecessary chances. Alex hadn't moved. She stood frozen in the narrow passageway between the door and the little TV room-cum-lounge. Pale-faced, she was staring at the tail which had slipped to the floor. Jackson walked past her to the kitchen where he pulled out a zip lock bag from a door before returning to her. With his dirty rag, he pouched the tail in the bag and cleaned up the small bit of blood that had leaked onto table and floor and then, as delicately as he could, he manoeuvred Alex to the kitchen nook. With her seated, he fetched the envelope and joined her at the table. Jackson looked at Alex and waited for her to acknowledge her assent before opening the bloody package. She nodded and Jackson flipped the unsealed lid of the paper package open. He pulled out a clean folded white sheet untouched by the cat blood. Gently he put the envelope aside and unfolded the paper on the table before them, angling it so they could both read it at the same time.

Alex!

You need to remember! I can help you; I can show you.

Don't call the police, they are pawns, you are not! It's always been you and I and it can continue like that if you allow it. Don't be scared, it will all make sense soon. I am finally free; you can be too.

Trust me – F

Alex grabbed the piece of paper and re-read the message several times over.

"What does this mean, what is he going on about?" Alex was losing control; Jackson could see it. As delicately as he could, he praised the paper out of her hands and laid it on the table.

"He is sick Alex. The note sounds like something a madman would write. Please don't read too much into it. I think he is alone, he is scared, and he is just reaching out to the person that was, is, closest to him!" Alex was nodding furiously, grabbing at the lifeboat of rationality that Jackson was offering while holding back the tears.

"May I read the note again?" Jackson picked it up and gave it to her again. While she read it, he moved across the kitchen to put the coffee on and busied himself with its preparation.

He believed everything he had just told Alex but he was concerned. Fred was clearly unstable and seemingly deteriorating at pace. He was getting more and more worried that he was involving Alex in this, targeting her. Jackson was worried what Fred would do next, with Alex, and he was worried that he didn't know how to protect her. Fred was pulling his sister into this mess and Jackson was deathly afraid where it might lead. Taking two steaming cups of coffee back to the table, he handed one to Alex who accepted gratefully. She had put the note aside but kept her hand resting over it, like a prised possession she was afraid would be stolen. Jackson noted this with concern before speaking.

"We need to tell the police Alex. Fred is dangerous!"

"No, not yet Jackson. We can't scare him away now that he has reached out. We could lose him before we have a chance to help him!" she replied with fervour.

"Help him, Alex?" Jackson asked.

"You know what I mean Jackson, we need to catch him so as to help him." Jackson wasn't so sure that was what she meant but he left it alone.

"Ok Alex let's see what happens next, but if I feel like you are in danger in any way, I'm going straight to Ben or Detective Levi. Nothing will stop me from doing that! You are too important to me to be offered up as bait." Alex smiled at him and moved over to sit in his lap before kissing him.

"I love you Jackson, just in case you didn't know!" That caught Jackson by surprise, pushing all thoughts of danger and murderous brothers' aside. It was the most wonderful thing anyone had ever said to him. He looked into her eyes and kissed her back.

"I love you too just in case you didn't know it!" He picked her up and carried her to bed. Over his shoulder, Alex eyes focussed on the letter still on the table as she was carried away.

Jackson was alive. His feelings for Alex over the next few hours were enhanced, deepened, and taken to a whole new level. She became a part of him, a part he had not known was missing until now. Everything from the last few weeks was swept away in a tidal wave of emotion and sensation and Jackson gobbled it all up. He was insatiable, drinking it all in like a man who had just found an oasis in the desert. There was a part of his mind that nagged at him, told him to focus, told him he needed to concentrate, but he brushed it aside ruthlessly. Whatever it was, it could wait. With selfish abandon, Jackson threw himself into the experience of the evening with Alex. It was only later, lying in bed next to her, the evening breeze drying the sweat off their bodies that he once again became aware of that nagging feeling of something missed. He turned over and checked on Alex's steady breathing before getting up and shuffling through the darkness to the kitchen. The note from Freddie was still on the table and like a shining beacon in the night and it pulled Jackson towards it. Sitting down, he picked it up and re-read it. What was he missing here? What would Freddie have to gain by sending it, why not just catch her alone somewhere and face her directly? Jackson kept on reading the note, over and over until he was chanting in his head like a catechism.

Eventually he threw the note down in disgust. He was getting nowhere, he was tired, and reading under the dim lights of his kitchen was giving him a headache. Getting up again, he quietly shuffled back to the dark bedroom and slid under the covers next to Alex, he asleep in seconds.

Jackson opened his eyes in the Dream. After trying so long and so hard to get back here, he could scarcely believe it, but the familiar sense of fear and panic was immediately noticeable. Before investigating his surroundings, he went inwards and partitioned his mind, cutting off the emotional input and enhancing his sensory awareness. Jackson opened his eyes in the Dream was again, this time with focus and clarity. He waited for the Dream to reveal its intentions. The room around him spun, he at its centre while the spinning

252

room moved faster and faster until it blurred his vision. He was a rock, in a vortex of spinning colours. With a lurch, everything ceased moving. Jackson closed his eyes and suppressed the sudden nausea that threatened to escape from him, violently. Under control now, Jackson refocused on the room, it was a nothing place. There were no borders, no walls, no features. Just infinite whiteness. Jackson looked down and saw his feet; he was standing on the same nothing, the same whiteness, seemingly floating. He took tentative steps forward and held his arms out for balance. It was so disorientating that Jackson became dizzy at the movement. He immediately stopped moving his feet and remained still and the dizziness passed. A simple, brown, wooden chair appeared in front of him and suddenly it was filled with a sitting man.

Had Jackson not had his mind guarded; he would have been shocked at the suddenness of it. As it was, he stood watching, unmoving, waiting for it to play out. The man in the chair was featureless, a white oval above a collared green shirt. As he watched, features began to appear and before he knew it, he was looking into the emotionless face of Freddie Harver.

They stared at each other for an age before Jackson eventually spoke.

"Fred, what are you doing here? How did you get here?" Fred continued to stare at him blankly, as if deciding the best way to answer the question. After a short while he spoke.

"I am not sure. I was asleep, then I was here, as he said I would be."

"Who is he, who said that?" Jackson asked straight away.

"The man with the hat, the manipulator. I didn't care to ask him his name, although I think he did tell me somewhere along the line. It's no longer important, but what is, is that he is a mutual acquaintance of ours. It was he that set up this meeting, even though he promised to stop interfering. Regardless, I am thankful as it gives me a chance to talk to you without my sister around. I need to explain to you, I believe you will understand where she might not." Jackson knew exactly who he was talking about and dismissed it, trying to understand those intentions would drive him mad. What he found extremely disturbing was Fred's countenance. He was hollow, empty, a vessel devoid of any human qualities. Much like Jackson imagined himself to look like but with one startling difference; he was still Jackson, a small part of him remained. In Freddie, nothing of that was present. *"I needed some time to understand who I was, Jackson. Who I was after the man in the hat revealed his manipulations to me. You see, it was the wrong question! It was never about who I was but why I was, my purpose! I discovered my purpose, Jackson, and that is why we are here today, for me to help you to understand what I must do."* The line of conversation was making Jackson feel decidedly uncomfortable. He tried an experiment and imagined a chair before him, in front of Fred. It appeared. Even in Fred's strange state of mind, his eyes widened in surprise. Jackson moved deliberately and sat down in front of him. The successful experiment gave Jackson a jolt of confidence. He motioned for Fred to continue. Fred had immediately regained control and went on blankly. *"Purpose is everything Jackson. Without purpose we are nothing but animals foraging in the dirt. Just living for the sake of living. Its purpose that separates us from the animals*

you see. My purpose is now clear, I help people to see and help them to understand. I must make Alex see, Jackson, she cannot go on as she is, living a lie!"

"What lie Fred, what are you talking about?" Jackson asked.

"It's not for me to tell you Jackson. She needs to learn it herself; it is the only way she will accept it. Me simply telling you is hollow, useless, easily dismissed," Fred elaborated. Jackson took a moment to think.

"So why are we here Fred, why are we talking? Why the note and the cat's tail. Why so cryptic?" He doused Fred with an avalanche of questions. Fred smiled back at him. It was terrifying to see, a smile attempted as if something from memory.

"We are here because our mutual friend thought it was necessary. We are here because I want to explain the realities of what's going to happen post this meeting. The note was our friend's way of getting your attention for this meeting. You see, it wasn't just for Alex, although that served its own purpose. It was also for you. The man tried to explain to me how, but I wasn't paying too much attention. Suffice to say, he needed you in the right frame of mind to find you and bring you here." Jackson digested that in silence while he waited for Fred to continue. "Jackson, you are here to guide Alex to her understanding." Fred stood up and loomed large over Jackson. "She must understand, and if she doesn't, she must die! She cannot live like this. It's is an anathema to the universe to be so completely unaware of yourself, of your true purpose. She must come into this state with your help, but it must be soon. I cannot allow for her ignorance much longer. I will kill her Jackson. I will do her this favour where no one

else would. I will do it with joy knowing that I am correcting the path the universe had chosen for her, the path she cannot yet see!" Jackson was becoming increasingly alarmed at the fervour pulsing off of Fred. It was without doubt that he had gone over the edge, he had completely lost his mind and that made him even more dangerous.

Where Jackson was previously worried about some random people that Fred might hurt, he now worried for Alex, the person, only person he cared about in the world. Cared deeply about. He stood up and faced Fred eye-to-eye and with a stiff finger poked Fred in the chest.

"Do you really think I will just allow you to threaten her and not do anything about it? Do you really think that I will not do everything in my power to hunt to down and destroy you? I will not let you harm even a single hair on her head you sick bastard!" Jackson was panting with fury and jabbing his finger repeatedly into Fred's chest, but it had no effect on him whatsoever. He merely looked slightly upwards at Jackson, a hint of a smile twitching at the corners of his mouth.

"You won't find me Jackson, even with your... abilities – nothing of me is here for you to trace. Once this meeting is over, you won't even have a starting place to begin looking. I, on the other hand, know exactly where you and Alex are and I can find you in a heartbeat. Help her Jackson, or I will!" With that, Fred simply vanished. Jackson stood there panting, between the two empty chairs, feeding his rage and his fear. He hadn't noticed his mind box imploding; all he could think about was the threat that had just been delivered to the one and only person he cared for. The whiteness of the room started to reflect his mood. Out of nowhere, storm clouds, *thick, grey and heavy started rolling in from above. The air became heavy, humid, and static, thunder rolled out and lightening flashed. The ground beneath him started to crack in red lines with colour and heat escaping from the fissures. It was all greens and reds. Screams echoed across the nightmare scene and in the middle of it, stood Jackson, alone, a man apart. Coming back to himself, he suddenly realised what was happening around him. Sucking in deep breaths and taking back control, Jackson partitioned his mind. Immediately the clouds started rolling back, the sky/space reverting back to its previous whiteness. The cracks in the ground sealed up and shut out the eldritch red and greens. In a moment, the scene of white was restored, and Jackson was calm. An unseen voice suddenly rang out from everywhere at once.*

"You learn fast Dream Stalker, very impressive!" before Jackson could respond, everything went black and there was nothing more.

The morning broke through bedroom window of Jackson's first floor apartment and landed softly on the side of his face. Jackson awoke. The Dream conversation was still fresh in his mind, but it seemed like it had happened years ago. Normally, after such night-time events, he would wake feeling groggy, almost hungover, but today was different. Today he felt like he had been supercharged. On quick reflection, it was his worry and concern for Alex that was driving him. He needed to act, to save her. He had no doubt of the seriousness of threat that was put forward by Freddie last night. Jackson had looked into the eyes of madness and was afraid. He had sensed a divine-like certainty within Fred and he knew if he didn't do something, Alex would die. He turned his head to the side and looked at her. Alex was still out, her blonde hair a tangled mess, her mouth just the smallest bit open against the pillow. He watched her for a while, letting all the feelings he had for her wash over him and then decided on the spot that he wouldn't tell her of the meeting with Freddie last night. She had been through so much already that Jackson felt he didn't need to add this one additional worry to her plate. Besides, he convinced himself that there wasn't too much she could do about it. While he continued to stare, Alex opened her eyes and smiled.

"You trying to stalk my dreams again mister?" Jackson smiled back. He loved these early morning moments, briefly free from life and its surprises.

"Only when you let me. This time though, was just confirming how beautiful I think you are." They spent a good portion of the morning lounging like that, not talking of anything relevant, and just having the sort of hushed, private, carefree conversations that relationships were built on. Eventually though, the real world intruded, like it always did.

"You've kept me locked up in this apartment all morning mister, I need to get to my shop. Feeling like I can start thinking about opening again but need to get it ready. Don't you have shift today?" Alex asked while getting dressed.

"Yup, but only in a few hours. I think I'm going to check up with the police, see if they have any leads… no don't worry, I won't mention the note from last night!" Jackson caught the question before it was posed. At the mention of the note, the true, real world came crashing down on Alex. Her morning of playful banter and carefree fun was gone. The new Alex had returned. The one with the permanent frown etched on her face, not the one with the dimple, the other one, the worried one. Suddenly it seemed like she had the world on her shoulders.

"Ok, thanks Jackson. I'm sure Fred will connect again, and I don't want to scare him off.

Please, it's my only chance to reach him right now!"

"I know Alex, I promised I wouldn't bring it up and I intend to do that. If things change, and its starts getting serious enough to become dangerous, the deal is off though, just so you know." Alex looked up at him solemnly and then stood up on her toes to kiss him on the cheek.

"Bye you, see you later," she said. Hiking her bag onto her shoulder, she turned and left.

Jackson waited for the door to close behind her before returning to his room. He had no intention of going to the police today, he had other, more supernatural (he hoped) plans. In the Dream, Fred had said that there was no way he could be found because he wasn't actually there, nothing of him was there. But Jackson remembered something that only occurred to him this morning. He had met Freddie in real life, he had spoken to him. Jackson was hoping he could return to the past Dream, perhaps he could go back there and pick up Fred's tune, his vibration. Much like he had did with Alex before he entered her Dream. There was such a slight chance of this actually working that Jackson didn't even stop to think of the possible consequences. He had taken the time to, he might have thought twice about entering the head of a homicidal, and recently confirmed, maniac. As it was, Jackson tried to prepare himself to go back to sleep. He only had a couple of hours before work, so he reset his alarm to wake him up. He felt so full of energy at the excitement of the idea,

Jackson started to doubt if he could fall asleep again. Perhaps it would've been better if he didn't fall asleep within minutes.

The alarm on his bedside table screamed at him. Jackson reached over and smacked it. He didn't want to get up, he had never felt so tired in his life. Unfortunately for him, when he hit the old-fashioned alarm, it didn't have the desired effect of shutting the damn thing up.

Instead, it now was screaming from a distance away on the floor. Cursing, Jackson swung his legs over the side of the bed, got up, and muted the awful contraption. The time read 11:40. 11:40? It took a while for it all to come back to him. His plan to find Freddie in the past Dream. When it did, it confused him even more. Jackson couldn't remember anything, not even the smallest detail. He remembered, setting his alarm and then… nothing. A new problem immediately announced itself, in the form of someone banging on the door.

"I'm coming, I'm, coming!" Jackson screamed at the door while trying to put his arms through a shirt. Not looking too much better for the shirt, he opened the door, to a snarling Randall.

"I don't want to hear it, you're four minutes late! In light of everything that's happened in the last few weeks, the time off I've allowed, and now you choose to sleep in for the beginning of you shift!" Jackson tried to say something but Randall held up a finger to stop him. "You have fifteen minutes to get behind the bar! If you can't do it, don't expect to keep your job!" He didn't wait for any response, just turned on his heel and marched to the stairs. Jackson watched him leave before remembering he only had, what, twelve minutes left to get ready. Now in hyper drive, Jackson hauled his tired body into action and made it downstairs with a few minutes to spare. Randall said nothing, just eyed him while cleaning a glass with a rag. Seemingly satisfied with what he saw, he replaced the glass on the shelf and walked out of the bar. Jackson released a breath and set to work. With the way he was feeling, it was going to be a very long day indeed. He started to feel the beginnings of a headache forming behind his eyes and dreaded what that might mean. He thought about partitioning his mind, but he didn't want to scare any customers away. Even those that chose to drink at 12:00 would be alarmed at 'robot' Jackson. Instead he went about his day as per normal, trying his hardest not to think of his mid-morning nap.

Meanwhile Freddie was caught in his own predicament. He couldn't wake up; something was holding him in this state of constant dreaming. He briefly felt as if someone had been watching him but that soon passed. In his dreams, he was murdering Linda and the campfire kids again, over and over again, like afternoon TV repeats. In one strange sequence he was suddenly at home answering questions from police, but that was very quickly replaced with the murderous ones, again running their loop. If Freddie could have felt anything, it would have been panic, instead he watched on impassively. If anyone had to have walked in on Freddie asleep, they would have seen a thrashing, sweating and shivering mess. A mess with his eyes silently mouthing, 'No, no, no!' over and over again. Fortunately for him, he had found a place to hide out that was out earshot and view of any interested parties. He had had to as the whole country seemed to be on the lookout for him. The place he had found was dark, wet and mouldy, perfect for him and perfect for keeping people away. He would soon be on the move but before he could, he needed to wait, the right moment would reveal itself and Freddie would be ready. Right now, he was lost in a dream that at times he thought was real, at others fully aware that it was a dream. He silently thrashed on the single mattress in the abandoned building.

Behind the bar, the day passed Jackson by with a monotonous crawl. For the first time since he started working, he missed old Bob. At least with Bob around he would always have something to do, even if it was only by fetching him another beer. There were just enough customers coming and going to make it worthwhile staying open. It gave Jackson all the time in the world to dwell on what could have happened during his morning nap, which made the day even worse to bear. He couldn't remember anything, but he knew he had dreamt. The fatigue was not the only indicator of something having happened. Internally he just knew it.

His gut was never wrong. It was nearing the end of his shift when Randall walked in at about 08:00.

"Jackson," he said by way of greeting. "Shelley is down with the flu; can I count you for the double tonight?" It wasn't really a question and Jackson knew it. If he wanted to keep his job and if he ever wanted to be on more cordial terms with Randall again, he knew what he needed to say.

"Of course boss, no problem." Jackson would've sighed if Randall didn't take a seat in front of him.

"Great. Since you are still here for a bit, could you organise me a rum and coke?" Jackson did. He tried a little small talk with his boss after that, but it fizzled out. Both of them weren't really interested in what each had to say today. Jackson returned to cleaning surfaces and Bob to reading the paper while nursing his drink. The door to the street opened and Alex appeared and headed straight towards the bar.

"Hey. You still working? I thought we could get a bite to eat. I'm starving." Jackson smiled and nodded at her.

"Sorry Al, working a double tonight. Shelley is sick. This is my boss Randall. Randall, Alex," Jackson finished the introductions and then went to serve another waiting customer. Alex and Randall appeared to chat briefly, if not awkwardly, while Jackson worked.

"I'm sorry if I interrupted your dinner plans Alex, I needed Jackson to fill in," Randall told Alex.

"Uh, it's no big deal really. Quite relieved truth be told, I'm exhausted," she replied.

Randall could see she was just being polite.

"Tell you what, the meal is on me tonight. Order what you want and I can get Jackson to run it upstairs for you once it's ready."

"Really? Thank you, that's very kind of you," Alex said, she was genuinely touched.

Jackson returned and raised an eyebrow at Randall while he took her order.

"Getting soft there Randall? That's the first time you ever gave away a free meal that I can recall." Jackson risked the joke.

"If you don't get back to work sonny, I can still change my mind," he retorted. Jackson laughed and went to serve another customer. Alex stayed for a while and finished the whiskey that's she had ordered. When her food was served by Jackson, she took it and her bag upstairs, wishing Randall goodnight on the way up. "What did you do to land that?" Randall asked Jackson once Alex was out of earshot.

"Just won her over with my wit and charm boss," Jackson replied. Randall harrumphed and returned to his paper. To Jackson, that little interchange between Randall, Alex and himself was the most thrilling part of his day. As the evening wore on and the bar emptied out, Jackson got more and more bored. Randall had already left for the evening and Jackson had cleaned everything down in preparation for closing. He was leaning his hip against the counter, swinging a dishcloth absentmindedly while he watched the TV across the room. He was wasn't thinking of anything in particular when he felt himself slip into that state where he could slip into mind-partitioning. It happened without conscious thought. The moment it was done, he felt an amazing jolt of pain that shot out from behind his eyes. He dropped the cloth he had been holding and clutched at his face. The boredom he was just now experiencing gone, replaced by agony. Without realising it, he had dropped to his knees, still clutching his face. Then he started to remember. This intrusion of the memory helped him gather his wits. He put the pain away, locked up the box then stood up. With the memory suddenly available to him, he closed up the empty bar and doused the light. He took a booth in the darkness, closed his eyes, and revisited what he briefly glimpsed. His heart was beating rapidly, and he was trying in vain to control the way his body was shivering. With his partitioned mind, he wouldn't miss any detail.

Jackson was in the Harver's House. He could see himself sitting next to Alex on the couch, watching while Fred was being questioned by the police. Detective Levi was sitting across from Fred, leaning forward slightly while balancing a notebook on his knee. While he talked, he waved a cheap ball

264

point pen in the air like a conductor. Jackson wasn't interested in the conversation this time around; he had brought himself here with one goal in mind-finding something to trace Fred's Present Dream whereabouts. Jackson zeroed his focus on Fred, he started at him with all the attention he could muster. He tried to look at the whole picture that was Fred, tried to take in everything at the same time. With a force of will, he looked and listened. After a while, be it his imagination or not, Jackson believed he could see Fred's frame shiver, as if vibrating and with that he heard it. Jackson heard the unique hum he had heard when he tried this experiment with Alex. This sound was much like Alex's, except so much different. Without knowing or being able to pinpoint what was not the same, Jackson knew he would forever be able to identify Fred by it, it was his soul signature. He would also never forget it. Jackson had what he had come for but wasn't sure how to use it, or what to do now that he had it. The scene before him was unfolding much like he remembered it. Without anything else to go on Jackson refocused on Fred and his vibration. He strained as he concentrated on it and as he did so, everything started to fade and move in slow motion.

Eventually it was just Freddie, sitting in a sea of blackness. For Freddie's part, nothing had changed. He was still acting his part of the memory, oblivious to what Jackson was seeing. Jackson then watched as Fred stopped moving and then froze all together, like an iceberg in a black sea. He stared in amazement as the image of Fred disintegrated into a million pixels and started streaming away at pace. For a while, Jackson watched as all the remaining colourful pieces of what was once Fred, slowly disappeared, then he followed. He didn't know how or why, but there was a sense of movement. It started getting faster and faster, the thin stream of pixels stretched out before him. They were headed for a point of light in the far distance. As Jackson watched, that point of light grew in his vision until it became painful to keep looking at. The pixels were being swallowed up by the light. All at once, Jackson was in the light and was blind. After an indeterminable amount of time, the bright light faded, and Jackson was able to look around. He was on a roof of a rectangular building and there were no doors and no other features apart from what you would normally see on the roof of tall building. Looking around, Jackson could see every corner of the roof top without obstruction. Moving to the edge, Jackson looked over. He might have been about 20 or so stories up. He didn't recognise anything of the street below him, but it did ring a bell. Something he saw screamed familiarity. Jackson put it away for now, he would refocus on that point later. He needed to focus on the Dream. Jackson turned around quickly the moment he sensed movement. There on the far ledge was an empty chair, balancing precariously on very feeble looking legs. Jackson looked behind him, someone was coming. As he watched, a figure came into view and much like his other Dreams, was stilted in his movements. His face was a blank white oval but as Jackson watched on, it shivered with a familiar vibration, and resolved into a snarly Fred Harver face. Knowing that it wouldn't do any good, Jackson lunged at Fred, but he was stuck, unable to move. In impotent rage and frustration, Jackson mentally tried tackle Fred, with the same useless effect. It took immense effort, but Jackson reinforced his mind box and took back control of himself. He was now able to watch on dispassionately.

Tracking Fred's movements, Jackson looked back at the chair and was horrified to see Alex sitting in it. She was bound and bleeding from the corner of her eye. She was wearing the exact same clothes Jackson had just seen her come into the bar with. Her arms were secured together behind the chair with cable ties and each leg was fastened to the front legs of the chair. She was completely panicked and constantly looking over the edge of the roof at the ground below. Jackson was screaming but nothing was coming out. He had never felt so useless in his entire life. There was a rope tied around her body, with a length of it leading back to Fred's hands. Fred put his foot out and tipped the chair back on two legs, Alex teetered over the edge and screamed. When her voice broke, he started sobbing and panting.

"What do you want from me Freddie? It's me Alex. Why are you doing this?" she managed to croak in between sobs.

"You need to understand sister, you must remember your true purpose! I brought you here to help you see this. I know you see it. I know you know who you really are. Just say it and I'll let you go! Say it! I can't let you live against the laws of the universe; it would be an abomination. Say it Alexandra, say it!" Fred roared at her while he strained on the rope holding her and the chair above the drop.

"Wha… what? Fred, I have no idea what you are talking about. You are sick Fred, it's me Alex, please don't hurt me." Alex cried back at him. For a moment, doubt crossed Fred's face before the anger returned.

"You won't say it Alex, even though you know it. You won't even acknowledge it in this small way?"

"What are you talking about Fred? You aren't making any sense!" Alex was screaming now; the chair had slipped on its *hind legs and she almost went over. Jackson couldn't breathe, he was dying inside.*

"Bye Alex, I always loved you the most." Fred let go of the rope. Suddenly Jackson could move, and he was running to the edge. He got there just in time to see Alex falling backwards, a silent scream etched on her face. The chair turned slowly in a circle as it fell, trailing the rope that Fred had been holding. Jackson watched on helplessly as the chair continued its downward journey.

"You will only see this when I feel the time is right Dream Walker. Go now!" Jackson heard the voice boom out from everywhere but ignored it. He watched on as the love of his life fell the street below her, just before she hit, the blackness engulfed him, thankfully.

Jackson leaned over the edge of the booth and puked. By now he had lost complete control. The shock of what he had just witnessed was still resonating through his body, leaving him hot and cold at the same time, with gooseflesh running up and down his arms in waves. He had to wait out the nausea before he could move. There wasn't even a thought to partitioning his mind, he doubted he could have pulled it off in any case. Jackson remembered that Dream as if he had just woken up. Then at the end, the voice saying he could only see this when he chose to. Why, what could it hope to gain by delaying his vision? Delay! Jackson shot out of the booth, paying no head to the puddle of puke he ran through. He was being delayed, delayed from taking action. He remembered noting the clothes Alex was wearing in the Dream, the same clothes he had last seen her in. This was going to happen now! He had been delayed in preparing, while he had been sitting here. Fred was going after Alex; he was sure of it. Heart in his mouth, Jackson bolted up the stairs. He was relieved to see the door closed as he bashed though it. Perhaps he had gotten back in time. His optimism at the thought was dashed away as he looked around the mess that was his apartment. Jackson called out Alex's name in desperation as he searched under fallen and broken furniture, hoping, but not expecting to find her. He moved to the window that led out to the landing of the fire escape, the same he used when trying to avoid Randall downstairs. The window was still open, the flimsy white curtain blowing into the apartment. He jumped though and looked below, there was nothing. He was too late, Fred had taken Alex, right from under his nose. Choking up, Jackson returned to his apartment and saw a small white piece of paper stuck to the TV, like it had been licked and glued on with spit. Fearful at what it would say, he reached out and peeled it off the screen and read it with shaking hands.

I realised you couldn't actually help. No one but I can! She is with me now Jackson, I will make her see. Don't bother trying to stop me, there is nothing you can do.

The note wasn't signed but it didn't need to be, Jackson knew who had written it. He gently lowered the note to the floor and sank to his knees. For a brief time, he allowed himself to feel and he cried in fear for Alex. It didn't take long but Jackson regained his composure and with it, his determination. He picked up the note, placed it in a zip lock bag and stored it with the now rotting cat's tail. No reason why, but he supposed the evidence could come in handy later. Right now, he had a job to do and the clock was ticking. Alex was out there with a madman and only he was even aware of it. He was going to find her, and he was going to kill that sick son of a bitch brother of hers! Jackson moved some furniture away to clear space on the floor. He sat down cross legged and adopted a meditative pose. He was doing the only thing he cold think off, he was focusing on Fred's vibration. He was going to find him, even if he didn't yet know how.

Ben was a tired and very frustrated man. He had absolutely no clues and or leads on the Fred Harver case and it was starting to take its toll. The case had been formally moved from Detective Levi to himself, to free up the older man's his time to address his own caseload.

The barrage of people demanding his attention, from reporters, to the general public and even his superiors. He had the resources of the largest police force in the world available to him, but he had nothing, absolutely nothing. Each day he would hold a briefing and report the same progress as the day before.

"We are following up on all available leads but at this point, I have no new light to shed on the situation." He could say those words while asleep by now. Even Jackson, with is abilities had nothing to offer, Ben had just recently realised how much he was hoping Jackson would come by and drop a major clue in his lap. The fact that he hadn't yet, was more depressing that it should have been. Ben shook himself upright. This would have to be done with old fashioned police work. He decided to start at the beginning, the Linda Gerard case.

He knew that Detective Levi had been working case and made a note to stop by his desk. If he could find some link between the Linda Gerard murder and the campfire massacre, perhaps it could link up to whatever was going to happen next. He suddenly remembered the ring that was found at the crime scene and with no small sense of hope, decided to go over to John's table right away. He found the untidy, greying man exactly where he expected. At his desk, scribbling furious notes with a cheap pen. Ben liked John. It was not just because of his well decorated career, it was his ability to get straight to the point, to suss the important parts out of the usual white noise.

"John, you got a minute?" Ben asked. John looked up and then motioned to the chair on the other side of the desk.

"How can I help you today Ben, any news on the Fred Harver case?" Ben shrugged his shoulders in resignation which was very unlike him.

"Nothing yet, it's why I am here actually. Need to go back to the beginning." Detective Levi nodded in agreement. "That ring you found during the Linda Gerard case, did anything ever come of that?" Detective Levi didn't need to consult his notes, he remembered it clearly.

"Well, we traced it back to a place called Jyms, with a 'J'. A gym if you needed any help, apparently. They gave them out to loyal customers or something. But it was a dead end, place was closed. In fact, quite strangely, it seemed to have just closed, like days before I got there. I confirmed that with a local bum that had occupied a place nearby." Ben noticed the slight shiver John had when he spoke about the bum, but he put it aside. "Maybe the guy wasn't the nicest example of homeless community. Any connection between Linda family and the gym?" Detective Levi shook his head.

"Didn't follow it up. After we discovered Fred Harver's involvement, there wasn't any need. The investigation

271

basically fell to you after the campfire deal. Not the most professional job I ever handled I'm afraid to say but, you know… limited resources mean I am working several other cases that needed my attention," Ben smirked, he knew what John was talking about, he also had several other cases needing his attention.

"Ok, if you can think of anything else that might help, please pass it by me." Ben said as he stood up to leave.

"No problem Ben, sorry I couldn't be of more help. Before you go, any updates from our mutual psychic friend?" asked Detective Levi.

"No, I had hoped for it, but nothing yet," Ben replied sadly.

"Might be worth checking in on him sometime, my gut tells me he is still playing some part in this." Ben agreed and made a mental note to do exactly that.

"Thanks John." Ben was already lost in though and didn't hear if John said anything back to him. Find the link. He needed to find the link between Linda and Fred. He pulled his laptop closer to him as he sat down at his desk. He typed in 'Jyms' and scrolled through the results. He had to keep closing off those annoying adverts that popped up on his screen, he needed to ask IT to block them somehow. On Jyms website, he noticed a big CLOSED sign had been virtually stamped across the screen. However, the website was still up and functioning. As he continued to scroll, one of those annoying adverts popped up. It was a fancy one, with music, making it all but impossible to ignore. It was some sort of flute music and it worked on him. Going against everything that he normally did, he clicked on the pop up. It was for a fruit company that specialised in providing smoothie ingredients, in fact it provided such ingredients to the now closed gym. This wasn't of interest in any way until Ben noticed the face of the smiling salesman on the advert. He was holding up a box of diced fruit and below the picture, it read; 'Joseph Gerard, Head Sales Rep'. Ben sat back. In just a few minutes, he had found the link between the ring and Linda Gerard. Her father had been at the gym. It was such a simple piece of police work and he started to wonder why it hadn't been picked up before now. Ben thought it through. How did this help him find Fred though? How could he find out if Fred ever visited this gym? There were two thing he needed to do.

He needed to question Joe Gerard and then he needed to speak with Alex, maybe even Jackson. In Ben's few dealings with Alex, he had come to understand the depth of the relationship he had with her brother. If anyone knew if Fred had been at Jyms, she would.

On his way out, John caught up with him.

"Ben, do you have a lead on the Harver case?" he asked.

"Of sorts. I found the link between the gym and Linda and am off to see her father. Might pop in to visit Alex and Jackson after that," Ben answered in his no fuss manner.

"You mind if I tag along? I can't sit at that desk any longer and to me, it feels like this Harver thing needs to be wrapped up." Ben could see that the detective as battling something.

"Everything alright John?" John looked at him, surprised to have been caught out.

"I'm not sure Ben, but this Harver case has me all twisted in knots. Ever since I officially handed it over to you, I can't stop thinking about it. I thought that maybe, in whatever why I can, I could help bring this thing to a close so I can move on." Detective Levi's confidence in newfound direction grew as he spoke, as if he had convinced himself by saying it out loud.

"Well, happy for the company John," Ben said. They moved through the PD, down the stairs to reception and then further down to the underground parking lot. Once in his car, Ben entered the address for the Gerard's house into the navigation system and they drove up and out the building onto the street. Detective Levi was a quiet passenger. He focused on his little notebook, seemingly checking for anything that could help. For his part, Ben paid studious attention to the road in front of him. It was nearing early evening, around 17:30 when they pulled into the Gerard's driveway. Walking to the door, Ben looked over at John and raised his eyebrows. The silent question was immediately understood by John.

"Yup, your case, you lead," he confirmed. Ben nodded and then knocked on the door. It was jerked opened quite suddenly. Mr Gerard stood there, in his underwear and a robe. He wasn't wearing a shirt and he looked like he had just woken up.

"I said no more questions!" he roared at the two new comers standing on his landing. Not taken aback but the hostile welcome, Ben reached into his pocket and displayed his badge, detective Levi doing the same. Still caught in the aftermath of his rage, Mr Gerard breathed through his nose, nostrils flaring, as he examined their IDs. He nodded to himself and held the door open for them to enter. "Sorry gentleman. We've been hounded by reporters and loonies ever since you found Linda's body. It gotten much worse since the supposed link to Fred the Freak. Was it really him, do you know for sure?" He hadn't bothered putting on his shirt but hurriedly herded them to seats at the dining room table.

"Yes, we do believe it to be him, but it's not yet confirmed. It's why we are here Mr Gerard," Ben said as he looked around the place. The room had a claustrophobic feeling; the windows were shut and all the blinds were drawn. It was a mess and it had the rank smell of sweat permeating it, the smell of unwashed bodies. It was obvious no one had bothered cleaning up for the last while. "Mr Gerard, your wife, is she around? It would be good to have both of you present for questioning as it would save a potential trip back here later," Ben said.

"No! Since the Freak murders and the hounding of the reporters, she went to stay with her sister. She hasn't taken this very well and we thought it best for her to get out of town," Mr Gerard said this dismissively. Ben looked at him and thought that he could use some time out of time as well. He didn't mention it however.

"I understand," Ben said simply before getting straight into it. "Mr Gerard, I need to understand your business relationship with Jyms. Have you ever seen a ring like this before?" Ben held out the plastic evidence bag with the ring clearly visible inside.

"Please, call me Joe. Yes, that gaudy piece of jewellery was worn by the pre-paid member, part of the extended program. They wore it like some kind of trophy. Anyway, I supplied them with fruit for the Juice Bar. I would be there at least twice a week for deliveries. They weren't big enough for the truck to go out, but they were near another client, so I had no issue dropping their stuff off for them. Why, what had Jyms got to do with Linda? Was that strange little place involved somehow? I never did trust that owner… Robert I think his name was. He creeped me out."

Ben looked across at John, who nodded back before asking, "Joe, what was strange about that place… and Robert, you said?"

Joe shrugged his shoulders, "Nothing I could put my finger on really, it just seemed unreal, sorta like being in the middle of a live gym commercial. The colours were all so bright and the patrons all looked like they just bought their gear. Don't know why half of them were even at the gym, they were all very fine-looking people already. Unreal or not, I was always offered a free smoothie after delivery, so I tried not to notice the fake smiles around me."

John wrote a few notes, "and the owner, Robert?" he asked.

"That guy was bizarre, always polite and always helpful but I could never shake the feeling that he was mocking me, like as if he knew something about me that no one else did. Like I said, he never was overt about it, but I just got the feeling that he looked at me… with contempt," Joe finished. Ben immediately shot another question at him.

"Any reason people at the gym would know of or recognise Linda, did she ever join you on one of your deliveries or something?" Joe looked confused for a second, then blushed with embarrassment and then, alarmingly, with concern.

"No, she never joined me for work, wasn't her thing but… well, I was very proud of her you see… I would flash her picture around at the bar to whomever I was talking to. She is the best… was the best thing in my life…" he took a moment to compose himself. "Did I do something that lead to Linda's death detectives?" He had tears in his eyes, and he was nearing breaking point.

Ben reached across and grabbed his shoulder, "No Mr Gerard, nothing like that. Just making sure we are being thorough." The little lie wouldn't hurt anyone. For Ben and John, they now had the link between the killer, the gym and Linda. Mr Gerard was not openly crying and with nothing left to accomplish there, they bade farewell and left, showing themselves out.

"Poor man," John said.

"Yup. Just need to place Fred at that gym now. You keen on one more trip to see Alex Harver and Jackson Brandt?" Ben asked his makeshift partner.

"You bet, nothing like a conversation with Jackson for additional mystery," John joked.

Ben smiled but didn't laugh, he knew how the detective felt. Ben remembered where Jackson lived, it wouldn't take them long to get there.

It was 18:15 when they entered the bar. They walked straight to the person serving behind the counter.

"Evening miss, Jackson in today? They both flashed their badges." Shelley took her time to examine the gold ornament before answering.

"What did Jackson do now?" she asked. When the officers didn't answer, Shelley shrugged her shoulders and said, "No, not since last night. He didn't show up for his shift again. I think Randall is going to fire him, poor thing. I called his place upstairs and knocked on the door but nothing."

Ben looked at the stair and said, "Do you mind if we take a look. We really need to speak with him. Maybe he is just bunking off work?" Shelley highly doubted that but didn't say it out loud.

"Sure, just up the stairs, then left, first door you see." Ben and John thanked her and made their way upstairs. They knocked on Jackson's door but there was no answer. Looking up and down the hall, John pulled out small leather sleeve with some metal instruments in it, lock picking tools.

"Put that away John, the door isn't locked. Keen to doing little illegal investigating?" Ben said as he pushed the door open. John didn't answer him, just walked past him and into the narrow hall of the apartment. Ben followed closely behind, silently closing the door after them.

"Dear god, what happened here?" John said and walked ahead of him. The place had obviously been overturned, signs of struggle everywhere. The open window leading to the fire escape was allowing the breeze to blow all the lose items everywhere, adding to the confusing mess.

"Look at this," Ben said to John, who came over to him immediately. Ben was holding the zip lock bags with severed cat's tail and the little note.

"Looks like Jackson has been holding out on us Ben," John said.

"Looks that way John," Ben agreed. "Fred had obviously been in touch with him… and Alex. This note was addressed to her. She must be staying here." Ben had recognised Fred's handwriting straight way.

"Ben, Ben, get over here, I think we have problem." He hadn't realised John had moved away from him. He was on his haunches, poking at another scrap of paper lying on the floor of the lounge.

"What do you have there John?" Ben said joining him in pose in the lounge. John leaned away and positioned paper with his pen, so that Ben could read it. "Dear god, Fred has Alex! This note was obviously for Jackson," Ben exclaimed, while pacing. He was worried that events were outpacing him. "All this looks recent. Jackson was still here last night; we can assume he was here today. He must have left just before we got here. We need to figure out where he is going John… feels like there is clock ticking on this!" To accentuate his statement, a little electronic beep sounded from the bedroom. Ben checked his watch, 19:00. "What are we missing here John?" Ben asked, hoping he didn't sound too desperate. Detective Levi didn't answer, he was searching around, looking for something to help them. Ben joined him the search, not knowing what they were looking for.

After several minutes of seemingly pointless searching, John shouted excitedly, "Got it! I least I think I do!" Ben hurried over to him. They were in Jackson's bedroom, John siting on the bed. He had a little leather notebook clutched in his hand.

"It was open on this page when I found it Ben. It's the address of where we found Linda Gerard's body. It's been circled in blue ink. It must be where they arc! Is it enough?" John asked, breathlessly. Ben had been around Jackson long enough to know to not disregard these signals that got left behind him. In answer, Ben radioed in backup and listed the address. This could come back to bite them in the ass, but he was not going to be taking any more chances. It was a slim lead, but cases had been broken on less in the past.

"Let's go catch our bad guy John!" Detective Levi nodded and smiled. They hurried out of the building, past a bewildered Shelley and out to their car. Ben hit the siren on and plopped the emergency light of the roof of the car before speeding off. Shelley watched from the doorway as the car the detectives were in squealed away in flashing red and blue strobes.

Chapter 9 – The Puppet Master

Jackson focused! He concentrated like never before. The panic he felt for Alex was overwhelming and hindering his ability to partition. Sucking in great breathes, with his eyes squeezed tightly shut, he slowly started relaxing his body. He started with neck, moved down to his shoulders, and continued on until he reached his toes. By this time, his heart rate and breathing had evened out and his eyelids were resting calmly. He judged the moment well and then attempted to partition his mind. This time it happened without any difficulty. The panic receded and with it leaving, the clarity and sharpness of unhindered observation and logic flooded in. Jackson opened his eyes and from his sitting position on the floor, looked around. He categorised his apartment and its contents against what was in his memory. It was a time-consuming exercise going through everything in this level of detail, but a necessary one. It seemed as if everything was in place, nothing was missing and nothing pointed to where Freddie could've taken Alex, despite the general mess. Jackson closed his eyes and returned his focus inwards. He brought up a picture of Fred in his mind and tried adding as many details as possible to the image from his memory. He needed it to be as perfect as he could make it. With his mind in the state that it was in, he managed a pretty good job. In his minds-eye, he had produced a photograph like image of the man, smiling sinisterly. The smile wasn't a conscious addition, but one borne of his own fears. Jackson shored up his little mind box, the fear disappeared and the smile on Fred's face, in his mind, vanished. Jackson played around with the image, committing it to all his senses. He imagined it walking, and it did. He imaged it talking, and it did. He imaged the smell of the image, and suddenly he could smell the cologne he thought he remembered Fred wearing. Next, within his mind, he reached out with a spectral arm and touched the image. He grabbed imaginary Freddie's shoulder, and suddenly he could touch the image. With all his senses actively engaged, Jackson added the final touch, the vibration, or the soul-sound of Freddie that he felt he knew so well. It had a remarkable effect. The lifeless, puppet image of Fred in his mind suddenly came alive. It was no longer a thing of imagination; this was a living entity that Jackson was now looking at.

Without a shadow of doubt, Jackson understood that he was now looking at the real Freddie. He had tapped into that silvery stream of consciousness of the man he was looking for. This was the real Fred. Jackson had found him! It was an incomplete picture though, it was just the man himself, and although he was moving around, doing something, Jackson had no view of his surroundings. Jackson took another deep breath. He was about to move from the land of the strange into the universe of the absurd, but the desperation of the situation demanded it.

In his mind, he shifted forward towards Fred. He needed to change his angle of perception. He moved from a third-party view into a first-person point of view. He wanted to see through Fred's eyes. The moment he moved into the image of Fred, everything went momentarily black and an icy coldness swept through his body, from his head, down towards his feet. It must have been mere seconds but to Jackson it felt like he had just dived into a frozen lake. When the cold sensation departed, Jackson was smacked full on with new sensory information. In a moment of panicked confusion, Jackson almost lost control of the little box in his mind. He felt split in two. For a terrifying moment, Jackson completely lost his own sense of identity. In the moment between breathes, Jackson was a hybrid of Fred and himself. He was overwhelmed with a lifetime of someone else's memories trying to blanket his. In that same moment, Jackson and Fred became aware of each other! It was such a shock experiencing that sense of recognition from two points of view that Jackson/Fred nearly blacked out. A moment later, it passed, to inconceivable for the Jackson/Fred brain to process so it was just ignored. Jackson took a deep breath and used the moment to strengthen the mind box once again. He had become aware how precious that box suddenly was. He imagined it opening up while he was still inside Fred. The thought was too terrible, he knew it would probably cancel out each of their own personalities, wipe them both out. There was only space for one consciousness in each mind. Now, more mentally prepared, Jackson looked around. He couldn't control the movement of the body he was in and he felt the same nausea he had once experienced while out sea fishing. Just another thing he mentally had to control; Jackson suppressed that as well. He/Jackson/Fred was looking at a space he though he recognised but could not yet place. It was late afternoon and the sky was clearly visible, they weren't inside of a room. Thankfully, that moment of recognition hadn't seemed to alert Fred of his own presence, he was completely unaware that Jackson was there. Jackson knew this, as he could sense the determined work Freddie was doing, focused on the task at hand and not concerned about anything else around him. Jackson suddenly felt his breath catch; he was looking at Alex. She was clearly unconscious, lying on her side on the grey concrete floor. Her arms were tied behind her back and her ankles were similarly bound together. He watched as her chest rose as she took a breath. Jackson almost cried out with joy at seeing she was alive, but of course he couldn't. The scene shifted around, and he was now looking at a length of rope trailing away, to a chair that was on a ledge. It was Jackson's Dream from earlier! This was it, happening in real time! Jackson/Fred walked over to the chair and attached the rope to its legs. As he did so Jackson caught a glimpse over the edge. He was on a roof. In the evening light he thought he recognised where he was. It had taken a while to make the connection seeing it from this point of view, but now he was certain. It was the same street below from which he and Alex had watched the police remove the dead body of Linda Gerard. 'Got you, you Bastard! Jackson thought triumphantly. It was so powerful in fact, that the alien thought must have been registered and felt by Fred because Jackson/Fred suddenly dropped the rope and looked around in alarm. Jackson took a second to enjoy this panicked alarm by Fred, who was looking this way and that for the unidentified threat, before he withdrew from him. The icy wave passed through him once again before the scene went black. Jackson opened his eyes in his own apartment. He was sore all over, legs stiff.

He tried to stand but his legs were locked. He slowly stretched them out and waited for the feeling to return to them in a wave of pins and needles. Lying on his back, he shifted his position to look at the clock on the wall. 18:30! He had lost the whole of last night and an entire day! No wonder his body was protesting so much. With that he realised how thirsty he was... and hungry. Forcing himself up on protesting legs, Jackson moved like an old man over to the kitchen and drank straight from the faucet. With his thirst quenched, he rummaged around in the fridge and found a couple of old apples. He put one in his mouth, between his teeth and the other in his left hand as he made his way to his room. There would be time to eat something later. Right now, he had to move, Alex had little to no time left. He found his little notebook in no time located the address of the Linda Gerard murder scene. He triumphantly circled it with his pen as he committed it to memory. Within a few moments, he was down the fire escape and hailing cab. It wasn't too far; he should get there in about 20 minutes he thought, as he gave the cabbie the address.

Feeling like he was in an action movie he said, "Fast as you can please!" The Indian cabbie just nodded back at him through the plexiglass screen. He had seen this sort of thing before, crazy Americans who watched too much TV. He would go as quickly as the law allowed him to but no more, regardless of what the crazy-eyed passenger wanted.

Alex woke up. She was lying on her side on a bare concrete floor. She tried to move but soon realised she was bound, her arms behind her back and her ankles strapped together. Both hands and feet were already numb, so she must have been lying, tied up like that for quite a while. Her head pounded and judging by the trickle of blood, mostly dried and scabbed up, dripping into her eye, she had been hit on the head with something. Becoming fully aware, she started to wriggle around on the floor in panic. Freddie had played her. When she had gone upstairs to wait for Jackson and to eat her dinner, nothing had seemed out of place. It was only when she was seated on the couch in front of the TV that he announced himself. He had been sitting on the fire escape landing and had knocked on the window right behind her. For Alex, her heart had nearly jumped right out of her chest. Before she even knew it, she had dropped her food and rushed to open the window for him. Lying on the cold ground now, as she was, she admonished herself for being so bitterly naive. She recalled how she suddenly realised what she had done as Freddie stepped into the room. She had backed away, although by then it was obviously too late. The look in Freddie's eyes was so disturbing, so alien to her that she finally conceded to what was the truth all along. She didn't know her brother, perhaps she never had. She had hoped against hope that this was all some terrible mistake, but right then, in Jackson's apartment, facing the man who was slowly advancing on her she finally accepted what all the evidence had being saying...Fred was a monster! A monster that was now coming for her. Alex remembered how, when that thought had hit, she tried to turn and run. Fred had dived for her, catching her by the ankles. As they fell over together, she tried to grab at anything around her to stop the fall. The TV toppled over with her. Lying there on the floor, with Freddie's hands gripping her ankles, she shifted to a position that allowed her lie on her back. Frantically grabbing at anything around her, she found a decoder box that had been attached to the TV. Bringing that over her head, she swung as hard as she could and brought the little thing down on Freddie's head. There was a grunt, and the hand gripping her relaxed. She kicked out at his head and shuffled away on her bottom. The blow the head had only momentarily halted him. Like the predator that he had become, Freddie jumped up to his feet, cat like, and caught Alex before she could even get up herself. Alex remembered that terrifying moment when he had looked directly into her eyes. Alex saw nothing she recognised in them, just a fanatical glow born of madness. She had been about to cry out when something smashed into her chin, completing knocking her out. She couldn't quite move and the numbness in her limbs was beginning to become painful. She tried to cry out but for the first time she realised she was also gagged. She was helpless and could only watch as Fred busied himself with rope and chair. From her position, lying flat on her side, she had a limited view to basically what was directly in front of her. She could see Fred, the chair and the rope but also now noticed the evening sky. So, she was on a roof, somewhere. She worked her tongue around the cloth gag in her mouth and after a few moments, had loosened it enough to spit it out.

"Freddie, what are you doing? It's me Freddie, Alex! Why are you doing this to me? You're my brother Freddie and I love you!" Alex cried out. She was tearing up and had to shake her eyes to clear so that she could see. Fred dropped the rope he had been tying to the chair and moved over to his sister. He grabbed her shoulders and pulled her up so she could sit and look into his eyes as he squatted in front of her.

"Alex, you are living a lie and you need to see! I am doing this is because I love you too Alex. You cannot be allowed to go on like you have, spitting in the universe's eye. You need to acknowledge who you really are Alex and I am the only one that can show you the way." The speech was said in a cold monotone, the features of his face hardly altering as he spoke. Alex started becoming deathly afraid. This truly wasn't Fred anymore, it was something else, something cold and detached. There was no question about it, he was mad, crazy, perhaps beyond help. He had been staring at her to see if she had been following what he was saying. "I see you do not yet understand, but you will. You need to be shocked, to be put in mortal danger to see. It is the only way the body will free the shackles the mind has created to keep you safe, to keep the truth hidden from you. The body needs to see its existence face being extinguished before it is strong enough to force the mind to reveal to you what I already know. It is not enough to merely tell you; you have to feel it." Fred had already stood up and was walking away from her before he finished talking. Alex looked around desperately, there was no one near that could help. There was nothing around her she could use to cut her binds. It was getting dark and she started losing hope. No one was coming to save her, it was impossible, how would anyone know where to find her. She had one hope left, Jackson. It was such a tiny, miniscule hope that it barely even existed, but it was enough for her. She clung to it like a drowning man would to a lifejacket.

"Jackson will come for me Freddie; you don't know what he is capable of!" she said with as much confidence as she could muster. Fred once again stopped what he was doing and looked over his shoulder at her.

"Actually, I have a fair idea of his abilities. Unfortunately for you, none of them will help in this situation. The only people who know we are here are you and I Alex, no one else.

No one is coming." He moved over to the chair and balanced it on a ledge, the rope he had tied to it training away on the floor behind him. Alex started to cry. When he was done with the chair, he moved over to sit next to her. He didn't say anything, just sat and waited.

"What are we doing here Fred, what are we waiting for?" she asked him in a whimper. He frightened her so much she hadn't realised she was flinching away from him as they sat there.

"I will know when it is the right time." Fred said. He noticed her shifting away from him and moved across to reapply the gag. Alex cried silently as they both sat there, waiting, as the sky darkened, and the air got colder.

The drive took forever. In Jackson's mind, he saw Alex falling to her death, over and over again, while he watched on helplessly. His constant urging for greater speed had no effect of the driver whatsoever so he gave up on that and watched on through the back-seat window. It was already getting dark. Jackson thought about how much his life had changed since Alex had first walked into the bar. Before her, he had just been existing. Breathing in and breathing out, day after day. Life had passed him by without him even having paid attention. With Alex, his perception of the world, of life, had been thrown into multicolour, sharp contracts from his normal sepia view. He would wake up more energised each morning, looking forward to the day, regardless of the fact that it would probably just like any other day. He had discovered a purpose outside of himself. It made what had previously just been existing, into living. He lived now, properly. He lived to make her as happy as she made him. His fear kept on building during the short commute. The more he thought about Alex, the more he began to worry until his was literally squirming on the backseat of the taxi. It was a new sort of worry for him as he had never cared to worry about anyone else apart from himself before. It was a much more intense sort of worry, all consuming, overriding all rationality. When his destination came into view, he had the car door open before the car had stopped moving. Not bothering to stop and check the amount, Jackson took whatever bank notes he had in his wallet and shoved it at the cab driver. He didn't wait for him to check the amount or even for change. He bolted towards the front door, looking towards the roof as he ran. In his panic, he didn't stop to prepare himself, he just forged on forward. The glass double front doors were shut with chains run through the handles. Jackson grabbed both handles and pulled as hard as he could. He didn't need to, the doors swung open with a loud creak, the chain falling to the ground between them. If he needed further proof that Alex and Fred were here there it was, a cut chain. Jackson dashed inside and immediately pulled up. It was very dark, with no power, it would be extremely difficult to find his way around the building. Jackson found himself tending motionless in the dark, just passed the entrance, trying to figure out a way forward while his anxiety grew. A scream suddenly echoed throughout the building. Jackson suppressed a scream of his own and bolted outside. A second scream came from the roof.

There, he could see Alex on a chair on the ledge, her back to him. He could just see her in the dim light.

"Alex! I'm here! I'm coming," he screamed as loudly as he could. He didn't wait for her reply. He knew what was going to happen, he had seen it already and he didn't want to waste a moment. He half ran half stumbled to what used to have been the reception desk. He figured the elevators would be to each side of the main desk, so he tried the left first. There was still enough moonlight or starlight coming from the doorway to distinguish basic shapes and when his hand touched the cold metal of elevators doors, his heart lifted. Trailing a hand against the wall, he moved forward past one, two, three metal doors. At the end of the three doors, deeper into the building now, Jackson continued, hoping the stairs wouldn't be too far away. He could see a door with a hollow rectangle for handle sticking out. As he grabbed it, he looked up and could just make out a little sign above the doorway with a white stick man walking up the stairs on what he imagined was a green background. A staircase! His joy at finding his route upstairs was short-lived as another scream rent the darkness. Jackson groaned and moved as fast as he could into the dark pit of the stairwell. He felt for the railing with his left side and then snatched at it when he thought he had found it. Now that he had a guide, he moved up the stairs with more confidence.

"Jackson! He's going drop me, please hurry!" Alex screamed from the darkness somewhere above him. Jackson was heartened by the fact that Alex had heard him outside but terrified at the sound of her pleading. She expected to die at any moment, and it was clear in her voice. Jackson pushed on faster and immediately regretted it. He missed a step and went crashing into her first and then onto the stairway in front of him. He felt his nose squash against the metal, protective rim of one of the stairs; unprotected by his hands as he had tried to break his fall with them. The crack sound in between his ears confirmed the break.

Panting, Jackson rolled onto his back and pulled his hands up to his face, riding out the pain. When Alex screamed again, Jackson was up, broken nose forgotten, as he continued on his looping, dizzying run up the staircase. Run, climb, turned left, on and on. He estimated his must be around the fifth floor when he hit a wall in front of him. Luckily, had had been walking at an angle to protect his face, so his shoulder banged into the dead end. Roof? He fumbled in the darkness and found a door handle and pulled as if his life depended on it. It didn't budge.

In a panic he screamed, "Alex, are you there! I'm right here baby, I'm coming!" He pulled again, no luck. He heard footsteps running towards them on the other side. Jackson sucked in a quick breath, stopped what he was doing and looked at the door. Tentatively, he pulled the door handle down and pushed. The door swung open silently. Thinking about what an idiot he was, he shoved his way onto the moonlit roof. Freddie had given up trying to reach the door when Jackson broke through. He looked from Jackson to Alex and seemingly made up his mind and returned to the position he had come from. He picked up a rope tied to a metal pipe jutting out from the floor that could have been a chimney or something. It trailed away to the base of the chair holding Alex over the edge. To Jackson, it was the Dream all over again. It was an exact replica. Jackson could see Alex falling away from him, over and over again. Jackson groaned and made to run towards her.

"Stop! Stop Jackson! I'll drop her!" Fred said calmly from across the expanse of the roof.

Jackson skidded to a stop. For a moment, they stared at each other before Jackson spoke. "What are you doing Fred?

That's your sister there, what sort of mad scheme are you trying to pull off?" Fred was about to answer him when his face suddenly went slack. His muscles seemed to tighten and lock in place. He was suddenly a statue. Confused, Jackson looked around, Alex was also unmoving, her face a mask of terror. Before Jackson, he could see a frozen Fred holding a rope, about six metres long, attached to the chair holding a similarly frozen Alex above the drop. Echoes of flutes, faint, dim but recognisable filled the air. Jackson watched on as ankle high fog rolled over the still forms of Fred and Alex, continuing until his own ankles disappeared under the silky whiteness. The tune of the flute intensified, forcing Jackson to cover his ears. Panic infused his entire being, he wanted to run. Jackson tried to partition his mind, but the panic was too strong. He lost consciousness.

"Ah, welcome back to the world Dream Stalker!" a voice giggled from somewhere in the mist in front of him. As he watched, the form materialised in front of him, the fog parting as he approached Jackson. With the music now faded, Jackson was able to concentrate and immediately partitioned his mind. The fear, the panic, the anxiety all faded. He welcomed the rush of observational stimuli and clarity. He quickly looked around and surmised that he couldn't have been unconscious for more than a few moments. The scene in front of him, Fred, and Alex joined together by the rope, had not altered at all.

"What have you done to them?" Jackson asked, motioning to the siblings.

"Ah, well done Dream Stalker! That mind trick of yours is so impressive. Pity you didn't think of doing it before you rushed up here like a maniac!" he giggled in response. "Them?" He swept his arm behind him like a circus MC.

"Nothing that will hurt them. I have just caught and am holding their minds at a certain point in time. I can release them at any time without damaging them. So, Jackson, what do you think of my little production?" The man asked. He was suddenly right in front of Jackson's face, the rim of his hat touching Jackson's forehead. With Jackson's perception so extraordinarily enhanced by the partitioning, it surprised him that he still couldn't make out any of the person's features. He needed to buy time; he couldn't let this 'thing' in front of him dictate how things were going to run. Jackson looked at the man calmly before responding.

"Who are you exactly? You say this is all your doing, but to what end? Why?" Jackson tilted his head and folded his arms as he waited for an answer, just a normal Sunday afternoon conversation around the dining room table. The man spun on his heel and walked away.

"Why? You ask why? Bahahaha. To begin to explain to a mortal like you would be like trying to teach mathematics to ants!" The man found this extremely funny and laughed while clutching at his sides. "As for who I am, I think you know. I have watched on as you dug up facts disguised as stories, disguised as myths on me! I am the Green, Jackson, Pan! I have many other names but those are my favourites. For you, you can call me Bob. I enjoy the sound of it, single syllable for emphasis." Jackson took it in his stride that he was now conversing with a god from the stories.

"So, Bob. You haven't answered my question… why? Why all this? Why stoop to the level of ants? Don't you have more important things to be doing?" Bob giggled furiously.

"Oh where have you been for the last few hundred years Dream Stalker? Oh the fun we could have had. Hang on, let me try something." Although Jackson couldn't see his mouth, he clearly sensed it opening. The man screamed, the sound of it sent gooseflesh running up and down Jackson's arms but left him otherwise unaffected. "Remarkable! You would have been a fine adversary in another time Jackson. Look at your colleagues, look at the puppets you mix with." Jackson did. Both Alex and Fred were still frozen, but their features had altered slightly. They both now wore masks of sheer terror, their eyes opened wide, blood dripping from their ears. "That scream Jackson, the one I just produced, has for millennia scared the shit out of your folk. Trust me, I have had much fun with it. However, it has no effect on you. Actually, you are the first I have ever encountered that is possibly immune to the shriek.

Hmmm…" The man walked around contemplating what he had just said. Jackson tried to inch closer to Alex, he wanted to get into apposition where he could yank her to safety. "I wouldn't do that if I were you, we haven't finished our conversation yet!" the man said with his back towards him. Jackson stopped trying to move closer to Alex.

"Why then?' he asked simply and waited for Bob to respond. Without seeming to move, Bob was suddenly again in front of him."

"Experience Jackson. Experience and emotion are the building blocks of life. You might not remember it, but we have a similar conversation around this before. However, I digress, let me continue. What you see, what you feel and interpret as the little beings you are, is what is essentially life. Everything that makes up life is coded from experience, emotion, perception. The greater the experience or emotion, the greater the quality of life. You ask why Jackson? Why am

I doing this? I am a god! What better food or sustenance for a god than experience or emotion. I build these stories to suck on the sweet fundamentals of life. It sustains and enhances me; it makes me whole and more at the same time!" The man was walking and swinging his arms theatrically as he spoke. "My brethren didn't understand this. They preferred to remain aloof, apart from the humans. They preferred to be worshiped and admired from afar. They were too short-sighted Jackson. What they required depended on hand-outs from the humans, even if the humans didn't know it. It would only be a matter of time before the hand's outs dried up… before the human's stopped believing. My brothers and sisters, fantastic, fearless, indomitable beings, through their own narcissistic tendencies had turned their food into their own masters. By withholding their worship, intentional or not, humans started to hold sway over the gods. They are all gone now Dream Stalker… yes, yes some of the smaller, lesser ones still hold dominion of this world but to a far lesser degree than they once did. Not I Dream Stalker! I was looked down upon by them all. Seen to be lessening myself by playing with the food. I was playing the long game Jackson. I knew then what it was that was core to my survival, they didn't. Too bad for them. This world is mine now. I play and lord over it, even if most of you don't know it!" The man was in the throes of fervour and fanaticism, lost to ideas of his own grandness, speaking up to the sky. For all the scorn he displayed for his brothers and sisters, he was as big a narcissist as they were, perhaps the biggest!

"A God you say?" Jackson spoke up, breaking the man from his grand reverie, "You think you are better than us because you play, manipulate, drive us according to your will? Do I have that right?" The man nodded at Jackson, as if he felt he had gotten through to him. "Right, well there is another term for you that comes to my mind Bob. There is something else that lives off, preys off others without their knowledge or consent. Do you know what that is Bob?" Jackson didn't wait for an answer but pushed right on ahead. 'A Parasite, Bob! You are a parasite! The man stared disbelievingly at Jackson.

"Wha… how dare… who do you think… how dare you!" the man spluttered in rage. In the moonlight before him, the darkness gathered, and the fog thickened around the man. He was still spluttering incoherently in his rage, oblivious to the effect he was having on his surroundings. The flute tunes were ringing louder and louder. Jackson was struggling against the onslaught of panic music, wind, darkness, and fog. The man was suddenly before him again. "Let me show you, Jackson! Let me show you what a god is. Parasite! Bah!" With both hands, he grabbed Jackson's head. There was a sudden bright light, then there was nothing. Then…

"Jackson! You with me buddy?" Jackson looked around the white space. 'Ah good, welcome!' Bob appeared before him, giving a body to the voice that rang out from everywhere. "This is my world; it's is everything and nothing. It is the fabric holding all worlds and times together. From here I can create, destroy and watch… everything! Parasite you called me. I'll show a parasite!" The world revolved into colour around him. Jackson seemed to lose his own form. He imagined himself as a pair of floating eyes. He quickly checked inwards to ensure his grip was tight on his little mind box, he needed to be prepared for anything. He looked

297

around, he was in a hospital room, the scene before him revealed a woman sitting up, in the throes of giving birth. A doctor was before the woman, hands between her knees, frozen in encouragement. A pair of nurses stood to either side of the doctor. "Behold! The birth of Jackson Brandt!" The man said, his disembodied voice echoing around the room. Jackson stared wide-eyed as the scene before him came to life. The woman, his mother, was screaming and clutching at the rails of the hospital bed on either side of her. In his current mental state, Jackson idly wondered where his father was. He had never really thought of his parents much, they had never featured in his life so why bother to. If he was honest with himself though, a deeply hidden part of him had always wanted this, a chance to meet her, to understand why. Why he had been abandoned, left alone. His earliest memories had been at the home where he had grown up. There they had only said that he had been given up, at their front door, without explanation. They hadn't offered any further information if they had any. Jackson took a deep imaginary breathe and watched on, he felt his mind box vibrate, as if it were going to split open. He took grip of it and held on tightly. "You see my Dream Stalker friend, I offer you the truth of your own beginning, something no one else ever bothered to do for you. Watch, watch how you came to be." Jackson did. He couldn't take his eyes of his mother's face even if he wanted to. Even in the grips of the terrible pain of childbirth, she looked beautiful to Jackson. He drank her in, committing her features to memory. The emotion of seeing his mother for the first time in his life was too much and Jackson had to release his grip on the mind box. Love, longing, and happiness flooded through him. Even though he had no body in this place, he knew he was crying, he could feel the tears streaming down his face. It was such an unexpected gift, he actually felt thankful to the man that brought him here. "Watch Dream Stalker, watch," the man said. Jackson did. He watched as his mother's face strained for one final push and then the grateful release. She fell back on the bed panting. Jackson didn't hear what the doctors and nurses were saying to each other, but he could feel the tension. He watched on, his mother still had her eyes closed, her breathing had slowed but her face was losing colour, strands of her hair were plastered to her forehead with sweat. Jackson felt the alarm before he saw it. The doctor had given little Jackson over to the nurses and was frantically administering something to the drip attached to his mother's arm. She was finding breathing difficult, it was irregular and laboured. Baby Jackson was whisked away to another room. There were beeps and flashing signals from the monitor at the head of the bed. The doctor was now opening his mother's eyes and shining a pocket flashlight into them. Jackson could see no response from her pupils, they were wide and staring blankly from her blue irises.

"No! No… help her man… do something!" Jackson implored at the man he knew was there but couldn't see.

"Do something? Like what exactly Jackson? You know as well as I that in the past Dream we can't change events. We can change our perception of it, move back, forward, pause and so on, but we can't change the event itself." Jackson could feel the man smiling, enjoying himself. Jackson looked back at his mother; she was lifeless, clearly dead. The doctor was administering CPR but on closer inspection of his face, he could see that he had already given up. Jackson felt his world crumble around him, the agony of the loss of his mother, a

mother he had never even known until now came crashing down on him. Thirty plus years of secret pining for knowledge of her, and then the sudden loss, right after seeing her for the first time was too much. Jackson broke down in tears, holding his face in his hands, even if he didn't have a body here.

"Why? Why are you showing me this?" he managed to breathe out between sobs. "Because my little Dream Stalker friend. I wanted to show you who the real parasite was!

Look closer Jackson. Closer! Open your eyes and understand what I am saying. You killed her! Your dream wanderings weren't confined to yourself in her womb. With no real form yet, the moment baby Jackson gained consciousness he started visiting and playing in the dreams of his mother, of his host! You are a parasite Jackson, you killed her with your own unique abilities. Your infantile wonderings of the Dream worlds used her a proxy, used, and drained her of her own source of energy Jackson. She used the last of her life force giving birth to you. You're a monster Jackson. The people you have been chasing up to now had nothing on you." The man had appeared in Jackson's vision. He was standing right in front of his face, breathing heavily while he spoke, almost panting with feeling, with hatred and malice, in and out with every breathe.

"Noooo!" Jackson screamed. He turned away, not able to look at his mother's dead face any longer, the mother that he had killed! "No, I don't believe you!" he said even though he didn't' believe it.

"You know its true Dream Stalker! Matricide was your first act in your present world." The man was smiling now, enjoying the effect his words were having on Jackson. For Jackson, his world had just broken, he couldn't face it. In

300

desperation he tried to gather all that he was, he needed to box all of this up, he couldn't deal with it. Unfortunately, he was too much of a mess. The emotional turmoil of the experience had completely incapacitated him, he couldn't do it, and he hadn't the energy. In a final desperate move, he gathered everything of himself into one tight little ball and held it fast in his mind.

Just before it unravelled, he hurled it outwards, "No more! OUT! I want OUT!" He screamed and unleashed the mental force of his emotion outwards before him. Jackson had a momentary glimpse of the surprise on the man's face before everything went white again.

Jackson was back on the roof. He lay sprawled on his back, exhausted. He slowly sat up and looked around. Fred and Alex were still frozen, the former holding the rope attached to Alex's chair which was hanging over the edge of the roof. It seemed that Jackson's little adventure back in time lasted only mere moments in the present. Sitting up, he quickly scanned the roof top for signs of the man, of Bob. There, in the corner furthest away from him, was an unmoving black mound. Jackson approached it cautiously. Everything screamed at him to rush over to Alex and pull her to safety, but he knew where the real threat lay, he needed to neutralise that first. As he walked, he partitioned off his mind, the image of his dying mother still fresh and agonisingly painful. Thankfully, Jackson seemed to be back in control of his ability and the emotions he was experiencing were silenced. With clarity of mind and purpose, he zeroed in on the god, yet still unmoving. He focused his mind as he had never done before, he submerged himself in all the details of the man, everything that he could see. Listening now too, he walked and focussed, Jackson stripped away at the projection of the man, listening for his core, his signature. In short order he had it. Unlike the others he had already identified, the god's soul sound was fundamentally different, the sound of a blue whale's heartbeat compared to that of a hummingbird. It wasn't a vibration, but rather a gong, belling regularly. With this new layer of understanding of the man, Jackson overlaid that on top of his mentally created image of him. The world opened up its secrets before his eyes.

The man, God, the thing before Jackson was revealed to him in its truest form. Jackson looked down at the dazed form and saw a pair of hairy goat's legs ending in hooves. The stringy, tan hair continued up his body up until it reached its belly button, after which, bare dark brown skin replaced the coarse hair. It was lying in the foetal position as it stirred back towards consciousness. Jackson continued his cold observation of the god thing in front of him.

Around its neck, hung with a length of raw hide, was a pan flute the likes of which he had seen in his research. Its head was that of man, dark brown, matt skin. A small white, wispy goatee, in stark contrast to his dark skin, surrounded a pinched, triangular, thin-lipped mouth. The bottom of which ended as the point of the V. A pair of grey horns curled behind hairy, pointed ears.

"I see you, you son of a bitch. I see the real you! How little, how small and irrelevant you really are!" Jackson said with feeling. The goat god opened his eyes, intense lilac coloured iris's slatted in a black line down the middle. They were blazing with an intense fury. Intense and, much to Jackson delight, wariness. He had to strike while he still had an advantage. He focused on the being's soul sound and once again and allowed his inner eye the sort of intense focus only a partitioned mind like his could bring to bear. A mass of differently coloured, incandescent energy lines flowed across the god's body in some sort of predetermined pattern, covering his whole form. As Jackson watched on, he could see where all the lines gathered together at the nape of his neck, following over and into each other, building in a small point of indescribable light. The point trailed away into the air around it in a twisting rope, ending in a mass of sparks that seemed to dissipate into nothingness. Without understanding anything he was seeing; Jackson focused his mental force on that rope twisting away from the being's body. He felt his mind touch it and he immediately recoiled, as if shocked. Gathering his resolve, Jackson mentally attacked the rope again, touching, and holding this time, riding the shock, absorbing it. Once over the immediate feeling of shock and pain, energy unimagined infused Jackson. He felt all powerful, he felt godlike and he felt like the sun! Resisting the temptation to further enjoy the sensation, Jackson mentally pinched at the rope, strangling it. He opened his eyes and looked down at the man. Bob's own eyes were wide open with shock, panic emanating from him in a wave as he lay still on the ground.

"Stop it! Nooo! Stop doing that… how?" he spluttered and tried to push himself up to a sitting position. Jackson pinched at the rope, tightening even further. Bob sank to the ground again, as if he had no remaining energy to get up. Jackson could feel the god before him withering, fading. "You think you have won Dream Stalker! Perhaps you should look once again to your friends, have you forgotten them?" Bob smiled weakly from below. To Jackson immense shame, he had forgotten about them. He spun around to see what was happening, involuntarily letting his mind grip of the rope go as his concentration focused elsewhere. In a flash, Bob was up on his backwards jointed goats' legs and had his long-nailed fingers around Jackson's throat. "You can't destroy me, you meaningless worm!" he hissed. "I spent a long-time planning this, you didn't think I would reveal everything at once did you?" Bob had completely lost whatever humour he had started this evening with. He looked ready the kill puppies in his current rage. "Let me show you the true meaning of despair Jackson, look and know my power!" Bob released his throat, allowing Jackson a brief moment to suck in a grateful mouthful of air. He was manhandled, as if a child before being turned around and shoved forward. As he stumbled away, Fred and Alex re-animated. If Fred was confused by the sudden positional change of everyone, he didn't show it, so intent was he on Alex, "Time to see sister!" He released some of the rope and the chair Alex was sitting on tilted backwards alarmingly. She screamed out in fear. Jackson didn't hesitate. Using his momentum from being shoved forward, he pummelled into Fred. As he hit him, he grabbed the rope. They fell together in a mass of swinging arms and legs. As he hit the ground, Jackson felt the weight of the chair pull at him, Alex was falling. Her weight pulled Jackson across the floor of the roof and he was sliding at pace towards the edge. The rope had seared away a good portion of the skin on his palm before he brought the other hand to double his grip. He hit ledge with his feet, immediately halting his slide. The weight of the Alex on the chair hanging over the edge almost pulled his shoulders out of joint as her fall was halted, but Jackson held on grimly. He was on his back, now, feet pressed toward the ledge, holding the rope before him. Jackson could feel his strength wavering.

"Noooo! You will not leave me Alex!" he screamed. With almost super human strength, Jackson started pulling the rope up, hand over hand. With agonising slowness, her head appeared over the edge, then her shoulders. When the back end of the chair was in reach, Jackson let go of the rope and grabbed the chair behind her before she could fall again. They were stuck there like that, face to face, noses almost touching, while Jackson held on for dear life. He had no leverage to pull up further, they were stuck in that position until Jackson's strength gave out.

"No! What are doing, she needs to see!" Jackson heard Freddie running towards him from behind. Without being able to do anything else, Jackson waited and strained against the weight of Alex hanging over the drop. Gathering the last of his strength, he judged the moment with perfect accuracy. As he heard Fred's final footstep land behind him, Jackson heaved and somehow managed to throw Alex and the chair to his left, over the ledge and back onto the roof. The force of the manoeuvre caused Jackson to fall back violently, straight into the legs of Fred. At pace, Fred hit the back of Jackson shoulders with his shins, propelling him into a somersault, head over heels, and right over the edge of the roof. Fred fell to his death without a sound.

Jackson lay back panting, he was pretty sure he had dislocated his right arm. The pain was unbearable but he didn't dare try and move it. He was sure he could hear sirens in the distance and hoped against hope that Ben and Detective Levi had somehow found them. A shadow appeared over him.

"Well done again Dream Stalker! Not the end that I had planned but still very satisfying I must say." It seemed that the goat man had regained his sense of humour as he was talking in giggles again. Jackson couldn't move, he could hardly breathe from his excursions. He was completely helpless. The goat man suddenly stopped giggling and leaned closer to Jackson who was lying prone on the floor. "Is it the end though? Is there more, maybe one last act?" he said menacingly. Dread filled Jackson. It was enough to fill him with the required energy to stand up before the god.

"What more could there possibly be!" Jackson asked wearily. The man before him twirled away and tittered.

"The final reveal my friend, look, look to your love!" With steadily increasing apprehension, Jackson ran over to Alex still lying where he had thrown her. Once he reached her side, he fell next to her and started undoing her bonds. She was squirmed, eager to be free of the chair, her tear steaked face revealing all the horrors of the evening. He had just removed her gag when Alex screamed. She screamed and screamed, a soul wrenching sound that hurt Jackson physically. He reached for her, but she pushed him away with force and shuffled backwards away from him.

"Don't touch me Jackson, don't come near me!" she screamed at him. Hurt and confused, he tried reaching out for her again. "I said back off!" Alex screamed once more. Jackson obeyed, hurt, confused and without direction.

"It's me Jackson, it's me! It was not Fred; I am the monster Jackson!" Alex was crying and screaming at him as if in mortal agony. "I remember now, Jackson," She pointed a shaking finger at the man behind him "He just showed me, opened what was previously blocked, showed me what I am!"

Jackson didn't understand, he sat there watching her with something approaching horror. "I planned it all Jackson. I caught the cat the Fred butchered, a planned the abduction of Linda Garver and her eventual murder... I planned the campsite massacre... I called Fred on the night and gave him the go-ahead Jackson. I did all those things... and many others." The last was said in a whisper, as painfully remembered as it was said. "I used Freddie as a tool, he was my assistant Jackson. The Linda Garver murder broke his mind I think... but still we continued on." She had stopped crying now, she had become pale and withdrawn, accepting. Jackson moved over to her and tried to embrace her as she sat on the ground. She didn't respond, she was a dead weight as he tried to wrap his arms around her.

"No, it wasn't you Alex, it was him... he made you do it... you didn't mean for any of it." Jackson was now crying himself, trying to position her arms around him. It was like trying to hug a sack of potatoes, for all intents and purposes, Alex appeared dead, lifeless.

"No Jackson, he might have manipulated me to into it, but I still did those things. I still watched and participated. I forced and manipulated Freddie into doing all those terrible things. I am worse than a monster Jackson," she told him tonelessly. She got up suddenly and pushed him away from her. Jackson stumbled at the unexpected shove. "I love Jackson, you at least were real to me, maybe the only real thing ever!" What remained of her was expressed in that last sentence, a final tear escaped her eye. Jackson had just regained his footing when Alex turned on her heel, ran to the edge of the roof and dived over, headfirst.

Without thought, Jackson sprinted and jumped after her.

Somehow, through force of will he caught her mid fall, and as they plummeted, he embraced her and whispered in her ear, "You are my life Alex, I love you. I will follow you wherever you go." Time slowed in those final minutes. She smiled at him and closed her eyes, pushing her face against his chest, they fell to the ground together. With Alex in his arms, Jackson finally relaxed. He was at peace for the first time in his life and was completely and utterly without regret. In his mind, he opened his mind box one last time.

This time he enlarged it, making it as big as he could imagine it and then threw his whole self into it, not even leaving that part out that usually maintained function of his body, he went into the box totally, completely, forever.

The man on the roof looked down on the two bodies sprawled on the sidewalk below, a little away from the broken body of Fred. It had been a most interesting story that had sadly left him feeling incomplete, unfinished. If he had been capable of feeling anything, he imagined it would be regret. He giggled to himself as he laughed it off. There were always other stories, other worlds, perhaps even, other Jacksons. If anybody had been staring up toward the roof of the building, they would have noticed fog gathering in from its sides towards a lone figure in the centre. It continued to gather in a sphere around the man until it condensed to the point of bursting, which it eventually did. In a flash, Bob and the fog were gone, leaving behind an empty, abandoned building, and three dead, broken bodies strewn below it.

The End